COMPLICITY

COMPLICITY

THE DANGERS OF DREAMING: BOOK 2

CHLOË L BLYTH

ISBN: 9798839362031

Independently Published

*For everyone left wanting answers after reading Duplicity.
Here we go again!*

~

Is love always right,
Or sometimes wrong?
I thought it was right,
Perhaps, I was wrong.

25 December

Adam

I don't have a clue what to do or where to go, all I know is that I need to protect Ella.

Moments earlier we were sat around a dining table at Cherry's house, finishing our Christmas Dinner. I was accusing Kyle of impregnating Ella, possibly through rape, and then the doorbell rang. Jeremy peered through the window, and we ran. But not before I noticed Ella's reaction.

"How do you know the Minister's son?" I ask as I hold open another gate for her to run through, though I don't really want to know the answer. Jeremy has a reputation. The Minister, Francis Krunk, might be old and geeky looking with mad-scientist hair, but his son is a blonde-haired, blue-eyed, six-pack possessing, womanising Adonis. At least Kyle looks like me. If she's slept with Jeremy, it's over.

I'm sure I see a blush rise in her cheeks, but it could just be from her exertion in the cold. It'd better be. Shit, would I really leave her if she has?

"He was one of the directors at my old job," she answers without meeting my eye. I didn't realise the Minister had allowed his son to work outside of the community. He's not

4

one of us, of course, but he knows. And I also know the Minister paid for him to have a very expensive education – one that I would have expected he'd want to make the most of.

"Why do you think he was there?" she asks, out of breath.

"He was probably sent to get you. We did break you out of his daddy's facility after all." It's the obvious answer.

"Yeah, but why? I thought they decided I wasn't special. Is this really about keeping the Dream-Walker secret?" She slows to a walk and pushes her left hand into the right of her body, then covers it and pushes harder with her right hand. "I've got a stitch, can we stop?"

I look around; I don't think anyone's following. My stomach doesn't feel great either. Christmas Dinner isn't the best pre-workout meal.

"Okay, let's rest for a minute."

I lean back against a garden fence and raise my arms to try to stretch out my stomach.

"And, I don't think this is about keeping the society a secret, I think it's about your new talent," I answer her initial question whilst trying, once again, not to think of the images that fill my brain when we have sex.

"But how would they know about that?" she asks innocently.

"I don't know, but the Minister is sneaky and maybe he saw something I didn't understand on your blood report. Maybe he knows why it happens. Maybe you're not the first person with that particular skill that he's come across."

"I'd hardly call it a skill," she says, looking down at her feet.

"No…" I reply, neither would I.

We stand in awkward silence, me thinking about how the most special moment of our relationship was ruined by images of her and Kyle together, and her… blushing? There's no doubting it this time, she's embarrassed.

"What? What are you thinking?"

She hesitates.

"It's just… If the Minister does know what I am, and his son Jeremy does too, then it might explain a few things…" She bites her lip and starts scraping dry skin off with her teeth. Why do I get the feeling I'm not going to like what she has to say next?

"Jeremy, um... He, we… Um, you remember when you didn't call me for like two weeks after that almost rape incident?"

"When my mum was in the hospital?"

"Yeah…"

"Go on," I encourage, feeling as if my heart is in my throat. I try to swallow but I can't get past the giant lump. First, I found out she had a dream relationship with my brother before we met, now what, she fucked the Minister's son?

"Well, I didn't know if you would call because you'd said it was dangerous and it'd been a week already. So, when he turned up at my flat and invited me on a date, I said yes."

She looks back down at her feet and starts trying to scrape some mud off the side of one of her boots. I try to be patient and wait for her to continue.

"He was very handsy and I tried not to, but he was so, I don't know, 'keen' I guess. I felt wanted and it had been a long time since I'd been with a man in real life, and I didn't know if you would ever call, so I…"

"So you what? Go on, spit it out!" I snap. I couldn't hold it in any longer.

"We kissed. We almost did more, but I stopped it because I didn't want to risk ruining things with you before they'd even started."

6

I start walking again and Ella struggles to keep up. I can't believe this. Was I the only one who didn't try to sleep with her? Foolish Adam, who tried to keep her safe whilst his twin brother had sex with her in her dreams, and bloody Jeremy threw himself at her in the flesh.

If only I could walk away, leave her to figure out all this shit on her own. If anyone else had been through what I have been through over the past few months, they would. But not me, not good, reliable Adam. I'm the type of guy you bring home to meet your parents and they think 'aw, he's harmless.' I'd never get your daughter pregnant and then disappear because I'm too darn caring. I'm responsible. Nice. (And I'm not an idiot).

Ella runs up and pulls my arm to slow me down. I stop and look at her.

"Do you think he knew? Do you think that's why he tried to have sex with me? To see what happens?"

I know she's trying to help me focus on the bigger picture, but I can't help it. I'm spiralling. I loved her so hard, even before we met. I knew she was special. I used to watch her go about her daily life knowing that we'd be perfect together but also knowing we could never be. I didn't want to put her life in danger. Knowing about Dream-Walkers has consequences and it's not easy to keep secrets from a partner. When I decided I couldn't take it anymore, that I had to speak to her, to be a part of her life, I also made another difficult decision: no sex.

If a Dream-Walker has sex with a human then, through 'transference', the human bears witness to all the dreams and nightmares that Dream-Walker has ever had, any dream-manipulations they've ever partaken in, all sorts of terrible and confusing things, right at the moment of climax. Way to ruin the moment, hey? And once they know, the Human Justice Department can come for them at any time, because we can't have just anyone knowing about us. It's a highly regulated secret.

By some miracle, Ella and I fell in love despite my unspoken 'no sex' rule. It was hard to keep my secret, but the more I loved her, the more I knew I could never put her in danger; that I had already done too much. But then of course, I found out that Kyle had dream-dated Ella for three months before I introduced myself. He'd known I liked her, and he claimed it was all for my benefit, so that she'd recognise me and want to date me in real life, but they had sex during that time. Dream-sex, anyway. So, despite my abstinence, my girlfriend had already had sex with my identical twin brother in her dreams. Oh, and soon after I found out the full extent of Kyle's dream wanderings, our mum's battle with cancer ended and I had to arrange a funeral whilst Kyle urged Ella and I to run away because the Human Justice Department was coming for us because somebody tipped them off about our relationship. It doesn't rain, it pours. Right?

Well, that was only the start. I am ashamed of my behaviour after that. I was hurt and disappointed by Ella and Kyle, so I abandoned them and attempted to face the Human Justice Department alone. I didn't expect us all to end up in court, and later at the Medical Investigation Unit, but there were a lot of motives at play and revelations to be learnt.

Ultimately, my dad, who just so happens to be the most powerful and feared Dream-Walker of our time, escaped from a secure MIU cell with help from Kyle and our newly discovered identical triplet brother, Damian. But Kyle soon found himself bound and gagged and realised that Dad was never going to help him like he'd hoped. He ended up helping me to free Ella, who had wound up stuck in an MIU cell herself since Damian had made her seem dangerous to a bunch of jurors in court. They nearly drowned in their sleep. But even once the Minister realised that Ella wasn't responsible for that, she was detained simply because she's a human, and the Minister really doesn't like humans knowing about Dream-Walkers. Even though he is one too.

Anyway, after all that drama, we were finally back together, and I realised I had missed her a lot. I was willing to do my best to look past what had happened between her and Kyle in her dreams, because she really had believed they were just dreams, and she really did think they were of me. Until she met Kyle, anyway. But feelings don't just go away, and what we had, what we have, is real. We fell in love with both eyes open, I wasn't going to let that go so easily. I was ready to risk having sex.

The risk was that she'd be scared by what she saw, but I already knew she loved me, and there wasn't any more danger that could befall her from doing it than was already there. She was already on the run from the HJD.

Little did I know she was bringing her own nightmares to the table.

It was only a few days ago, just before Christmas, and the anticipation couldn't have been greater. I knew Ella wanted it too, she'd never understood why I made her wait.

Now that I think about it, perhaps I shouldn't be surprised that she nearly jumped into bed with Jeremy, she really did want to have sex with me. I was always fighting her off. But she waited for me because she loved me. She didn't understand why I made her wait, but she loved me enough to wait anyway.

We finally did it on a wintery morning when I hoped for a whole day of sexy shenanigans in bed. Or perhaps in various locations, as we had a lot of sex to catch up on. But for that first time, we were in bed. I kissed her and she kissed me back and the longing was palpable. We didn't waste much time. I knew it was going to be deep and meaningful.

9

Oh, it was deep alright. Bottom of the ocean tied to a rock kind of deep. Just as I reached completion, as she trembled beneath me letting out a noise of pure pleasurable release, it happened. Flashes of her with Kyle, random scenes presumably from their dreams together. Snapshots of them playing board games, strip-poker, walking a fluffy white dog, eating strawberries and cream off each other. It felt like I was watching clips of home videos and it made me want to puke. Luckily for Ella, I was able to make it to the bathroom first.

She denies the scenes I saw were real, says they're just my imagination. Apparently, they didn't do those things. But how would I know? Kyle's a liar and Ella, well, she loves me. She would deny it just to keep me. And now I know she nearly slept with Jeremy too, I don't know how much more my heart can take. Ever since I let her into my life, ever since I ignored my gut instinct to stay away from her to keep her safe, my life has snowballed.

Sure, I was unhappy before. I was miserable. All I did was care for my terminally ill mum, of course I was miserable. There was no light at the end of the tunnel. Not my tunnel, anyway. All I could do was make Mum as happy and as comfortable as I could for her remaining days. After that, I had no plan. I didn't know what I would do once she was gone, but I was safe; there was no running. Nobody cared what I was up to, whose son I was, because I didn't draw attention to myself. I left that to Kyle.

I thought Ella would make me happy, and she did, she does, but if I had never played along with Kyle's plan to get us together, if I had never physically introduced myself, my dad might still be locked up. Maybe Ella would be happily dating Jeremy now instead. Maybe he would have kept her safe, away from the Dream-Walker community.

Then again, if she was dating Jeremy, she would still have caught the attention of the Minister. Perhaps she'd still have ended up in a cell in an MIU (Medical Investigation Unit). Perhaps she'd have even been stuck there, without us to help her escape. Jeremy might have left her and moved on.

Ella tugs at my sleeve and tries to put her fingers between mine, dragging my attention back into the present.

"We should keep moving, they might catch up."

For a moment I consider letting them. Letting Jeremy have her, letting him have a go because it's fucking traumatising knowing that your dream girl isn't so perfect as you thought. I know that sounds mean. I don't mean she's meant to be 'perfect.' I know about what happened in her past, mistakes she's made. But she was meant to be mine, not Kyle's, not Jeremy's, and I don't like to share. Raised as a twin, that's not the best trait to have, but it's fine because Kyle doesn't share either.

He's always been a pain in my arse, but this was a new low. I don't know what to believe anymore. He says he did it all to set us up, to make me happy, but I know that's a lie for two undeniable reasons: One, because he let his part in Ella's dreams go on way longer than was necessary to make me feel 'familiar', and two, because he wanted the Human Justice Department to come after us. He wanted us to get caught, because he wanted to be sent down to a Medical Investigation Unit in my place as a 'favour' so that he could help our father escape. Our criminal father. Gerome Clarke. Voldemort incarnate.

And why did he want to free the most powerful and dangerous Dream-Walker? To get revenge on the man who killed his fiancée. And didn't that work out well? Instead of getting me a girlfriend and getting revenge on a murderer, he fucked up my relationship with the only girl I've ever loved, possibly even fell in love with her himself (though he'd never admit it) and freed a dangerous criminal who has no intention of helping him.

11

I need to stay focused. From tomorrow, Kyle is leading the mission to find our dad, capture him, and put him back into a secure underground MIU. He's learnt the hard way that Dad will never help him, he only looks out for number one. That should mean Kyle's giving up on his revenge plan, but I know him better than that. He'll have something up his sleeve. He always does.

Whilst Kyle's focus is on finding Dad, mine is to stop the HJD getting their hands on Ella. Again. I'm sure they want to run more tests on her and they may already know about her 'condition' or whatever she is. If she's not just pregnant with Kyle's dream-baby as per my initial conclusion.

"Come on!" she pulls my arm again, scared.

My perfect girlfriend. It's not her fault.

"Okay, let's go," I squeeze her hand and lead the way.

Ella

I pace the hotel room looking at Adam, fear and adrenaline running through my veins. I can't believe I fessed up about Jeremy, now he hates me even more. But we weren't even together! The well-known Ross and Rachel words repeat over and over in my head, "we were on a break!" Except we weren't even on a break because we weren't even together yet! His mood is so unfair.

"So, what do we do now?" I dare to ask him.

"I don't know. Do you think you've done it before?"

He looks up at me from his position on the edge of the bed. Well, there's no right answer to that question.

"Given that none of my exes have ever stuck around, I would say that's likely. But they never told me if something happened, or what they saw…" I trail off.

We've never discussed my previous relationships before, but they're what led me to him, or Kyle, I suppose. If I hadn't had such a disastrous relationship history, I probably wouldn't have been so eager to fall in love in my dreams. A dream man, a dream relationship, a dream body. He was perfect. I remember telling Kristina all about it, how I had finally found my rom com hero and could step away from the TV screen…

13

I miss Kristina. I didn't realise how much I would miss talking to her, but ever since I left that job and my life contorted into some kind of action movie with trials and labs and, for want of a better name, 'super-heroes and super-villains', I do miss the normal life. Drive thru coffees on our way back from work in the rain. Gossiping about Jeremy. Bloody Jeremy. Another beautiful specimen with another hidden agenda. Was he really only into me because of what I can do? Did his father send him?

"Well we need to figure out what you are, because the Human Justice Department probably has a name for it already; I doubt you're the first. Until we know what the Minister knows, we're on the back foot. That has got to be our main focus." I'm relieved he's started to accept that I'm not just pregnant with Kyle's dream-baby. That theory was ridiculous.

"I agree. Now, how are we going to do that?"

"I'll make some calls, see if anyone has ever heard of anything like it, see if we can find somebody else like you." He feels in his pocket for his phone and then remembers he doesn't have one anymore. We threw them away when the HJD started chasing us the first time. "Damn it!" He rests his head in his hands.

I've never seen him look so tired and stressed. I hate that I'm doing this to him. Not just me, his dad, Kyle, Jeremy, Damian... He really has had the worst end of the deal. My poor boyfriend, everything seems against him right now. I stand in front of him next to the bed and rub his arms, trying to get him to look up at me. I cuddle him into me, feeling his head rest against my chest.

"I love you, Adam. Please don't lose hope, we can get through this. We can figure out what I am and how to avoid that happening again, and we can go on to live happy lives together. I know it. Kyle will deal with your dad. We can do this, I promise."

14

He looks up and I see his face is wet. I kiss him softly on the lips, they taste salty. The kiss deepens.

"I love you too," he says as I pull away to position myself across his lap. "But I don't think it's going to be that simple, you have no idea what my dad is capable of."

With my thighs around him I want to have sex again, but I daren't suggest it; he'd never agree. It's a wonder he made it through the few times he did. I've traumatised my own boyfriend. The fact the others all ghosted me finally makes sense.

No, there will be no sex tonight. We will spend the night cuddling in the hotel's double bed under smooth white bedsheets which are so much better than my bobbly over-washed ones at home. That's one benefit of being on the run, I suppose.

26 December

Ella

"Hi honey, sorry I'm late, the traffic was horrendous," I say, slamming the front door behind me and walking into the apartment I visited once last April. The floor to ceiling windows frame the incredible view across the water and I breathe in a lovely fresh fragrance. Heaven. I remove my heels and place them into a shoe cupboard, appreciating the organisation. I've barely straightened back up before I'm presented with a glass of chilled white wine. I take a large sip. Ah.

"Thank you, I needed that!"

"I thought you might," says Jeremy, his blue eyes twinkling. "Dinner's in the oven, but we have a little time, if you want me to help you unwind further…" He sinks towards me. We kiss and he lifts me onto the clean worktop and stands between my open thighs. His hands caress my spine, relaxing me and tickling me slightly at the same time. He undoes my bra strap and sneaks his hands around to the front. I gasp as he squeezes my right breast.

"Should we-" I start to say but I don't even need to finish my sentence. He knows what I want. He lifts me and carries me to the bedroom. I lie on my back, watching him longingly. He is soon undressed and ready to continue. He

reaches for a red silk scarf and ties my arms to the bedframe. He kisses me again before slowly making his way down my body, removing my skirt and panties in one smooth move. His mouth trails kisses down my stomach, along my inner thigh, and finally –

I jolt awake shocked, embarrassed, sweating, and relieved Adam is still asleep and didn't witness that. What the hell?

I wipe the sweat off my face and neck with the duvet cover and turn on the TV to distract myself. I switch to the news channel, watching on mute. Gerome Clarke's freedom is highly evident already.

He's been out for what, a few days? A week? Already the headlines are rolling in, battling for the 'top story' spot. There are a few 'strange' incidents like spa goers drowning themselves in hot tubs; dog walkers jumping off cliffs; rollercoaster passenger restraints malfunctioning and sending adrenaline seekers to their death or lifetime disability.

Then there are the bigger ones, train and plane crashes set up as accidents but raising fears of terrorism throughout the country. We are now at the highest level of the terrorism threat scale; the government are scared. The events seem unrelated, but too much of a coincidence to really be.

Adam told me that some of our human government know about Dream-Walkers, they are entrusted so that they can maintain the secrecy, but they don't know the full story; they don't know the level of destruction one angry escapee can cause. I'd thought Gerome Clarke was more into dream-raping and paedophilia, manipulation on a smaller scale, for individual pleasure. Clearly, I was wrong. He plans to take revenge on the entire population of England, and then some.

I look at Adam, still fast asleep. I want to wake him up so we can talk, but I know he needs the rest. I turn off the TV and snuggle back into him. I'll rest my eyes whilst I wait, but I won't risk sleeping again so soon. If Adam caught me dreaming about Jeremy, it would destroy him. I can't let that happen. I don't even know why it happened that time, it's not like I was thinking about him. Much. But I only want to know why he asked me out and if he knows what I am. I don't care about him; I don't like him. He's overly confident, he's slick and smooth and annoyingly handsome, he's so not my type, even if he is nice to look at.

Adam

"Mummy, what's wrong with me?" I ask, my little legs dangling from the chair.

"What do you mean, darling? There's nothing wrong with you." She smiles sweetly, passing me a napkin and then stirring her drink.

"My friends don't like me anymore. They said I'm bad." I pick up the lemon iced bun. It's so big in my little hands. I take a bite and my nose touches the icing.

"You're not bad, Adam, it wasn't your fault," she answers, unconvincingly.

"But no-one else did it! And it was really nasty. Nicholas said I'm going to be a cereal killer." I lick my lips, enjoying the lemon curd's usual tang.

"You don't even like cereal!" She laughs. I put the rest of my bun down.

"No! Not that kind of cereal! He said I'm going to be a bad man, like the clown." A frown takes over my little face.

"What clown?" she asks softly.

"The one in my dream!" I shout, frustrated.

"It was only a dream, Adam, it doesn't mean anything." She nudges my plate back towards me. I don't want the bun anymore.

"But only bad people have bad dreams!" I shove the plate away from me.

"You can't help what you dream about, Adam. Nobody can," she tries to reassure me. She's not very clever.

"Kyle can."

"Did he-"

"-He gives me dreams all the time. He said he's going to be just like daddy."

I wake up and am surprised to see Ella curled up next to me. I attempt to lean up slightly to read the clock. 10am! I didn't plan to sleep that long. I shake her gently and kiss her cheek.

"Wakey-wakey!"

Her eyes open quickly and she smiles at me,

"Oh good, you're awake."

"Hey, I just woke you up!" I poke her.

"I was just resting my eyes!" she replies indignantly.

"So you weren't…?"

"No, I wasn't an involuntary spectator of your dream. What was it this morning then?" she asks, sitting up.

"Just a semi-memory of sitting at Cherry B's café with Mum, but it made me think."

"Okay, what did it make you think?"

"Well, when we were kids, Kyle used to practice on me. Dream-walking, dream-watching, you know? Now I know my dad didn't need a brother for that, because he was raised in a cage and trained and all that, but we're twins, no, triplets, and don't things like that run in families? So, it stands to reason that, whether or not he knew it, my dad might have been born a twin or triplet too!" I grin.

"I'm not sure how that's supposed to help us find him or work out what I am though," she says, seemingly disappointed.

"No, neither do I. But I've never thought about it before; I could have relatives out there I've never met!" It's an exciting prospect.

"Join the club," she says sarcastically. Shit. I didn't mean it like that.

Ella was adopted as a baby, she doesn't know any of her blood relatives, doesn't even know her biological parents' names. It's all part of the mystery of why she is the way she is. Or what she is. Human with a nightmarish sex twist?

"I'm sorry, I didn't mean it like that."

I open my arms and she snuggles into me. I love the feeling of her against me. Her small body, so fragile and in need of protection. I've always felt protective of her, even before I introduced myself. She looks up at me.

"Maybe instead of worrying about your relatives, we should be looking for mine."

I nod and kiss the top of her head.

"That's a great idea, but where would we start?"

She sighs into my chest.

"With the ones who adopted me."

"Are you sure?" I gently direct her chin so I can look into her eyes, and she nods, biting her lip.

Okay, I guess it's time to meet the parents. Ella's adoptive parents. And their daughter, whom Ella disabled in a car accident. I should be nervous to meet my girlfriend's parents, but I don't think of them like that. They effectively abandoned her after what happened, blamed her and made her feel even more unwelcome than she already did. But Ella's right, they are the best place to start. They must know something about where the baby they adopted came from, babies don't just arrive by stork.

"What's their address?"

Ella tells me but then says we can't go until tomorrow because they won't be there. She hasn't spoken to her adoptive parents in years, so there is no way she knows that, but I don't doubt her. We'll do this when she's ready. There's no hurry, so long as the HJD don't find us.

For the meantime, we can snuggle and chat and maybe go pick up some clothes from the supermarket. Christmas jumpers won't be seasonally appropriate for much longer, plus mine stinks from running here yesterday. There's a reason sportswear isn't knitted.

27 December

Ella

Home, or what used to be home; before. I've delayed this moment long enough.

I stare up at the small semi-detached house. I'm surprised they never moved, choosing instead to have a kind of 'granny annex' built on the side, taking up half of the driveway, so that Viva could live downstairs. I wonder what it's like to live in a house and never go upstairs. I'm sure they've had to make other alterations, widen doorways, probably special things to help her use the kitchen appliances safely, but they'll have had funding for that. There are always people who want to help the disabled and keep them independent, even if they do still live with their parents. Viva is 21 now, I wonder if she plans to leave anytime soon.

We should have called ahead. I look at Adam and I can tell he can feel how nervous I am. My palms are sweating. But if I had called, Mum would have made excuses. She would have invented something crucially important that she absolutely had to do so that she couldn't be here. My dad would have quietly agreed with her that it 'wasn't a good time', and Viva, well, we kind of cleared the air back in April so I'm sure she'd see me, but she'd be of absolutely no use since she was just an unfertilised egg in Mum's ovaries back then. No, this was the only way to ensure that I get the answers I need. We need. To move forwards.

I imagine what they're going to think when they hear I am 'special', 'different' but in a nightmarish way. Not the dancer or gymnast they planned for Viva to become, but instead a woman who terrifies the men who sleep with her. Something impossible to be proud of.

"Are we going to knock then?" asks Adam, rubbing the small of my back. My arms are crossed, and my scarf flips angrily in the wind. I'm surprised they haven't sensed my presence standing outside, the darkness shadowing their perfect lives. Or not perfect, ruined-by-me lives. Can't they sense the impending doom of my arrival? Why isn't Mum peeping through the net curtain? Or Viva? If Viva saw me, she'd open the door, wouldn't she? I thought we made up, but if she didn't tell Mum then perhaps she won't make that obvious, perhaps she'll pretend. She does have to live with them after all.

I look at Adam and he nods at me encouragingly. I'm scared. I don't want to knock. I don't want to see Mum's disappointed face again, the blame, the hate, the disgust. It was an accident! I don't want to have to defend myself again, I won't put myself through it.

It's normal to be nervous about bringing a man home to meet your family, but I couldn't care less what they think about him. And besides, I know they will love him like everybody does. It's me that I'm scared for them to see, how I've grown up. The woman I've become without their influence, without their love, without anyone.

It was their blame that led me to move away and become that girl who drinks wine and watches rom coms every night. The kind of girl whose only friend is her ex-colleague, who was technically beneath her on the company hierarchy. The kind of girl who had unsuccessful relationship after unsuccessful relationship until she finally found solace in her dreams. The kind of girl who thought she made up her dream man out of some kind of sad desperation to finally be happy, and then believed she had met him in real life and dated him, only to find out he wasn't the one who'd been in her dreams – that was his brother. And feelings about said brother are still rather conflicted. It's a good job he's taken off to chase their dad, I needed a break.

My point is, it's my parent's fault that my life took that path, if they had believed me when I said it was an accident, or if they had forgiven me for what happened, I would never have moved away at eighteen, lived alone and worked my way up in a career I didn't even like. Maybe I would have gone to university or stayed at home until I knew what I actually wanted to do. Maybe if I –

Before I can finish that thought, the door opens. I can't speak. It's my dad. His hair is almost all grey now, a little tufty, and he has big, black-framed glasses above his grey beard. He looks larger than I remember, as if his evenings are also spent in front of the TV now.

"Ella-Rose, is that you?" His eyes flit from me to Adam. I still can't form words. My eyes are threatening to spill. I don't know what to say. We should never have come here. I can't do this.

Adam takes hold of my hand and guides me closer to the door.

"Hi, I'm Adam, Ella's boyfriend," he holds out his other hand to shake my dad's.

"Would you like to come in?"

We follow him through to the lounge. It's almost exactly how I remember it, only the carpet has been replaced with some type of wood – presumably because it's easier to navigate on a wheelchair and doesn't get worn out by wheels. One of the armchairs has gone, and the TV is finally one that goes on a bracket on the wall rather than the old chunky one that used to sit on a table and stick out halfway into the room it was so fat. The walls are still the same magnolia, and the school photos of Viva and I still lead the way upstairs.

It hadn't even occurred to me that Adam might see childhood photos of me whilst we're here. I'd imagined all signs I ever existed would have been burnt or shredded long ago or put in a box in the loft at the very least.

"I'll put the kettle on," says Dad. He begins pottering away, leaving me to compose myself. I look again at Adam.

"Are you okay?" he asks quietly. I nod.

"Your mum and Violet are out shopping, but they'll be back in a while, if you want to see them." Dad explains, carrying in a tray with three steaming mugs of tea. He didn't even ask us if we like tea, or how we take it, but it appears we are getting milk no sugar, regardless. And who doesn't want tea when they are seeing their adoptive dad for the first time in over seven years, or when meeting their girlfriend's estranged adoptive dad? We're British, tea is the solution to all of life's problems. I sip it and try not to flinch as I swallow. It tastes like dishwater; I imagine.

"You're probably wondering why we're here," I state bluntly.

"I hoped you'd come back some day, I didn't like how we left things." Dad says, earnestly.

"Well, we're not here about that, and I'm not here just to show off my new boyfriend either."

He frowns,

"Okay."

"I need to know where I came from, who my biological parents are. Something has happened, and I need to know who my real family are."

He leans forward in his chair, placing his mug back down on the tray.

28

"Are you okay? Are you ill? Is it something genetic? Do you need a donor?"

I sigh. How the hell do you tell someone you're a freak without sounding like a freak? And my thing, well, it's not something I want to talk to my dad about anyway. Sex. How do I tell him that when I have sex, I make the men see horrible visions without a) admitting that I have sex, b) admitting that I have had sex with several different men and c) talking about sex?

I loosen the scarf around my neck, suddenly feeling very warm.

"Um, so, this is going to sound strange, but I've recently realised that I'm not entirely normal. There's something that happens when I… um, have um, coitus that er, um…" I look to Adam for help. Coitus? When have I ever used that word in my life?

"What she's trying to say is that when Ella has sex, her partner sees things, strange things, like their worst nightmare. It happened to me, and we think it has happened to others."

My dad blushes, this is worse than the sex talk! Who doesn't talk to their dad for seven years and then pops round to talk about sex?

Before we arrived, we agreed that we can't mention Dream-Walkers to them because we don't want to put them in danger but, as we don't know what I am, we can talk about that because nobody has told us not to.

"That's why I need to know about my biological parents. They might have the answers I need. Maybe that's even why I was put up for adoption, maybe they split up after they had sex because my mum has the same issue I do, and my dad couldn't put up with it." I finish the rest of my lukewarm tea and wait for my dad to speak.

"Well, I didn't see that coming!" He chuckles. "Nice to meet you Adam, by the way. You look like a lovely man; I should be proud my daughter has you. Thank you for bringing her home." He looks at me and I swallow nervously.

"Ella, we meant to talk to you about this when you turned eighteen, but with how everything was back then, it just didn't happen. Your mother and you couldn't even be in the same room."

"So, you do know something? Names? A photo? A letter?" I ask eagerly.

"Not exactly. Wait here, let me get something." He heads upstairs and then returns with a shoebox. "This isn't all about them of course, this is just a box of mementos Mum kept for you. Your first shoes, your baby teeth, though why you'd ever want those I'll never know, a snip of hair from your first hair cut... all sorts. She thought you might want them someday. Because you were ours, you know, right from the beginning. You weren't born to us, but you were handed to us to raise, and we really did do our best. We never expected to have Violet, as you know, so I'm sorry how that played out. We never meant to leave you behind, but Audrey got so caught up in making her child a superstar, we inadvertently left you to blossom on your own." He pulls out a hanky and dabs his eyes. "Here," he says, passing the box to me.

"Is anything in here from my birth parents?" I ask, removing the lid and peeking inside.

"Only the blanket you arrived in. The only thing we know about your parents is that they chose us. About a week before you arrived, Audrey, sorry, your mum, had a dream that a baby was coming. She told me, '*We have to be home on the 25th at 3pm, our baby is coming!*' I thought she'd gone mad, you know, after all those years trying. We'd finally accepted that we weren't able to have our own child, and here she was telling me that our baby was due to arrive on the 25th at 3pm. It didn't make any sense. But you

30

know what I'm like, I do as I'm told. So, on the 25th January we put on our finest and we sat right there on that couch, waiting for something to happen. I was sceptical, of course, and I had done nothing to prepare for a baby. Your mum had been busy all week, buying a cot, and clothes, and nappies, and blankets; little rattles and squeaky toys. I thought if nothing happened, I was going to have to get her some serious help. 3pm came and went, and nothing happened. We sat there waiting, like children waiting by the fireplace on Christmas Eve, expecting Santa to materialise before our eyes. Then at 3:15, Audrey stood up, opened the front door, and there you were."

"What?"

"You arrived on our doorstep. Probably at 3pm, but we didn't think to look straight away because we thought somebody would be delivering you."

"So there were no adoption papers, no hospital tags or whatever? No paperwork at all? I was a random baby on your doorstep?"

"You were our miracle baby." He blows his nose, a loud hearty blow.

"So, you don't know anything either! This was a dead end." I say, crestfallen.

"Well, I wouldn't say that. We know one thing, you're special. And if your parents made Audrey know you were coming, they were special too. So it doesn't surprise me that you've got a new, erm, side effect."

"Do you think Mum might remember more?" I ask, clinging to my last shred of hope.

"Maybe, but how well do you remember dreams you had last year? Never mind a quarter of a century ago!"

"True." I sigh.

"They'll be back soon if you want to wait. I'm sure Viva would love to see you."

"Ha, but Mum wouldn't?"

31

"You know how she is."

"We'll get going but, thank you." I say, standing up. I open my arms and offer him a hug. He squeezes me tightly and rubs my back.

"Don't leave it so long next time, okay?"

"Okay."

"And Adam, as Ella's only 'known' father, I'm telling you to look after her, okay?" He points his finger at him and smiles with a twinkle in his eye. "It was lovely to see you both."

"You too," Adam and I say at the same time, then laugh.

"Bye!"

Ella

When we arrive back at the hotel, someone's waiting for us. He holds his hands up,

"I come in peace!"

Jeremy. Still hot, in that surfer-esque way. His sun-bleached hair seems out of place against the long winter coat and statement/probably cashmere red scarf.

The scarf reminds me of my dream, of where we left off. I was tied to the bed…

Adam moves to stand in front of me, protectively.

"What do you want?" he demands.

"I want to help. I'm not working for the Department, I swear. I have the answers you're looking for."

Adam eyes him suspiciously then looks around the lobby.

"Fine, come up to our room, we can't discuss it here."

The lift is intense, Jeremy's scent overpowers us all and makes my nose itch; he should probably hold back on that a bit. But now's probably not the time to tell him.

Once inside the room, that also feels too small for the three of us. Jeremy carefully removes my neat pile of yesterday's clothes from the only chair in the room – knickers on top – and places it on the dresser. He throws me a smile and then sits down, having removed his coat and folded it neatly over the back of the chair. He looks so expensive, unlike us in our supermarket clothes that we picked up yesterday 'on the run.'

But what does that matter? We need to find out exactly what he knows, and what that means for me.

Adam and I sit down on the bed opposite him.

"Presumably you've discussed who I am with each other since Christmas Day?" he asks confidently. Is he proud of his almost conquest? I try not to think about it. It was a stupid mistake, that's all it was.

"Yes," Adam answers for us both stone-faced, giving nothing away.

"So you know that I'm the Minister's son," he looks at me, "and you know that Ella and I had a… dalliance," he looks at Adam.

"Yes," Adam confirms.

"Well, what you might not know is that I, too, have seen the inside of a Medical Investigation cell. I, too, have been experimented on and tested. The Minister's wife is my stepmother, but my real mother was a Dream-Walker."

"Are you a Dream-Walker too?" I ask, breaking my silence.

He must be a cruel one if he is, sleeping around and making all those human women experience Transference. Then again, I suppose if you've never had a bad nightmare, or never had anything bad done to you, would Transference even be so bad? If the partner 'see's everything' dream related, would that not be sort of okay if you've led a boring safe life? It might be a little jealousy-invoking if you saw him dreaming with his exes, but in the grand scheme of things, not that bad. Not as bad as my issue, anyway.

Or maybe there are more Dream-Walkers around than I realised. Maybe all the women he's slept with were Dream-Walkers too, so they didn't experience it.

"No, I am not. I'm what my father calls a P.I.N.S. and so are you, if rumours are to be believed."

"And what is that exactly?" I ask eagerly. I am something! I have a classification!

"A Pessimistic Instigator of Negative Stimuli. It's an awful name, I'll give you that, but it's hard to name what we do, isn't it? Nightmare-giver? Jealousy-invoker? I'm the same as you, Ella, that's why I'm single. Or, mostly, anyway," he flicks his hair arrogantly.

"Did you know what I was when you asked me out?" My eyes narrow with suspicion.

"Yes, I've known for a long time. My father has a project running that specifically looks for people like us, because we're still very much a minority. I sneak a look at his files from time to time to see if he's found anyone else like me."

He clasps his hands together and clicks his wrists before continuing,

"Did you know he sent me to boarding school purely so that I was far enough away from him whilst he studied all my test results and tried to figure out what I was and if I was dangerous? My own father was scared of me! In his line of work!" He opens his arms expressively and waits for a response. I let out an awkward fake laugh which he takes as an invitation to continue.

"It was kind of funny when I figured it out first, with my 16-year-old sweetheart. Well, not funny, emotionally scarring. I thought I'd done something wrong, physically. Her biggest fear was drowning so, just as she climaxed, she started wiggling around on my dick making choking noises and crying. It was terrifying for us both.

"The next time I tried to have sex, the girl, who was very skinny, sprang off me making me jiz everywhere because she suddenly thought she was obese and was going to squash me to death. That's when I knew something wasn't quite right."

I notice Adam smirk, trying not to laugh. I guess I got lucky. The men I was with never told me what they saw, until Adam, and by comparison his fear is a lot more manageable.

"Wait, so, when you asked me out, was it because of what I am? Did you want to have sex with me just to see what happens if we're both whatever you called us?"

"Basically," he shrugs. "I'm not like my father, okay? But it's only natural to want answers, and I thought it would be useful to know what happens when two of us get together. Maybe we counteract each other, maybe we both suffer…"

"Well, I guess we'll never know," says Adam sternly. Obviously. We would never do that just for an experiment, would we? I keep my eyes down. "So, is that everything? Anything else you wanted to tell us?"

"I can tell you who her biological parents are too, if you're interested."

"Seriously?" I interject.

"Of course, how else did my father know about you?"

"So even if Adam and I had never met, I would still have ended up wrapped up in all this madness?"

"Most likely, yes."

"Well go on then, who are my parents?"

Jeremy lifts his coat from the back of the chair and digs into his inner chest pocket for a folded piece of paper. He unfolds it to reveal a printed photo of a woman who looks a lot like me but older and with an asymmetric bob haircut.

"This is your mum, Elaine Robertson. She was known in some circles as 'Nightmare' because she was like us, a P.I.N.S., and she was a prostitute. I don't have a photo of your dad, but I understand his name was David Watt and he

36

was a Dream-Walker. Average kind of guy. He was a greengrocer." I nod, and then pause.

"Wait a minute, you're using the past tense. Are they dead?"

"Unfortunately, yes, although it was only recent, and quite unusual."

"Typical." Of course I can't meet my biological parents. I could never be that lucky.

"Unusual how?" asks Adam. Jeremy adjusts his sleeves,

"Honestly, I suspect foul play. The police didn't investigate either of them too thoroughly, but they were weird. A bit too unlucky to be believable; especially considering they were both within the same week."

"Like, Dream-Walker suspicious?" asks Adam.

"Definitely, and they weren't even together, which makes it all the more unusual. These two people who hadn't seen each other in years, whose only connection was Ella, both died of freak accidents within the space of a few days, and both after your dad escaped." Jeremy looks pointedly at Adam.

"I don't think my dad had any reason to hurt Ella's birth parents, he's got a bit more on his plate right now, you know, taking over the world or whatever he's up to. I hardly think he's been going around killing Ella's parents 'just because.'" He sighs. "My dad tends to work with a purpose in mind. There would be nothing to gain from killing them."

"Hmm, so who do you think did have something to gain?" I notice Adam clench his jaw, refraining from taking the bait.

"How exactly did they die?" I steer us back to the point.

"I'd rather not say."

"Why?"

"It was unusual and beyond unlucky and, honestly, violent. Your mother's death was especially violent and

37

gory, and I just don't think I need to put that kind of image in your head."

"Well now you have to tell me!" I stand.

"Honestly, you won't believe me anyway. It sounds like something from one of those 'Final Destination' movies."

"Tell me, I want to know. If someone out there has killed my birth parents, I deserve to know how they did it." I walk over to the window.

Jeremy looks at Adam as if asking for permission.

"Erm, hello? I am a fully grown woman! I am not a child! You can tell me. I'm not going to faint! Come on! Spit it out!"

"She's right, just tell her, man," says Adam.

"Thank you!" I roll my eyes at him, then tilt my head at Jeremy and glare. I sit back down.

"Don't say I didn't warn you." He sighs. "Elaine was at the supermarket. There was a demonstration on at the cheese counter and the cheesemonger was slicing cheese with one of those sharp wires, and Elaine was watching."

"Don't try and tell me she had her arm chopped off, because that's not possible for two reasons 1) you can never get close enough to where they're chopping and 2) I'm pretty sure I read that it doesn't cut through skin. Not that badly, anyway. I'm sure it could do some damage, but to cause death would require a fair amount of force, and I don't see that situation occurring in a supermarket, however bizarre and unbelievable her death might have been."

They both turn to look at me. What? Who hasn't looked up whether cheese wire can cut through skin late at night? It practically jumps out at you after you look up how to cook bacon in the microwave, or eggs in the oven.

"Well I don't know if that's true, but no, she did not have her arm chopped off." Jeremy continues. "The cheese demonstration was just the reason she didn't see it coming; it was the distraction that prevented her from moving out of the way. You know those e-scooters people have now that go pretty darn fast, but are also pretty darn quiet?" I nod.

"Death by scooter?" I can't help interrupting again.

"Wait for it."

"Okay, but please skip to the point. I'm not going to react badly; I just want to know." I roll my head from side to side and try to click my neck.

"A young hoodlum came zooming into the supermarket on his scooter at top speed. People were dashing out of the way as he headed down the aisle towards the bottom of the shop where Elaine and a group of shoppers were standing watching the cheese. He made a sharp turn at the end as if he was aiming directly for the group. People began to scatter, Elaine was pushed backwards into some other shoppers, stumbling and reaching around to stop herself from landing on the ground. One woman fell first, then another, then soon they were falling like dominos and who was standing behind Elaine? A man who had just bought himself a new set of sharp kitchen knives, of course. The kind of guy who had already removed the packaging to check they were sharp enough for his purposes and so had them loose in his basket." He looks up at me to check I'm okay before continuing.

"So, in true slasher movie style, the basket tipped, Elaine fell, the knives went in her – more than one – and she died from those wounds. There was blood everywhere. Oh, and then one of those tall metal things the staff push around when they're stacking shelves was knocked over and tins of baked beans and spaghetti hoops crushed her, just to finish her off. See what I mean about unusual and extremely unlucky?" He looks at me and waits for me to react.

"Uhuh," I answer. "Where did you find all that out? Surely that's not in your father's files. That's quite a story."

"No, most of that was in the Dreamer Gazette two days ago. Are you ready to hear what happened to your father?"

"Go on, but please keep it short this time."

"Well, his death wasn't quite so dramatic. Short story, he was poisoned. But, more than once. It's as if someone didn't want to take any chances of him having an EpiPen nearby. It was his allergies that ultimately killed him, but they found traces of all sorts of chemicals he had seemingly been consuming for around a week. The coroner reckoned that if he hadn't had the allergic reaction, he would have died soon from the other toxins anyway."

"Huh. Now I bet that wasn't in the paper. By the way, where can I get a copy of this paper? I've never seen it in the newsagents."

"No, that information was via the Human Justice Department. As David was a Dream-Walker and died younger than expected, he fell into the category of people that my father insists have a thorough 'private' autopsy to check for biological mutations and deficiencies. My father is on high alert for anything that could cause Dream-Walkers to die out, as well as anything that could indicate higher powers."

It's a lot to take in. I look at Adam. What do we do now?

"Oh, and the paper, well, you just have to know where to get it, who to ask. It's there, you just have to know about it. Being a human, you would never come into contact with it accidentally. Even being a P.I.N.S. you won't be offered it. Adam should be able to get you a copy though, right mate?"

"I'm not your mate," Adam says through gritted teeth. Clearly story time is over and he is ready for Jeremy to leave.

"Well, thanks for coming and telling me all of that. It was… enlightening," I tell Jeremy, hoping he will take this as his cue to leave before things get heated. This has all gone much smoother than I thought it was going to; Adam really gave him a good chance to explain. Adam is such a good guy. Jeremy stands and places his coat over his left arm.

Just at that moment, the hotel room phone rings and Adam quickly answers it and waits for an outside line to be patched through.

"It's Kyle," he says, looking up, before continuing to listen. He frowns a lot, then seems to agree to something, then looks back at Jeremy and me. He puts the phone back in its holder.

"I can't believe I'm about to say this, but can you keep an eye on Ella and make sure nobody takes her?"

Jeremy's smile widens, showing his perfectly straight white teeth.

"No problem."

"And no experimenting, okay?"

Before I can respond or hug or even kiss him goodbye, he's grabbed his coat and swung out of the room.

Jeremy and I look at each other and my eyes fall back on yesterday's knickers, placed so closely by his side on the dresser. He sits back down and places his coat back over the back of the chair.

"What do you want to do now then?" he asks suggestively. "I won't tell if you don't," he winks. Shit. Oh boy oh boy am I in trouble now. Why did I have to have that dream?

Ella

The room falls silent with Adam gone; I don't think I dare to speak. But I've got to say something, we can't just sit here in silence until he comes back – he might be gone for hours, or worse, days!

"So, er…"

Jeremy looks at me, his blue eyes bright and alert.

"You should know, I would never have gone out with you if Kristina hadn't already suggested it."

"Really? Your little friend from the office?"

"She's almost as tall as you!"

He chuckles.

"Alright, don't get your knickers in a twist. I was only teasing, she's tall enough to be a model…" He raises his eyebrows and then strokes his chin as if in thought. I throw a pillow at him.

"She's far too young for you, don't even think about it!" He takes this as an invitation to move closer and sits on the bed next to me. I scurry closer to the headboard like a mouse. I need to keep some space between us.

"Are you scared of me?" He asks. I shake my head. "I'm not like them, Ella. Anything you do with me, will be entirely your decision. I can't influence your mind at all." He smiles, "now isn't that refreshing?"

"We're not going to 'do' anything. Okay?"

I stand up to put more room between us and start pacing, unable to keep still. I feel trapped, overwhelmed. I don't know what to do. All these men with their plans, chasing after the bad guys and all that bollocks, but I myself am what? Too weak to do anything useful? I have to be kept safe, stay put, don't do anything stupid.

That last thought strikes a nerve. Don't do anything stupid, especially with him. Why is he so calm? Can't he see I'm losing control of my life once again, there's a powerful monster on the loose and my birth parents might have been murdered?

"Ella, sit down. You're making me dizzy."

"Fine!" I sit in the armchair and glare at him.

"Why are you so angry?"

"I'm not!"

"Tell that to your leg," he responds curtly. I hold my leg to stop it bouncing like a rubber ball on lino.

"Is that better?"

"No." He comes over to me, crouching on the floor at my knees. "I came here to help you, Ella, not to stress you out."

"Well I am stressed out, okay? Telling me that going on a date with me was an experiment hardly helped matters."

I don't know why I said that. I don't care about that. Shouldn't I be thinking about my dead biological parents right now? He smiles at me and tilts his head,

"I see, is someone feeling sorry for themselves? That the director didn't want her for her body, only her ," he pauses, "oh wait, *only* her body?"

I push him away playfully.

"I thought you at least fancied me. Everyone said so, after I quit." I say quietly. What does it even matter now? I have Adam.

"I never said I didn't fancy you." He traces a finger gently across my thigh as he kneels beside the chair.

"You just admitted it. Earlier, you said you wanted to find out what would happen. It wasn't personal." I fold my arms and look away. He pulls at them to unlock them.

"I was hardly going to tell your boyfriend the truth, was I? He'd have never left us alone." He smirks, raising his eyebrows.

"You're too old for me, too."

"Or maybe I'm 'mature', 'experienced.'" He moves closer, both arms now on the chair around me. "I wasn't lying when I told you I wanted you."

"Obviously, because you wanted to know what would happen."

"No, Ella, I wanted you." He's so close, I try to avoid his eyes, but they're so in my face, so present, not looking away.

I close my eyes and screech.

"Leave me alone! Stop playing with me! I just want everyone to stop manipulating every bloody situation, okay?" He backs off.

"Alright, alright, but you should know, I don't give up easily. We could be great together, we just need to try. Age is just a number, and we, my dear, are two of a kind. It's a lot more destiny than a couple of guys who messed with your dreams."

After a bit more pacing, I plonk myself down on the bed and huff, but he doesn't even look my way. Perhaps he is finally going to shut up. I pick up the book I took from downstairs. They have one of those bookshelves visitors can put books they've finished reading on and pick up another one someone else has put back there. I didn't have

44

anything to offer in exchange, so I'll make sure I put it back before I leave. I can't read a full sentence before my mind starts wandering again.

I wonder where Adam has gone and what Kyle is up to now. Perhaps they are closing in on their dad. Perhaps it's nearly over.

Except, I know it isn't.

Getting their dad is only half the problem; it won't stop the Human Justice Department coming for me. But then again, if my dad really was a Dream-Walker then, surely, I'm allowed to know? Plus, I don't think the Minister has any right to detain me just because he's curious about me. And if he does have that power, then maybe someone should take it from him. Dethrone him.

"So how come you didn't enter the family business?" I ask Jeremy.

"I already said, I'd seen the other side and I didn't want to be a part of that."

"That's pretty brave."

"I'm more than just a pretty face, my dear, I'm also a bit of a bighead. I think it comes from my boarding school education." He puts on a 'posh' voice. "I have an unerring sense of righteousness, meaning I do what I want, when I want, and my father can't do anything to stop me."

"You do know that cocky attitude is exactly what I don't like about you?" I tease.

"Really? Well that is interesting to know." He drops that voice and puts on a rougher one. "Maybe you'd like me to level with you then, show a really soft and sincere side. Would that make you want to sleep with me?" Ugh, he almost had me then. I roll my eyes at him. He clears his throat and returns to using his normal voice.

"I can tell you about how horrible it was, my own dad observing me like a monster, an abomination, a freak. I wasn't even any different as a child, but he knew something

45

wasn't quite right. He just didn't know what it meant, what it signified. My mother was a Dream-Walker and I think he hoped I'd be a half Dream-Walker, so he was disappointed when I didn't show any signs of dream-walking. That didn't stop him testing me though. He was determined to figure out what was different about me."

"Oh yeah, I forgot you said Charmaine is your stepmother. What do you know about your real mum?"

"My birth mother died. She was gorgeous with long blonde hair and blue topaz eyes, much prettier than Charmaine, though my dad clearly has a type." He pauses and smiles as if remembering something amusing.

"I didn't tell him about my 'dalliances' with the ladies, so when my reputation started to make its way to him, he was furious. He said I was tainting the family name, so I changed my surname by proxy at eighteen. He thought I was a ladies' man, a scoundrel, a man-whore. By the time the other rumours reached him, much darker, the type he'd been eagerly awaiting since my birth, I was far beyond his reach. There would be no more experiments. My childhood in the lab had finished long ago. Perhaps there were signs he should have seen... I'll never know what went through his head once he realised, but I'm sure it was disappointment – Not disappointment at losing me, disappointment at not figuring me out in time and losing his chance to experiment on me, a P.I.N.S., the new area he so desperately wanted to explore."

I curl up in a ball.

"Do you want to talk about it?" he asks.

"What?"

"Childhood? Life? Whatever's bothering you. I can listen, I promise."

"Yeah, right, you seem like a great listener." I mock.

"What?"

46

"How long was that monologue just now? I nearly fell asleep. And earlier, telling the story of my mum's death – how many unnecessary details?" I tease.

"I was trying to give you the full picture but fine, you can sleep if you want. It is getting late, I suppose. And, like I said earlier, you're safe with me. I can't get into your head. Not forcibly anyway."

I gasp,

"What are you implying?"

"I'm not saying you won't dream of me, just that I won't be the one putting myself there. If you dream of me, it's because you want to. Remember that."

I lean back on the bed. It's a very good point, smoothly made. And until two nights ago, I had never dreamt about him. I was so wrapped up in Adam and Kyle, that was more than enough man for my brain to obsess over. Besides, I don't understand Jeremy. I understand coming to tell me (finally) what I am; but sticking around to watch over me? It's weird. He must be hoping for something, other than the obvious.

Perhaps he wants to team up, pins against the world! We could destroy bad guys, but only through having sex with them, one at a time... I shudder at the thought of having sex purely for the side effect of hurting the person I'm doing. It's the most backwards thing I've ever heard. Sex is for love, for lust at minimum. It's for enjoyment and pleasure. I cannot and will not ever do it purely to, well, stick a pin in someone.

POP.

Oh, it is such a ridiculous acronym. What does it stand for again?

"Hey, what does P.I.N.S. stand for again?"

"Pessimistic Instigator of Negative Stimuli."

Well, if that's what I am, I suppose I am destined to burst bubbles. Pop love with a sharp prick.

47

I can't believe I just thought that.

And with Jeremy right here.

Oh, Jeremy.

What would happen if two pins tried to pop each other? That really is the question.

Ella

I can't believe Adam still hasn't come back, it's been hours! I can't stay awake much longer.

Why would he leave me here with Jeremy, the man I only recently admitted I nearly slept with before we properly got together? Did he know he'd be away this long? He must really trust me. I wish I shared that faith.

The more hours we spend together, the less irritatingly smooth and well educated he seems, and the more convincing his argument that we should see what happens if we sleep together becomes.

But I can't do that to Adam.

I won't.

I'm not like that. I'm not that kind of girl.

I wish I had someone to talk to about all of this, someone I could discuss this with, who could help keep me on the right path. Kristina, Viva, even my adoptive mum – a bit of criticism might help my resolve not to live up to her perpetually low standards of me.

But I can't. If I told any of them, they'd be wanted by the HJD too. They wouldn't be wanted for experiments like me, but they'd be kept like lab rats or messed with until they couldn't think straight so as not to pose a threat to the secrecy of the Dream-Walkers.

If somebody had said to me a year ago that I could have a boyfriend, but I'd have to give up everything I had and everyone I knew, would I have agreed?

Honestly, yes. Probably. It's the mindset I was in. I was fed up of men always letting me down, ghosting me, and what friends did I have? I'd lost touch with Viva, deliberately cut ties with my adoptive mum, and any old school friends were long gone. All I really had was a crappy job, and Kristina, who, let's face it, was only really a colleague, despite our rapport.

But what if I'd had another option, whereby I would still lose my life as I knew it and everyone in it, but where I would also find the answers I've been unknowingly searching for since I turned eighteen and became sexually active? Where I could finally figure out what I am and why the men always disappear after sex. What if I could even find the one man who isn't affected by me, who could even heal me? Perhaps we could heal each other. An orgasmic explosion with no 'negative stimuli.' Two magnets attracted instead of repulsed. Pulled together. Hard to separate, unlike all those men I have repelled over the years.

Not that I was a whore, just a modern woman. A serial dater for whom the relationship always ended just as it was starting to get serious. But you know that. You know me. I fell for Adam in my dreams, and then in real life. Except it wasn't Adam in my dreams. And then there's the whole Kyle thing.

If there's one thing Jeremy has in his favour, it's being an only child. No identical siblings to pop up and confuse me. Not that I know of, anyway. There'd better not be.

Plus, he doesn't have a relationship with his mum either, so he understands me. We've spent hours tonight sharing theories about what our mothers might have been like. He's kind of a sweet guy, beneath the womanising exterior.

Now that I understand that he's like me, I understand the series of women. He's no worse than I am, and I refuse to judge myself for something out of my control.

Jeremy is watching me now as I return from the ensuite in my Disney Princess pyjamas. Thank God I picked up pyjamas, I'd joked to Adam that I wouldn't need them anymore. As I walk under the air con unit, I wish I'd kept my bra on. It's a little chilly and it feels as if Jeremy's eyes can see straight through the thin cotton blend. I rush to the bed and get under the covers.

"Do you want me to stay awake, or shall I try to sleep here?" Jeremy asks from the armchair. Well, I don't know where else he's going to sleep. He can't get in the bed with me, that's just asking for trouble. Even if he does keep pointing out that with him, I don't have to worry about him getting into my dreams.

That's not my biggest issue right now. My biggest issue is him getting into my pants. Of him being a horny red-blooded male. I can hardly allow him to spoon me, can I?

And besides, he's meant to be keeping me safe. I think we'll both be vulnerable if he drops his guard to have a cuddle.

Finally, I tell him to put the chair against the door and get in, but he must stay on top of the covers, fully dressed, and face away from me. He obliges, but it feels awkward. I roll onto my back and pull his shoulder so he lies on his back too.

"Fine, I give in, you can lie on your back," I tell him.

He rolls over further to face me properly.

"But I want to face you."

Those bloody sea blue eyes! I thought I was into Adam and Kyle's chocolatey brown eyes, but Jeremy's hit differently. It's like he can see through me. I suppose it's that darn 'understanding' aspect again. We know each other, even though we don't. There's some weird innate thing inside us that recognises something within each other. It feels like it's pulling me home.

I look at his pink lips, almost pursed as if he knows I want to kiss him. As if he knows I'm losing the battle.

"I'm good at keeping secrets, you know, if you want to find out. No strings attached."

I bite my lip. Adam would know. I know he would. And he would never forgive me. He can't even get over what happened between me and Kyle, and that was in my sleep. Mostly. If I do this, there's no going back. I swallow. Should I?

I want to know, but, what if there's another way? Is this the quickest way? What if there are negative consequences? It's not a hook up, it's an experiment. And nobody knows the side effects. It's an unregulated trial. But he's watching me, and he's not getting any closer. He's letting me decide, and he smells so good.

It's an oaky yet zesty and alluring scent, somehow manly yet with a hint of luxury spa shower gel. I close my eyes and breathe slowly, in, and out, like in yoga. I need to make a calm and rational decision.

Just as I feel myself slowly sinking towards him, eyes still closed, there's a bang as the door crashes open into the chair, forcing it further into the room. My eyes fly open and Jeremy springs to action and then immediately falls to the floor like Neville Longbottom in that Harry Potter film when Hermione puts a spell on him as they're sneaking out of the dormitory.

I scramble to stand up beside the bed, crossing my arms over my boobs. Now is not the time for a nipple erection.

There's a man looming in the doorway like something out of a horror film. He's standing there, waiting for me to scream or try to run or throw something at him. He's a predator playing with his prey, and I know who he is.

The man before me, trying his utmost to look like a bad guy despite his aging body, is none other than Gerome Clarke, Adam and Kyle's dad. I know not to underestimate his fifty-six-year-old body, I know he is powerful. Possibly the most powerful of them all. And him being here is no coincidence.

I thought I was insignificant to him, I thought only the Human Justice Department were after me; clearly, I was wrong.

I've lost the ability to speak. I don't know what to say. I'm frozen too, of my own accord, and I haven't blinked once. I've been practicing.

"So, you must be Ella," he says, slowly entering the room and stepping over the chair and Jeremy's flaccid body. "The pathetic human my boys love," he spits out the words. "Except, maybe you're not so human after all?" He tilts his head. "I've been here a while, watching, listening… You're not quite 'normal' are you? You're worse. You're like him." He kicks Jeremy's lifeless body. I'm still unable to speak. I open my mouth, but nothing comes out.

"You're lucky that I'm here. I don't know what you've heard about me, but I'm your best bet. Your best chance of finding out what you really are and who your real parents are. I'm powerful, I'm sure you know that, but I'm not all bad. I help those who help me. And I could use your help, Miss Thompson."

My eyes are getting dry, it's quite a strain not to blink. It's going to happen; I can't help it. I can't hold them open any longer. He moves even closer to me, but I stare straight ahead, focused.

"Ella, I know who your mother is. Your real mother, and your real father. If you help me, I will introduce you. Then you can play happy families, and you won't have to fuck

53

this douchebag. You can stay with my boys, they love you, I thought you loved them. Are you good enough for my boys, Ella? Do you deserve their love? Or are you more human scum that I should clean off the face of the earth?"

"I, I…" I still can't form words or even focus on what he's saying, my eyes are watering and taking all of my attention. I'm going to blink, I'm going to –

8 hours earlier…

Kyle

My chosen base of operations is discrete but well-equipped. It's one of the better sites used by The Resistance but was easy to obtain because everyone agrees that this mission is of top-level importance. Gerome Clarke must be recaptured before he can cause too much damage. We have some of the best technology, access to vehicles, and fast exit routes. This is not a place that suffers with congestion during rush hour, nor poor Wi-Fi. We have the fastest and most reliable connection in the country because The Resistance made some invaluable friends back when the internet was just starting to show its value. It really is all about who you know.

"What are you doing here?" My eyes narrow as the familiar red-haired woman stalks into my mission control room in a tailored plaid blazer with matching skirt, high stiletto heels and her hair carefully curled into perfect waves down her back. At least she's made an effort today, less crazed stalker and more psychopathic ex. She just won't leave me alone, Frankie-Lou, or 'Donna' as she introduced herself to Ella.

"I'm here to help of course!" She surveys my team. "By the looks of it, you need me," she says with her usual tone of disdain.

We do not need her getting in the way. I have everyone I need right here, people I have personally selected and trust to get the job done. No psycho exes and only one whom I suspect used to have a crush on me because, well, sometimes that can't be helped. Tasha receives a harder scowl from Frankie as if she knows.

"What do you know about where my dad is then? What do you have that can help us?" I ask her.

"Well," she saunters closer and pulls up a chair, "wouldn't you like to know." She giggles and sits down. Tasha shoots her a glare and Max and Jake smirk.

"Just cut the crap and say what you want to say or be on your way, we don't have time for this." I huff.

"We're closer than we thought," she raises her eyebrows at me. "You and I, we have more in common… Nothing too strong, we're not siblings, don't worry, but I may have discovered a connection."

"May have or you have?" I don't have time for her games.

"Fine, I have."

"And the connection is?" I snap.

"You're not your dad's first born."

I roll my eyes. It comes as no surprise that my dad played the field, and I don't see how that connects me to her in the slightest.

"And you know who is?" I ask, humouring her.

"Yep," she grins.

"And why do you expect me to care? Is my dad with them now?"

"Oh, probably not. I don't think he's seen her since he met your mum." I sigh.

"So why did you need to come and tell me this now? How does it help me? How does it help this mission?"

I flap open my arms, expressing my frustration to the room. I just want her to leave and stop slowing us down. I don't care if I have a half-sister out there. If my dad's not with her, then who gives a shit? He's probably got a load of love children out there if I wanted to go digging for siblings. Now is not the time.

"Because it's a pattern of behaviour and it leads us to new connections, who may or may not be helping him."

Okay, perhaps she has a point. He's been inside a long time, he might be calling on old acquaintances. I wonder whatever happened to Al', the one he said he escaped with originally.

Frankie comes to stand beside me then pushes me out of her way and points to the chair she has just vacated. She's hijacking my meeting.

"Who's ready to hear a story?" She clasps her hands together and doesn't wait for an answer. "It was 1985 I think, when Gerome Clarke met my aunt, Bethany Parker or 'Beth' as she liked to be called. She was one of his first recruits."

Kyle

"Shortly after escaping Herthmoor with Al', Gerome lured Beth and Jennifer when they freed more Dream-Walkers from other cages. Gerome told them his mission, and they were only too happy to join the cause. They were young and idolised this 'cool' and powerful older boy."

I stand to interrupt.

"Okay, so there's Al', Beth, and Jennifer. Where are they now?"

"Don't you want to hear the rest?" Asks Frankie, irritated.

"I think that's all we need, but get to the point if there's more you'd like to add."

"Well, long story short," she rolls her eyes, "Aunt Beth was a lesbian and after years of disturbing sexual dreams invoked by Gerome, he took things a step further. He raped my aunt and got her pregnant. He planned for them all to raise the baby together, but Beth refused to play happy families. She accused him of rape and threatened to kill the baby. She ended up spending a lot of her pregnancy asleep to the world so that she couldn't cause the baby any harm. Later, she found out that Gerome had twisted the story round so that Al' was the rapist, he was locked up, and

59

Jennifer was going to raise the baby with Gerome, after they committed Beth to an asylum." Her eyes scan the room in search of sympathy.

"So where's the baby now? Do you know who she is?" Tasha asks.

"Aunt Beth doesn't remember ever meeting her baby. She thinks it's a girl, but all we really know is that he/she is a couple of years older than Kyle and Adam, so about thirty."

"Hold on, so all you have to go on is your psycho aunt?" I scoff. Perhaps the whole family is crazy.

"She's telling the truth! Why would she lie about that?" Frankie stands her ground at the front of the room.

"Plenty of people came forward with stories about my dad, I doubt they're all true. Some people just crave the attention, the sympathy," I raise my eyebrows at her, Attention Seeker No. 1.

"I have proof! There are photos of the four of them, which proves they were a group, and my aunt has a scar from a caesarean so evidently, she's carried a baby. And doesn't it sound exactly like your dad to lock up anybody who threatens to go against him? Of those three early followers of Gerome's Resistance, one is in a psych ward, one got locked up somewhere charged with rape, and the other..."

"Yes, the other?"

"I'm not sure."

The room falls silent as I try to decide on the best plan of action. It's annoying always having to be the one who comes up with the plan. I'm a natural leader, I suppose, but I hate how it's always expected of me.

"Have you got any proof we can see right now?" asks Jake, who had been keeping quiet so far.

"They were in the papers in the mid/late eighties, leading protest marches. I'd try the Dreamer's Gazette or something, my Aunt has snippings."

Of course she has snippings! She probably also has a scrapbook of pictures of herself cut out and stuck next to my dad. She's probably just another obsessed lunatic like Frankie. The apple doesn't fall far from the tree and all that.

"Alright, Jake, you work with Frankie and follow up on these women, let me know if you find anything useful – especially who or where Jennifer might be now. Max and Tasha, you can help me try to find Al' and work out what really went down. We need leads to his current location, we can't spend too long looking into the past, okay? If there are no fresh leads, it's back to following the news for trends and working out my dad's next targets, okay?" Everyone agrees.

But Max and Tasha and I are going to do a bit more than I've just announced. I'm also going to scan the database for partial matches to my DNA. I'm going to find out if Dad had any siblings, or if my older half-sibling is on there, and I'll bet it's going to be a lot quicker and more successful than interrogating Frankie's crazy aunt.

*

"Do you believe what she just told us?" asks Tasha, in the car. She always seems too kind and gentle to be a part of The Resistance. She's a walking juxtaposition, a petite blonde you do not want to underestimate. Or meet in a dark alleyway. That girl can kick serious ass and all without smudging her lip gloss. Hence, she's on my team.

"Not at all, but you know Frankie, she'd never leave us alone if she thought we weren't taking her seriously, she'd chase us around the country getting in the way, so it's better to let her get on with it; let her think she's helping. Jake will keep her in check. And you never know, maybe there is some value in what her aunt has to say, if they dig deep enough."

"I wouldn't wanna be Jake right now," laughs Max. Max is a big guy, as is Jake, both chosen for their physical strength and unbreakable determination. But Max has always been able to crack a joke when things get tough, he's a great one for lifting the mood and making you come up for air. I also suspect he has a soft spot for Tasha, but he's yet to act on it. I think they'd make a good couple.

Our first stop is a Resistance building with backdoor access to the HJD's Medical Database, not far from our base of operations. The only reason we don't have this technology at our base is because we deliberately have different technology and capabilities at each site so that if ever one is discovered, the HJD will not be able to figure out everything we know. We'll always have a few secrets left to play with.

The lab is quiet and grey, and I feel uber-aware of Tasha's noisy heels clip-clopping on the floor as we enter. I nod to the techs, and they look back down, uninterested. They know who we are and what we're likely to be doing here. Everyone wants the same thing now, so it's somewhat of a free-for-all down here at the moment. You used to have to check in and be allotted a time.

We load my sample into the system and wait for it to run through looking for matches. Whilst it does, Tasha unlocks another nearby PC and begins working through all the Als on the system as I have momentarily forgotten what Al' is short for. Alan? Albert? Alexander? She adds search keywords: rape / dream-rape / Gerome / Beth.

"Okay, I think I might have something! Albert Fox. Brought in in June 1990, accused of raping a girl whilst she was unaware and in a dream state, believed to be dangerous and part of a secret organisation. Locked up indefinitely.

No visitors since 2001 – when did your dad get caught?" I don't answer. "If it's him, he's only twenty miles away."

"Great work, Tash," Max rubs her back, and she looks up at him and blushes. Perhaps she likes him too. That's cute.

The other computer pings, having finished searching for matches to my DNA.

"Alright guys, let's see who we've found!" We crowd around the screen.

57 decent matches. Bloody hell, maybe I have half-siblings everywhere! It's brought up Dad so we can then filter the results to show the ones which match the most with both of us. Then, looking at the ages of the matches…

"Okay, look there," I point at the screen, "there's a match that's sixty years old! And it's a super high match with my dad. That's got to be a brother, right? An older brother!" I grab a scrap of paper and scribble down his name, Marcus. Uncle Marcus. It says that he was born in the cage at Herthmoor, like my dad, but that he was released as he didn't show any signs of being a Dream-Walker. There's no current address, but he shouldn't be too difficult to track down. If the police can do it, I'm sure we can.

"Look!" says Tasha scrolling down the page and pointing at another name, Maria. Thirty years old and a reasonable match with both of us. "Do you think?" We all look at each other.

"Yep, I think we just found Frankie's cousin and my half-sister," I confirm.

"But it doesn't say where she is," says Tasha, biting her nail. We quietly read through the information on screen.

"I wonder," I say, taking over control of the mouse and keyboard and typing her Dream-Walker number into another search box. "Look, she was adopted!"

"Makes sense, one parent was locked in a psych ward, the other busy ruining lives. It was never going to work out with that other girl and Gerome raising Frankie's aunt's child. We know Gerome went off to have you, for a start. Who adopted her?" asks Max.

"Jennifer Carmichael, née Bridge. Current address, 19 Avondale Close, West Guilten."

"Carmichael? As in…" Tasha looks at me.

Tasha Carmichael.

Kyle

"Tasha, I think it's time you introduced us to Mummy and Daddy, don't you?" I tease. The poor girl is in shock. I've never seen her so quiet and fidgety.

"Do you really think…?" She looks up at me through the hair that has fallen over her face. I nod. Max puts his arm around her.

"But she's my sister, she's not, I mean, she can't be… She's my sister! And then, well, my mum… Jennifer, Jenny… Do you really think she's the Jenny from Frankie's story? The Jenny that was with Beth and Al' and your dad back in the eighties?"

"Maybe, it would make sense."

I let Max do the consoling, rubbing her arm and trying to make her feel like the rug hasn't just been pulled out from under her. I don't know what I can say to help. If we're right, her mum has been lying to her for her entire life, but for good reason. Tasha and her sister wouldn't have had the same childhood if people had known who their mum was, who she had been in the eighties. Helping my dad was a punishable crime by the end of it, and she was the only one left out in the wild, as it were.

I wonder, with Beth in a mental health facility, and Al' locked up for rape, how did Jenny get off so lightly?

Tasha and Max look great together, I should pat myself on the back for uniting them. First Adam and Ella, now Tasha and Max. It's a shame I can't help myself the same way. My true love is gone and all I have left is this pit of anger and emptiness and a lust for revenge. I want to make Philip pay for what he took from me. Not just a girl, my girl. My future.

Revenge was the only reason I wanted to free my dad in the first place and yet here I am tracking him down to put him back inside because he's too selfish, and dangerous. He doesn't want to help me because he's too busy trying to take over the world. I have to let my hopes of revenge go because once Dad is back inside, there is no chance. He's the only one who can help me.

Why does everyone else get to have a happy ending, and I get nothing? Ingratitude is what I get. I bet Adam's still mooning over what I did with Ella, too.

I wonder how different my life would be if Izzy was still here. If we'd got married like we'd planned, would we have moved away? Would I have left The Resistance? Would we have children by now?

Philip killed the only person who ever really 'got' me, so what hope is left for me now? I'll never meet another girl like her.

Even Ella, whom I'll admit I like considerably more than I should, is not the same. She doesn't have the vivacity, the wild side that I miss so badly. Izzy was the perfect girl for me, and she burned to death in her sleep.

I realise I'm clenching my fists and staring at Tasha and Max. I blink to break my gaze and shift my focus to the matter at hand, Tasha's mum, Jenny. It's time to find out more about her time with my dad.

*

When we arrive at Tasha's family home, Frankie and Jake are already there preparing to knock on the door.

"You figured it out too, huh?" I ask as we walk over to them.

"It makes sense, Tasha's sister's the right age, and her mum's name is Jenny. It doesn't get much simpler than that," says Jake.

"Did you get anything more out of the aunt?"

He twirls his finger beside his head and pulls a face behind Frankie's back.

"Nothing more to add, just a photo." He pulls it out of his pocket. It's a group shot of the four of them. Cute but, damn, I really do take after my dad.

"Right, are we going to do this then?" Asks Tasha, springing to the front of the group. "I think I should go first, so they don't run." She knocks on the door.

Tasha's mum looks just how I'd imagined with long mostly blonde hair and bright blue eyes. She's a good match for the photograph I just looked at, but also has a strong resemblance to Jeremy, the Minister's son. I know he has those same bright blue eyes. I wonder if she has a history with Francis Krunk which could explain her remaining free in the world whilst her friends were locked up in various facilities. I must remember to investigate that later.

She seems surprised to see us all standing here like I don't know what, a band of misfits? A few tough guys, her daughter and a random ginge? I shouldn't say that, I know, but Frankie doesn't mind. She's always embraced her red hair; she loves anything that makes her stand out from the crowd. She loves being the centre of attention. She welcomes the banter.

But now's not the time to tease her about her hair colour, she's being helpful for a change. I wonder what her motive is, besides hoping to meet her long-lost cousin. There's got to be one, she's Frankie. She's more conniving than I am most of the time. I think that's why we've fallen together so many times. We use each other. She's got nothing on my Izzy, but she does tickle that itch. You know, when you just want to 'be' with someone. Someone you can tease and piss off, and then make up with. She drives me mad, but I can never completely leave her in the background. Subconsciously, I wanted her to turn up and help on this search. I was waiting for her.

Fuck. That's not something I wanted to admit. Now, or any day.

We're going in.

It's a lovely house, it's big and modern, and it must have 6 bedrooms or so. I had no idea Tasha came from money, she could've put a bit more into our fundraiser last year! Although, I do wonder how they made their money. I feel bad when Dream-Walkers manipulate the systems of humans, making them look the other way whilst they take things for free. It's ruining their economy, and if their world crumbles, so does ours.

I think some of us forget that we all live in the same world, there is no 'other level.' We all live amongst each other. If the train from London to Canterbury gets cancelled, there are both humans and Dream-Walkers left waiting on the platform. Sure, the Dream-Walkers might have an easier time rearranging their travel plans to get to where they need to go, but that's not the point.

Maybe I've been spending too much time near Adam, I'm sure it never used to bother me so much. I really need to get out of my head and focus. They're already talking around me, and I'm supposed to be in charge.

Mr Carmichael is out, which is probably for the best as he may not know all his wife's secrets. Tasha has already started questioning her mum, so I let her continue. So far, I think she has admitted that yes, she was in The Resistance with Gerome and yes, Maria is Beth's daughter. She said she took her in to keep her safe, though she admitted that Gerome told her to.

"Have you heard from him since he got out?" asks Tasha.

"Got out?" Jenny frowns.

"Yes, got out. Gerome is on the loose. Have you not seen the news? Have you not heard about the strange incidents occurring? Did that not ring any bells with you, from before?"

"Honey, no. I haven't seen the news, and I try not to think about before." She smiles, but it doesn't quite reach her eyes. I don't trust her.

"Well he's out so, has he contacted you? Is he likely to? How did you leave things… before?"

Jenny

"How did you leave things… before?"

Tasha's words go round and round in my head. How do I answer that? He broke my heart, but I made the best of it. I did as I was told, I started a new life without him. I can't admit that I've been writing to him. I can't admit that I've been keeping tabs on what she gets up to with the latest 'Resistance' just in case she has information about him. She wouldn't understand, none of them would.

"He told me he had to leave, that people were going to take him, so I was to look after the baby – Maria – and start a new life, but never admit that he's her father."

"And that was it? You never heard from him again?"

The man taking charge now is clearly Gerome's son, Kyle. I've heard about him and worried that Tasha would fall for him when she first joined The Resistance. He looks so much like his father.

"Well, I heard on the grapevine that he hadn't been taken, that he'd married your mother and had twins, but that was all. I didn't have any direct contact. Just the usual gossip like everyone else."

"Can we trust you, Jenny?" he asks seriously. His gaze reminds me of his father's and sends shivers down my spine. That was a look reserved for those he tortured, he never looked at me that way.

"Of course, why wouldn't you be able to?" I try to appear nonchalant.

"When you were with them, the original Resistance, what was your relationship like with my dad?" His eyes narrow as if daring me to lie but I'm not put off, I'm used to it after all these decades. Lies slip off my tongue like ice, cold and slippery and impossible to take back.

"Like slave and master. I did as I was told, until he took things too far."

Kyle shakes his head.

"You mean, until he left. And you did as you were told even then, looking after Beth's baby and keeping her real father's identity a secret. Why did you remain loyal? Even after everyone turned on him and he was captured?" It's like he knows, or suspects.

"I did it for Maria. I didn't want her dragged into all this. She's always been such a kind girl. She's taken after my husband, Rob. She's a vet!" I tell them, proudly. Kyle nods slowly,

"And where is she now?"

"At work."

"Would you mind calling her please, to check she's okay?"

It's a reasonable request so I agree and reach for my phone. I can't help feeling a little nervous, it must be the tension in the room. I'm sure she's fine, but she doesn't even know who Gerome is. What if he has come for her? What if he needs something from her that he can't get from his sons? Although, if that is the case, why didn't he respond to my letters? Is he upset with me?

"Now please, ma'am." One of the other men steps forward. He's quite a beefcake.

I start scrolling and tapping my phone, mistouching everything. My hands are shaking. She doesn't know who he is. She wouldn't recognise him. She wouldn't have known not to close her eyes. Even if she did, even if somebody from our community had filled her in on the latest gossip, that this dangerous Dream-Walker was on the loose, he could make her do anything, no problem. She'd be clueless as to why she'd been targeted. So unprepared. I should have told her. I should have warned her. If she'd joined The Resistance like Tasha, at least she would have learnt how to fight. But my poor Maria, she's so gentle. She wouldn't hurt a fly.

I look up and show them my phone. The call has gone through to her voicemail, so she's probably with a patient.

Is that what you call animals at the vets? Patients? I'll have to ask. Gosh, I'm such a terrible mother, and wife. I should know that! There are two vets in this family, and I don't even know if they call pets 'patients'! No wonder Gerome's son is looking at me like that, I'm unbelievable.

"Send her a message asking her to call you, urgently," he orders.

I do as I'm told but I'm sure she's just busy. This is just a coincidence. Unless Gerome really has come back for her.

"I could call reception, just to check?" I suggest.

"Please Mum," asks Tasha, concern etched across her beautiful face.

Nobody picks up. I start to panic.

"Somebody always answers at the front desk, even if it's full-blown chaos in reception with dogs chasing cats and whatnot. Something's wrong."

"Give us the address."

Once again, I do as I'm told, even showing him the vet clinic on Google Maps.

"There's a car park right by it…" I start to explain, but they're already halfway out the door.

72

"If Gerome reaches out, call Tasha." Kyle provides his final instruction before they split off into two cars and drive away.

Before I can sit down, I hear movement on the stairs. I turn around and feel my heart rebound in my chest. He takes slow steps, almost teasing me. First, I see his feet in heavy boots, then his knees covered by black slim fit jeans made for a younger man, his waist, still slim unlike most men his age, his chest covered by a thin long-sleeved top, and finally, his head. He has aged a lot since I saw him last, but he still looks healthy; he still looks dangerous and ruthless.

"Thank you for getting rid of them, I almost believed you myself," says Gerome, coming to stand in front of me. I can't believe he's really here; I've dreamt of this moment. I had no idea he was upstairs. I would never have sent them away if I had.

Would I?

He brushes some of my hair behind my ear.

"I knew I could count on you."

He leans in to kiss me as my heart pounds, and I try to resist the innate impulse to close my eyes. *Don't do it, Jenn, don't do it.* But his aftershave stings my eyes, and I can't help it, as our lips touch, I blink.

One of his hands grips both of my wrists as he shoves a blindfold on me to maintain my visual darkness and his control. He ties me up and secures me somewhere as in my head I see Maria being chased by a pack of wolves.

"Gerome, please…" I whimper.

"Why are you acting so surprised? I told you I was coming back. You've done a great job raising my girl but, did you have to make her such a pussy? She was expressing a dog's anal glands when I got to the vets this morning and I thought, what is my daughter degrading herself doing that

73

for? She is a Clarke. And then I realised, no, she's a Carmichael. You made her weak like him."

He leaves me then, to sleep, or starve, or die. I hear his footsteps retreat and then nothing but silence. I don't think he's ever coming back.

How could I have been such a fool for so many years? How could I have ever believed that he loved me, cared for me, that we would be together in the end? He used me. He was always using me. I did everything he asked me to, and for what?

I lean my head back against the wall I feel behind me, and let the tears soak my eye mask before running down my face. I can't wipe them anyway.

Memories come floating back to the front of my mind, showing me how I got here, how I ended up in this situation. My foolish younger self taunts me. It's like Younger Me is narrating the scenes, explaining my previous actions; it's like I'm dreaming, but these events really happened, and I really felt that way. I loved Gerome.

How could I have been so stupid?

Jenny (1985)

You never forget your first love. That's what they say, isn't it? So, I'll never forget Gerome Clarke. I adore him. He's just so… him. He's masculine, confident, he knows what he wants and he's going to get it. I believe in him. I want him to succeed. Okay, he pushes the boundaries sometimes, but who doesn't love a bad guy? And he's not bad really, my mother wouldn't approve, certainly, but he's fighting for a good cause. He's fighting for us. For all of us. The Dream-Walkers. Everything he says is right and true.

I let the scene wash over me and allow Younger Me to tell our story. I see it through her eyes, with her narration.

*

I'm watching him, watching us. His little crew. The founding members of The Resistance. I wonder if he feels my gaze. I know he knows I love him, but he never acts on it. Not when I'm awake, anyway. I would love for him to hold me in his arms in front of everyone, perhaps on one of the platforms after one of his empowering speeches. I would love for him to embrace me and announce to the world that I'm his girl, his woman. The future Mrs Gerome Clarke.

But I understand why he can't. He needs women to fancy him, he thinks it will help lure them into joining us. Into fighting with us against the Human Justice Department. He needs me to lure men in, too. Neither of us can be seen to be dating, it would only hurt the cause.

I sometimes wonder if that's why he saved Beth, why he asked her to join us, to attract another sector of the population. She's a little younger than me, and my absolute opposite. I appear angelic with smooth blonde hair, good manners, and a 'sweet' personality; she's a lioness with a frizzy mane of red hair, an addiction to neon green clothes and accessories, wears thick eyeliner like a rockstar and oozes attitude. Oh, and she hates men. Including Gerome. We have never discussed her sexual preferences, but I guarantee she is more into me than she is Gerome, or Al'.

Al' is the other member of our crew. He was here before me. He escaped from a cage with Gerome, so he's been with him from the start. He's older than the rest of us, and I think he has already started to lose his way. He used to laugh when Gerome caused chaos, but now I think he's started to care for the humans a little too much. I see him wince at Gerome's laugh sometimes, like it physically hurts his insides; like he's pained by what he's released into the world.

If it weren't for Al' being placed in the same cage as Gerome, Gerome might never have desired to escape; we might never have ended up where we are now. It's all thanks to Al' and I think he feels that burden now. He worries if he's done the right thing.

Of course he's done the right thing! We've freed so many Dream-Walkers since we started! Okay, so Gerome has also incited some murder and we've stolen some money too, but we had to make a statement, right? And we needed the money to live, to fund our lifestyle of driving around the country and popping up where the HJD least expects.

"I think we're ready!" says Beth, adding the final painted sign to the pile. I finished the one I made for Gerome ages ago, hence I've been sitting here watching him ever since. I stand up and stretch my legs, folding myself forwards to release my spine and pointing my derrière in his direction. As I straighten back up, I glance over my shoulder and see him smirk and stamp out his cigarette. He noticed me.

We're protesting again today, hopefully making a name for ourselves in a new part of the country. It's nice here, a bit further away from a city than normal, with lots of trees. I feel like I can breathe. I feel like there's room for growth. I think we'll do good work here.

"Alright, here we go!" says Gerome, picking up the largest sign and leading the way. I follow quickly behind him, holding leaflets. "Justice for Dreamers!" he shouts, starting off a chant as he enters the street.

It's exhilarating. People come out to join us and prove that he does have a point, that we are fighting for good. Nobody wants the Human Justice Department to continue breeding Dream-Walkers like puppies, testing us and using us like slaves. The slave trade is over for humans, so why not for Dream-Walkers? Are we not as important? Shouldn't we be free too?

So many of the people here today have never seen the inside of a cage, they're the lucky ones. The ones allowed to live outside, provided they follow the rules. They have benefitted from their ancestors' obedience, but they understand our plight. They still want equality.

"No more testing!" shouts Gerome. The crowd cheers and starts to repeat it again, starting another chant. I begin handing out my leaflets, lovingly photocopied and folded last night. I smile and make eye contact with the men, *making them think they stand a chance, like my heart isn't already taken by somebody else; someone much more powerful than they could ever dream to be.*

Beth is raising her sign and stomping with spirit, her punk boots, once again, making quite a statement. Al' is bringing up the rear. He's doing what he has to, but his heart is clearly not in it. It's a shame, I figure Gerome probably counts on him to bring in the 'older' members of the community. If Gerome lures the younger women, I lure the men, and Beth lures the other women, then it makes sense that Al' is meant to lure in the rest: the mothers, grandmothers, and grandfathers... The people who look for a trustworthy face to believe in above all else. His look is less distinguished than Gerome's, and less versatile. His expression is one of permanent kindness. You can't not trust that face.

We've reached the platform now so the four of us climb up. Beth and I hurry to our usual position on one side of the platform, and Al' stands opposite us, whilst Gerome takes centre stage. The crowd quietens.

"Hello my glorious Dream-Walker community!" The crowd roars then quickly hushes again as if being controlled by an unseen force. "Who here knows what it's like to grow up in a cage?" Silence. "No one? Well, aren't you the lucky ones? There are people like us locked up and being experimented on every day under the cover of 'safety' and 'precaution.' Do we not deserve to be treated as equals? We are stronger than them! They are right to be afraid, but they are wrong to contain us. Who are they to tell us what we can and cannot do? Our people deserve to be free. We need to fight the system! Who's with me?"

The crowd cheers and whoops and Gerome grins, lapping up the attention. He throws me a wink and my knees buckle.

"We are strong, we are powerful, and we have a right to decide our own destiny. Did you know they used to use me on prisoners? I was only a child, and I was used to manipulate paedophiles into killing themselves! Can you even imagine what those people dreamt about? The HJD would never approve of a regular human child being forced to endure anything like that, so why is it okay for Dream-Walkers? Are we not also human? The Human Justice Department is corrupt, and we need to destroy it. Justice for all, not just for them!"

Gerome signals for Beth to pass him the poster of Michael, a young man with a beautiful face.

"Michael was a good man. A father, a husband, an honest man just trying to do right by his family. The Human Justice Department found out he was one of us, pulled him from his ordinary life and forced him to help them torture spies. Spies! The violence and death he witnessed in their heads was too much for Michael, it destroyed him. They used him to take lives until in the end, he took his own. All because he was one of us. Is that 'fair'? Is that 'justice'? No!"

The crowd shouts in agreement, but Michael was not so innocent as Gerome makes out. He was not a good husband. His wife was a human, and their marriage was unhappy and violent. I looked into it once when we were passing by her hometown. She is much happier now. But that is beside the point. It could be true. That's what matters.

Today's crowds are fully accepting of this information. They are mostly young men and women like ourselves, and they are excited like I am by Gerome's dynamic presence

He signals with his hands for quiet and everyone obeys. We're coming to the clever part of Gerome's rallies.

"I'd like us all to take a minute, bow our heads, and send our thoughts to Michael's family. They don't even

know the truth! One of us, a Dream-Walker, will have provided them with another version of events to vaguely remember. They don't know what he was, what he went through. They probably think he left them of his own accord!"

The crowd boos.

"Please, let us have a moment of silence." He looks around to check his audience is still obeying his every command. They are. "Bow your heads, close your eyes, and think about what we could do if we were allowed to be free. If we weren't bred like puppies, kept like slaves, captured like criminals. If there were no rules governing us. Evoke love if you want to, reap revenge if you need to. Our skills could make this world a better place."

The crowd quietens again and all that can be heard is the hum of cars and buses on the nearest main road. It feels as if even the birds are partaking in this moment of silence. Beth, Al' and I are the only ones with our eyes open. We don't need to see this.

We know what Gerome has planned for today, he told us last night. It's not the worst he's done, he calls it 'suggestive' rather than 'controlling.' It's down to the people to decide what they do with it.

Each person stood in that crowd with their eyes closed will see their doctor telling them that they have terminal cancer. The only way to save themselves, is to take the life of another. But not just any other. Not a Dream-Walker, a human. The only way to heal a Dream-Walker is by killing a human. They must reset the balance. There are too many humans. It's the only way if they want to survive.

I watch as the moment passes, and they start to reopen their eyes. Some start sniffling, others frown, they all look around confused at each other as the information sinks in. It will feel like a memory to them; they know what they have to do, but will they?

80

Gerome's methods are very effective, so I'm certain this will get the attention of the HJD by 'The Six O'Clock News', if they're not already on their way.

The Human Justice Department has a subdivision of particularly malleable Dream-Walkers whose sole purpose is to ensure the Dream-Walker secret is not divulged to humans. Every time we pop up, they follow us to make sure no humans have accidentally stumbled upon our gathering. It takes a lot of time and uses a lot of manpower when really there is very little risk of humans finding out. The locations are only ever disclosed via word of mouth amongst the community, and Gerome always chooses locations that are heavily populated by Dream-Walkers. He's considerate like that.

Once the HJD's subdivision has ensured there haven't been any leaks (or provided coverup dreams if there have been), they begin tackling the crimes Gerome has incited. It's a bit backwards if you ask me, they protect the Dream-Walker secret first, then the lives of the humans they are supposed to be protecting, but I'm not complaining. Their poorly thought-out tactics help to progress our cause, they allow Gerome's messages to sink in a little longer.

I don't mind Gerome's violent methods because we cannot allow the world to continue as it currently is. We, as Dream-Walkers, need to take our rightful place at the top of the food chain, and that isn't going to happen if we play nicely. We've been playing nicely for generations and all that has achieved is our presence being kept a secret from the vast majority of the population, and tests upon tests upon tests on us. There will never be an end to the secrecy and the testing unless we do something now. Gerome is the perfect person to make this change happen. We won't be slaves or 'political assets' much longer.

Before any chaos can start in front of us, Gerome ushers us towards him, puts an arm around Al' and I, and leads us back the way we came. Beth follows, carrying the remaining signs and leaflets. I breathe in Gerome's musky scent, enjoying this moment of closeness. This moment of being next to greatness.

The afternoon passes in an uneventful blur. We travel and live together like a family, the four of us, so we spend our downtime like a family too. We each split off to our preferred pursuits. I paint my nails and practice doing fishtail plaits in my hair. I pout in front of my mirror and try to think of ways to make Gerome notice me, really notice me. As someone special.

We hear a few sirens pass by, but nothing too dramatic. When the news comes on, we all convene in front of the television. Gerome has the armchair, I have the couch, Beth lies on her stomach on the floor with a magazine in front of her, and Al' leans against the windowsill.

It's the top story, breaking news. Gerome leans back and cracks open a beer as the news broadcaster straightens his papers.

"There have been mass casualties all over Wiltshire today, in a strange turn of events. People are calling it 'Murder Day.' Bodies have been found in taxis, at bus stops, on trains, in their front gardens, at their desks, all brutally murdered. The police have been inundated with phone calls and are so far unable to provide comment. We do not know what has caused this violent episode within our community and can only suggest one thing: stay home."

The news then moves on to something lighter, to keep the British public comfortable and not scared out of their wits, though we all know the broadcast has just increased the number of natural, untampered with nightmares that will be circulating the humans' dreams tonight. Gerome looks pleased, it's going to be even better than after an episode of Crimewatch UK and he loves watching the dreams (or nightmares) after that airs.

I settle back into the couch and bend my right knee up towards my chest to get to a snag I noticed in my tights earlier. I've never been able to resist making ladders worse rather than fixing them. This one is laddering higher and higher up my thigh.

"If you're not careful, you'll have no tights left," jokes Gerome. I look up and find him raising his eyebrows at me suggestively.

"Oh no! And then what would happen?" I reply, placing a hand in front of my mouth in mock-surprise. I blink and see an image of Gerome pushing me back, yanking my tights down, and entering me roughly. I blush. I wasn't expecting that. That was a very explicit image, I feel weird, and a bit turned on. Avoiding Gerome's eyes, I look to Al' and catch him glaring at Gerome in disapproval.

Beth is completely oblivious, flicking through her magazine and most likely daydreaming about Madonna. She always does that. She doesn't even try to hide it, she hasn't told us that she's gay, but she'll happily lie in a room of Dream-Walkers fantasising about Madonna for all of us to see. She's brave. It's something I admire about her.

Al' stops leaning against the windowsill and stands properly, moving the curtains and looking outside. A couple are walking past, arguing.

"Do you ever think we've lost our way?" he asks Gerome as he watches a police car speed past the arguing couple. "Getting Dream-Walkers to kill humans, isn't that taking it a bit far? We want justice, equality, not murder."

Gerome clicks his knuckles and stands to join him by the window.

"We're taking a stand, Al'. They can't ignore us now."

"They weren't ignoring us! They weren't ignoring us after we blew up that very first cage filled with humans

83

after we freed all the Dream-Walkers! They certainly weren't after the second, third, fourth, or fifth! And when you made that human politician who wouldn't give you the time of day tie a noose around her neck through fear of being outed as a self-hating lesbian who poisoned her husband just to be free from him, they definitely learnt the name Gerome Clarke. But those are innocent people dying out there. There must be another way."

I watch as Gerome smiles at the reference to the politician, now that was a statement. I know he's proud of that one.

"I'm sorry you feel that way."

He punches Al' in the jaw and pushes him to the ground before he can react.

"Maybe it's time for another time out. Beth! Can you pass me the ties?" She's closest to them and passes them promptly, clearly not entirely oblivious to her surroundings after all.

Gerome ties Al's hands behind his back and his legs together, then he places a mask over his eyes before returning to the armchair and closing his own eyes.

I know better than to join in that dream, he's about to make Al' pay for doubting him.

I will never upset Gerome.

Kyle

The vet clinic is a crash site, and there's no sign of Maria Carmichael anywhere.

"He's taken her, hasn't he?" screams Tasha.

I eye Max, silently asking him to help her to hold it together.

"Not necessarily, she may have escaped, or gone out before he got here. We don't know that yet. I know your mum said she never told her anything, but do you think she might have figured it out herself? She'd stand a much better chance if she knew what she was up against."

"Well if I didn't figure it out, why would she?" Her nose is streaming like two snot trains racing out of the station. Max holds her tighter and encourages her to sit down.

"Maybe because she's different? She doesn't look like you or your mum?" I suggest. She shrugs.

"We always said she got the red hair from Dad's rellies."

"Has she ever said anything to you, anything that made it seem like she suspected something?"

"No! Of course not!" she wails, "I'm just her stupid little sister. Now I'm not even that."

"Hey shut it, you. Stop moaning. She's still your sister. She doesn't even know she's my cousin." Frankie adds this last statement as if it is a great injustice. I sigh. For a moment there I thought Frankie was going to say something helpful.

"We don't know what she knows, okay? All we know is that she's not here. So where do we go now?" I look at the others for answers. "Anybody?"

"Back to plan A? Find Gerome. Or, we could go to visit Al'?" offers Jake.

"How about, you lot go to Al' whilst listening out for possible locations of my dad, and I'll attempt to track down my long-lost uncle."

"And how is that going to help us?" Frankie asks, posing with her hands on her hips.

"He's Dad's brother, maybe he'll have some tricks up his sleeves."

"Or maybe you just want to meet your uncle, like I want to meet my cousin."

"Touché Frankie, now on your way! Report back at the base tomorrow at noon!"

I hate to admit that Frankie is right, but she is. I am dying to meet my uncle, and I can't meet him without my brother. It wouldn't be right; we should meet him together. I wonder what he's like.

"If I can't get back tomorrow, I'll be in touch. But in the meantime, Tasha's in charge," I inform them. It's always good to have a backup plan. And they'll all listen to Tasha. Well, except Frankie. But she's not supposed to be here anyway, so hopefully she'll leave them to it soon.

I walk away and try to remember the name of the hotel Adam and Ella are staying in. This would be so much easier if we'd had time to buy burner phones and exchange numbers before we split up on our separate missions.

Jenny (1986)

The dream shifts to another memory, and younger me continues to narrate.

"Jenny, darling, I need you to do a favour for me," says Gerome gesturing for me to sit beside him on the end of his bed. I pause in the doorway, hesitating only for a second before rushing to his side.

I've never been inside Gerome's bedroom before; he keeps his room private from the rest of us. I regularly have to share with Beth, and even sometimes with Al' too, but Gerome always has his own private space. My heart pounds as I sit beside him. He places his hand on my lower back and rubs it. It feels oddly comforting and affectionate. It shouldn't turn me on, but I find any physical contact from him to be intoxicating and erotic.

He has been in quite a few of my dreams recently, and things have escalated, but he never shows me anything more than brotherly love in real life. He never wraps his arms around me, never even pecks me on the cheek. Oh, what I would give to taste those lips! I look up at him, finding his face closer to mine than it has ever been. I can see every little spec of stubble. I wonder how it feels…

"Jenny, I trust you. I know that you believe in the work we are doing here. I appreciate you and your hard work. What I'm about to ask you will sound strange, but I promise you it is for a good reason."

"Anything!" I say enthusiastically. I would do anything for him. He is my master; I am his servant.

"I need you to leave." His face remains solemn.

"What? Why? Where will I go?" I jump up, panic rising within me.

Have I done something wrong? Is he luring me into a false sense of security like I've seen him do to others so many times? Am I about to experience my first taste of torture at the hands of Gerome Clarke? He wouldn't hurt me, would he?

Where could I possibly go? I don't belong anywhere else. I don't know what happened to my family after I joined Gerome. Maybe they got recaptured, maybe they're living elsewhere. They wouldn't want me back, that's for sure. I deserted them.

Gerome takes my hand and pulls me, making me sit back down. My heart continues to pound as he starts to make small circles on the top of my hand with his thumb.

"It's not forever, Jenn. It's just for a little while. I need you to go and breed with the future Minister of the Human Justice Department." I pull my hand away.

"You want me to breed?"

"Yes. I want you to have sex with the future Minister of the Human Justice Department. As many times as it takes to get pregnant."

"But I, I can't, I… How do you know he'll want to have sex with me? How do you even know he will be the next Minister?"

I'm a virgin. I was saving myself for Gerome. I've had many sexual dreams, but I've never physically done it with him or with any man. Some call me a tease. Why is he *treating me like this? I thought he loved me too, in his way. Why would he want me to do that with someone else? With someone he despises?*

"Don't worry, I have already confirmed that you are Francis' type. He's a nice enough man, besides his obsession with caging us and using us for experiments. He won't hurt you. I just need you to have his child, and then I will come for you and bring you back to us."

"What about the child?"

"Never mind the child. You will leave it with him."

"You want me to have a child with a man I do not love, and then leave it with him? A man whom I know likes to experiment on Dream-Walkers, and to do that knowing that the child is at least 50% likely to be one?"

"Yes. You'll do it, won't you? You trust me?"

He stares at me so earnestly. Of course I trust him, I know he is doing good work. If he says this will help, then this must be part of some big master plan that I don't know about because I'm not important enough. I should be proud to have been given this role. He could have asked Beth, but he chose me. He trusts me to do this for him. I can do this. The future Minister can't be that bad. And if I'm his type, it won't take long, right? I only need to get pregnant. That should be easy enough. I'm young and, hopefully, fertile.

"Tell me about him."

My decision is made. When I come back, Gerome will be so pleased with me, and I'll be sexually experienced. Maybe he'll want me then, maybe then he'll see me the way I want to be seen.

Kyle

Adam meets me at the agreed service station, and I watch him get out of a taxi without paying. So, he wouldn't steal or 'commandeer' a car, but he will take a free ride. Typical Adam.

I let him in my stylish commandeered sports car, and we begin our journey towards our uncle. Marcus. Uncle Marcus. Here's hoping he's kinder than Father Gerome.

I fill Adam in on what I've been up to and what we've discovered so far.

"Shit, so we've gained an older half-sister and an uncle today?" he summarises.

"Yep. What've you found out about Ella?"

He explains the story of her birth parent's life and death, and I'm relieved it at least makes sense. A prostitute and a greengrocer would of course give up a baby, it was clearly an unplanned pregnancy. Then Adam explains that the information came from the Minister's son Jeremy, that he's like Ella, that she nearly slept with him before, and that he's left her there with him at the hotel, and I slam on my breaks as I almost drive through a red light.

"What? He's like her? And they almost…? Jeez Adam, why didn't you tell me? You shouldn't have left her there with him! What if he convinces her to have sex with him, to find out what happens? You don't need me to tell you they could be having sex right now!"

"I trust her," he says, but I can hear the worry in his voice.

"Well, that's one way to test your relationship." I try not to be disappointed. It's not like it makes a difference to me if they work out or not, but I am quite invested. I got them together. And, I like her too. I at least want to keep her in the family.

Is that weird?

Probably. But Jeremy? Yeesh. He's so… blonde. And blue eyed. A lot like Jenny actually, as I thought earlier. Could there have been a baby with Francis Krunk in her past? Could she be Jeremy's Dream-Walker mother? But she caved and told us everything, didn't she?

Could she have skipped the chapter where she slept with the Minister, or gave him her eggs? It's possible. My dad could have set it up. He always did hate the system. It sounds like something he would do, for revenge.

Adam looks at me curiously.

"Tell me I'm stupid, but I'm wondering if Tasha's mum might also be Jeremy's supposedly dead Dream-Walker mum. They share the same blonde hair and bright blue eyes, and it would explain how she managed to stay out in the world whilst the rest of the original Resistance were locked up or in a psychiatric facility, wouldn't it?"

He nods in agreement.

Oh Jenny, if that's another secret you've kept from us, what else are you hiding? I tap my fingers on the steering wheel.

Jenny (1988)

More time has passed. Younger me is older now, a mother.

Jeremy shares my blonde hair and bright blue eyes. He giggles at me when I pull faces at him. I love him, but I am trying not to get too attached because Gerome will be back for me any day now. My job is complete. But I can't help it, those chubby little fingers melt my heart.

Day in, day out, we live like a married couple with a baby. We are a married couple with a baby. I had no idea that Francis was a traditionalist. Gerome didn't mention that when he told me about him. But I knew I had to make a baby, so I did it. I married the future Minister of the Human Justice Department. A man I should hate, who spends hours musing over the capabilities of Dream-Walkers, the best ways to use us, to analyse us, all sorts of scientific plans.

And, honestly, I don't mind him. He doesn't treat me like an experiment, despite what I am. And he doesn't look at Jeremy any differently either. Well, okay, maybe a little. But I've told him if Jeremy is a Dream-Walker, he won't start showing it until he is much older. For now, he's just a baby, let him be. That seems to have done the trick.

I hope Francis won't use him as his own personal lab rat if he does turn out to be like me, that would be awful. I can't believe Gerome would have sent me here if he believed that would be the outcome. Doesn't Francis have enough Dream-Walkers to test? Why does he need one with his own blood?

I still haven't figured out why Gerome wanted me to do this, but there must be a bigger plan underway, I just can't figure it out.

Figuring things out has never been my kind of thing, I don't like the term 'dumb blonde', but it is a little true. I prefer to follow my heart rather than learn maths and science or how to argue in a court of law. And how much do you need to know to be a housewife, anyway? How to read a set of scales so you can bake a cake? I've yet to feel the urge to better myself education-wise, believing I'm much better as an asset on someone's arm, than I am on my own. I've got a sidekick mentality; I was never meant to be the star of the show. That's Gerome. That's always going to be Gerome. So, why bother?

Francis hasn't mentioned Gerome once. It's like he's oblivious to what's going on out there, the mass hysteria and murder being caused by one man on a mission, with the help of a couple of other miscreants. He's extremely focused on his path towards becoming the next Minister. I wondered before how Gerome could be so sure that this man would be the next Minister, but now that I know him, it's hard to miss. Nobody could be more dedicated to the Human Justice Department than this guy. It's his life's work. Maybe that's why Gerome wanted him to father a child who may or may not become a Dream-Walker: to put him in his place and make him more sympathetic towards our cause. Oh, I don't know. Maybe they have a secret alliance, though I don't see how that would ever work.

Jeremy starts crying so I pick him up and start bouncing him. I catch sight of myself in the mirror. What have I become?

I used to be so perfect, at least, that was the image I attempted to convey. Clean, smooth, a portrait of goodness and integrity. Now my hair is sticky with baby food, my clothes are creased, and I lost my lipstick months ago. I focus on my dry lips and remember the day I chose Jeremy's name.

I missed saying 'Gerome.' I still do. I used to whisper his name to feel closer to him, to feel less abandoned. I said it facing the mirror that morning and I realised, the mouth movement is almost the same with 'Jeremy' as it is 'Gerome.' It's only the ending that's different, and the name itself is so similar, it just felt right. Like home.

I miss the excitement of life on the road, the rallies, and all the chanting. Looking after a baby is boring. Francis doesn't let me mix with other mums much because he doesn't want anyone to know what I am. I'm lonely stuck here with a baby who can't even speak.

I wonder what's taking so long. I thought Gerome would come for me as soon as he heard I'd given birth, but it's been nearly a year since he was born and still, I've heard nothing. I place the now quiet Jeremy back in his bed and wander out to see my husband.

He's reading, as usual. Some medical journal or other, scientific and confusing. I sit the other end of the couch and carefully rest my feet on him as I open my own book, a saucy romance novel. He looks up and smiles at me, putting his reading material down.

"Is he sleeping again now?" he asks, pulling off one of my socks and proceeding to massage my foot.

"Yep, he's back asleep. He's such a good boy, isn't he? We got lucky."

"We did indeed."

Sometimes I wonder if he believes our charade. If he really thinks I turned up one day desperate to marry him

94

and have his baby, or if he knows about Gerome, and maybe even requested this as some kind of deal. I can't tell.

All I do know is that he gives really good foot massages, and I'm going to miss them.

Adam

We arrive at the address a little before 8pm. It's dark and uninviting.

"Are you sure this is the place?" I ask Kyle.

"Last known address," he confirms.

It's very small; a little cottage in the middle of nowhere. It's the kind of home that's filled with friends of the eight-legged variety. What type of person would ever choose to live here?

I suppose we're about to find out as Kyle isn't hesitating at all. I thought he'd be more careful than me, having walked into traps before, but it seems he is all too keen to get to the bottom of this and meet our mystery uncle. I just hope he's not like Dad. It's all very well the files saying that he was released and allowed to be adopted because he wasn't showing signs of being a Dream-Walker, but what if he was just a late bloomer? He was born at the start of the sixties; they could easily have made a mistake back then.

And we don't know whether Dad knows about him. He might not, but he could easily have had Damian run his DNA through the system. He could know the names and addresses of all his bastard offspring, and his long-lost brother. He could be here right now. Ready to mock us once again.

"Kyle, I think we should –" I start but it's too late. He's knocked on the door.

We see a light go on in one of the windows and a few minutes later, the door opens, slowly.

Marcus Clarke is definitely my dad's brother.

The eyes, the nose, the expression on his face, but that's where it ends. This man is old. Like, I know he's not that old, he's only four years older than Dad. But his hair is long and bedraggled, he has a beard which has seen better days and less Coco Pops, and a pot belly. Our dad would never have a pot belly, I'm pretty sure he was working out even when he was strapped to that rotating contraption, he'll have been tightening and releasing his abs to keep toned.

We all stand there, looking at each other in silence. I wonder what thoughts are running through his head. He must see the family resemblance, even if he doesn't know about Dad. He might think we're about to announce we're his sons.

Kyle doesn't appear to be ready to speak yet – so much for taking the lead. I step forwards and offer my hand to the stranger standing in his doorway, for second time today.

"Hi, I'm Adam, and this is Kyle, and we believe you're our uncle."

He doesn't move, only glancing from me to Kyle. We often get this reaction, being identical twins.

"We've come to -" Kyle starts but is interrupted.

"You've come to what? Why are you here? What do you want?" Uncle Marcus retorts. His teeth are disgusting. I suspect they don't have a dentist around here.

"Can we come in?" I ask.

"The hell you can! I don't know who you are or what you want from me, but I'm not stupid, okay? I'm not letting you in until you show me some ID!"

I look at Kyle. It would be so easy to make him let us in, but we don't want to scare him. We want him to trust us.

"Do you know you have a brother? Gerome?" I ask him. He stares thoughtfully.

"I," he pauses, "I think I did have a brother, but I don't remember." He frowns.

"It must be very confusing," I console.

"No! Don't you try that, Mr! I'm not confused, I'm fine here on my own. I don't need any help thank you very much. If you're here to worm your way inside and tell me I need help, that I can't live here, you can sod off!"

He's shaking now. I feel sorry for him, but I don't know how we can make this any easier. He needs to let us inside; he needs to sit down.

"Here, this is my ID," I say, showing my driver's licence and glaring at Kyle to do the same.

"We're your nephews."

"I don't have any nephews. I don't have anyone. And I don't need anyone, okay? Are you here for my money? I don't have any! Look at this place! Does it look like I have money? If you're here to kill me, you'll be inheriting debt, not money. Alright?"

"We're not here for money, we just wanted to meet you," I say.

"And?"

"And?" I repeat, unsure what he's getting at.

"And what? Why would you want to meet me? You must want something more than that! I'm not an imbecile!"

"We wanted to meet you, and to find out if you know anything about our dad, or where he might be. He's a dangerous man, your brother."

"Well, I don't have a brother, so you can be on your way!" He starts to push the door closed but Kyle sticks his foot in the way.

"I'm sorry Uncle Marcus, but we're going to need more from you than that." The old man's eyes widen. I look at Kyle. I know what he's going to do, but I don't want to be a part of it. That's our uncle; an old man. We shouldn't... but we need to. We need to know everything. All those years of being blissfully glad that Dad wasn't around anymore were foolish. We should have been learning more about him so we'd be ready for something like this, so we'd know where to look, his favourite tactics, everything.

I look away as Kyle confuses him and we're allowed inside to the small lounge.

"Marcus, tell us about your dreams."

Jenny (1990)

"Oh, it is so good to be back!" I exclaim, stepping out of Gerome's car and trying to ignore the incessant tugging on my heart strings. Jeremy will be fine; Francis will look after him. "I can't wait to see everyone!"

I practically skip up to the front door, playing my excitement up a notch or three, to compensate for the sadness I'm trying desperately to ignore. Gerome has changed in the time I've been away, he has a few more lines, and I was surprised when he said he'd decided not to take on any more members of The Resistance. It seemed as if maybe he'd tried that, and it didn't work. I don't know what's been going on whilst I was away, I'll have to ask Beth.

It was a long drive from Francis' place. I got the message from Gerome in my sleep last night, telling me when to sneak out and meet him. I left Francis in bed and kissed Jeremy's head for the last time on my way out. I'll miss him. I'll miss them both. But this is where I belong. This is where I'd been waiting to return to that whole time. I can't wait to get stuck back into this lifestyle.

"So where are we going next? What's the plan at the moment? The current strategy? I can't wait to hear

everything you've been up to!" I tell Gerome. He lets me inside but doesn't say anything else.

Fine, I'll go find Beth and Al'. I carry my rucksack inside and place it down on the floor out of the way, then I look around. It's a nice enough place, a bit gloomy, it's the wrong angle to get the morning or afternoon sun on the front room, but it's okay. It's temporary after all.

"Beth! Al'!" I shout and wait for someone to come and see me. They must have missed me too, right? They must want to know where I've been, what I've been up to.

Or did Gerome already tell them about that?

Well, I can't stand here waiting all afternoon, I'll have to go to them. Gerome heads to the fridge and I hear him open a beer as I make my way upstairs.

"Hello?"

I continue going up and find every door is closed. I knock on the first one on the left.

"Hello? Is anyone in there?"

Silence.

I try the next one. When there's no answer, I decide to try the handle. It's locked. I knock on the next door and finally I hear movement.

"Hello? Is anyone in there?"

"Just a minute," I hear Beth respond. I wait and listen as she flushes a toilet, washes her hands and opens the door.

Whoa.

"What um, what–" before I can string together the words to ask her what the hell happened to her, she wraps her arms around me and pushes a somewhat larger than it should be stomach into me as she says,

"Jenn! Thank God you're back!"

She leads me to what I presume is her bedroom, the final door I had left to try. Inside she has a single bed with a

101

patchwork quilt. She sits down, leaning back against the headboard.

She's wearing what is best described as curtains. It's a horrid shapeless floral dress which now that she's seated, more clearly shows her rounded stomach. I can't believe it. She's pregnant. But she's gay!

"Beth, what happened?" I ask her, concerned by this transformation. She was so spirited, so confident and punky. Where has her eyeliner gone? Her neon clothes? Her hair is scraped back in a greasy bun like she has given up washing. Like she no longer cares to live. She was always so oblivious before, so in her own world. What has turned her into this? Have things really been that bad without me? Have they been failing? Has Gerome tortured her like he'd started to do to Al'?

"Beth, talk to me. What happened? Who's the father?"

"Do you really have to ask?" She tilts her head at me. My eyes widen. Gerome? No, he wouldn't. He loves me. He would never impregnate Beth. He knows I would have done it willingly. I would have found it an honour to carry his child. Why would he use Beth? With her blatant love of the female kind?

"He raped me, Jenn. I thought I was dreaming. I'd been having these dreams for a while and I sort of suspected they weren't natural, like he was doing it on purpose to mess with me, but then I missed my period and my boobs started to ache and well, as you can see, I'm pregnant. He must have raped me whilst I was asleep."

"And you're sure it was him?"

"Of course it was him! You know what he's like. You know how much he loves messing with people."

"But -"

"-But what, Jenn? But I'm gay? Yes, I am. That's probably the reason he did it. Get the gay girl pregnant so she has to live the life she never wanted." She scoffs.

*"Jenn, you have to help me. I can't have this baby, I can't."
She reaches to grab my hand then lets it drop as Gerome
appears in the doorway.*

*"Got to help you with what?" he asks, entering the room
uninvited. "What's going on? Aren't you happy to see
Jenny?" He takes a few steps closer and then stops. "Oh,
wow, Beth! I had no idea! Who's the lucky father?"*

*"You piece of shit!" Beth screeches and throws a pillow
at him. I stand back, stunned.*

*"Careful now, you don't want to hurt the baby," says
Gerome calmly. I don't know what to believe. Beth looks at
me with pleading eyes.*

I turn around and leave them alone.

*

*Later that day, Gerome kisses me for the first time. He tells
me that he's happy to see me, that he's glad I completed my
mission, and he's got big plans for my future. I lose myself
in that one perfect kiss.*

*It's only afterwards that the fear creeps in. His last
mission had me leave; will his 'big plans' require me to
leave again?*

*I don't have a bedroom at this house, so I'm left to sleep
in the lounge. Once Gerome is in his room, I creep upstairs
and sit outside Beth's bedroom. I close my eyes and hope to
enter her dreams.*

"You look incredible," he tells her, licking his lips and
winking. She's wearing a skimpy ballerina outfit and she
frowns and screws up her face as she looks down and
realises. "Come here." She does as she's told. "Now do a
twirl!" She does. He smacks her on the bottom as she spins.
"You've been a bad girl, haven't you?" He sneers.

"N-n-no," she stutters.

103

"Oh yes you have, you've been looking at Jenny, watching her in the shower, haven't you, Beth?" He taunts her.

"No, I would never!"

"But you wish you had," he smiles.

"No, I…"

"You what, Beth? No, you don't want Jenn to lick your pussy?"

"Shut up!"

He moves to stand closer to her and lets his hands run down her body, pausing between her legs. I feel sick.

"This fire burns for Jenn, doesn't it?" She tries to push his hands and arms away from her as he increases the pressure, starting to lift her from the ground by her vagina. His face is red with exertion.

"I want to help you, Beth. I want to free you from your twisted mind; to show you what pleasure you could have if only you were more open." He releases her vagina but places his hands on her arms instead, holding her in place.

"Go away, I don't want to." She tries to wriggle from his grasp. He releases one arm briefly, and then the other, enabling him to pull the leotard straps off her shoulders and peel the outfit down her body, exposing her naked breasts. She's cold.

"It looks like you want to," he says, flicking a nipple.

He pushes her down onto a bed, holding her hands up behind her head.

"Get off me! Get off me! Somebody help!" she screams.

He pulls his trousers down and enters her roughly before beginning his rhythmic thrust.

"No!" I hear Beth shout from inside her room. She must have woken herself up. I slowly open the door, making sure it doesn't creak, and go in to see her.

"Is that how it happened?" I ask.

104

"Maybe, that's not the only dream I had like that, there were others. I keep reliving them." Her face is soaked from her tears.

"You should go," she tells me. "You don't want to upset him."

It's true. I don't. But I also can't believe what I've just seen is true. I know he's capable, but we're on the same side. Why would he do that to her?

I know that she believes it was him, but I see no real evidence. There's nothing to suggest it wasn't Al', for example. Trying to make Gerome look bad. Trying to make us turn on him.

I still haven't found Al'. I would like to hear his version of events.

Jenny (1991)

The next dream-memory starts almost immediately.

"Look at me, Jenny! Please! I'm begging you. I don't care how you do it, just do it soon! Please!"

Her desperation reeks of pregnancy hormones; she doesn't know what she's saying. She's just scared of labour. It'll be okay. I did it, I survived. She will too.

"Beth, I can't. I won't. You'll feel differently when you see your baby."

She shakes her head and wails, her skin is pink and blotchy,

"Please! Kill me and my baby. I cannot bring the next generation of Clarke into this world! Please, Jenn, you're the only one who can help me."

"Beth, I know you think Gerome did this to you, but he didn't. He promised me, it wasn't him. It was Al', pretending to be him. Trying to make you turn on him too. And it worked, didn't it?"

"Do you honestly believe that Jenny? After everything we've seen Gerome do?"

"Yes, of course I do."

"Then you're a dumber blonde than I realised! Can't you see he's playing you? He doesn't love you, Jenn. He's

106

using you, and you're letting him. Help me! Don't do what he says, for once in your life! Stand by me, your friend who was raped. Don't stand by the man who raped me. Please, Jenn!"

I stare at her.

"After everything Gerome has done for us over the years, how can you possibly believe he would do this?"

"Exactly, Jenn, after all these years, how can you not see that you are the only one Gerome hasn't hurt? What about all those dream manipulations, all the murder and violence you know he incited; the cages we helped him burn to the ground – we're guilty too, don't forget, but he's the one with the real power. He's the dangerous one. Why can't you see that? He's a rapist, Jenn. He raped me."

"No, he didn't! Gerome has done some bad things, of course, but only to make a stand. To prove his point, to make them take notice. And what he's done, most of it has been in dreams, he hasn't physically made anyone do anything."

"Oh, come on! Hasn't made anyone do anything? Errrm, the murders? Do you not understand what we are as Dream-Walkers? What we are capable of? That people take notice of their dreams? Especially dreams that feel really fucking believable! And, do I need to remind you what he made you go and do?"

"He didn't make me. He asked, and I went willingly, because I believe in what we are fighting for."

"And what exactly are we fighting for, Jenn? Dream-rapists?"

"You don't understand. Gerome isn't a bad person."

"Are you sure about that?"

"Yes!"

"Was Hitler a bad person?"

"Yes…"

"Did the Nazi soldiers think he was a bad person?"

107

"No, probably not."

"Well, do you see where I'm going with this? You are no better than a Nazi soldier. Following Gerome around like you're 'just following orders', eh? I bet if you ever get caught, you'll drop him like a dirty nappy!"

"I'd die for him!"

"Well, I'm sorry I can't stick around to see that. But since you won't help me, if you could just get out of my way, I have an appointment with the medicine cabinet." She moves towards me, but I don't budge from my position blocking her exit.

"I can't let you do that."

"Why? You can have your own baby with him, I know that's what you want. Just let me die, so I don't have to do this, and let my baby die too. If you don't let me, I'll only find another way."

"Not if I keep you here until Gerome gets back, you won't."

"And then what's he going to do, this good man you love? Do you think perhaps he might torture me until I give birth? Do you think he might steal my baby and kill me or lock me away somewhere?"

"You need help," I tell her, calmly.

"Oh I need that alright. I need some big fucking help. Dear Jim, I'm pregnant with my rapist's baby and nobody will let me kill myself or it. Please help. Love, Bethany Parker aged twenty-one and a half." She laughs maniacally.

"Seriously, Beth. Gerome isn't like that. He's kind to those he loves. He loves us. We're his family."

"Jeez Louise! You need to stop drinking whatever he's pouring you and open your eyes!"

"My eyes are open Beth. The only one who's acting crazy is you."

108

"Because you can't see what he's done to you! I know you fancy the guy, but seriously! He needs to be stopped!"

"So you don't want equality for Dream-Walkers?"

"Of course I want equality, but Gerome Clarke is not going to be the one who gets it."

The front door slams shut, signalling Gerome's return. Beth looks at me with the eyes of a deer about to be shot by hunters, afraid and frozen to the spot. It's over.

Gerome walks in,

"Well, well, well, what's going on here then?" He observes us.

"Beth is trying to kill herself and the baby again," I tell him. He shakes his head in disapproval.

"Beth, we talked about this. You're leaving me no choice." He sighs and she whimpers,

"No, please! I'll behave!" she begs. Gerome looks at me,

"Do you believe her? Do you think she'll behave?"

I hesitate and then I tell him the truth.

"She doesn't want to live, and she doesn't want her baby to either. I don't think anything will stop her from trying to kill them both." Beth gasps,

"You bitch!"

"Okay then, here's what we're going to do." Gerome explains the plan. Beth will be kept under close guard until the baby arrives, at which time she will be moved to a psychiatric facility and he and I will raise the baby. We'll be an unconventional family unit, raising Beth and Al's baby, but I can't imagine anything better. Maybe in time we'll have our own children.

That night, Gerome kisses me on the head and holds me tight. We lay together listening to each other's heartbeats until Beth's scream jolts us back into reality. The baby is coming. Tonight.

Adam

My uncle looks much smaller sat on the couch, he's hunched over, holding his arms. I realise he's afraid.

"Would you like a drink?" I offer, "I can put the kettle on." He looks at me like I just suggested dying his hair pink.

"What? And have you snooping around back there? I don't think so. No. You sit down. You wanted me to talk, I'm talking." He rocks slightly backwards and forwards.

"We need to know if you've had any contact with our dad," says Kyle.

"Well, I don't know anything about any brother, okay, but I do know something about dreams. Nightmares, I'd call them. I've been having awful nightmares for the past week or so." Since Dad escaped. Kyle and I nod to encourage him to continue.

"You can't tell anyone mind you, I don't want to be locked up in a loony bin," he warns.

"Of course, this is just between us," I assure him.

"It's like I lose control of my dreams. One minute I'm riding a bicycle through woodland and the sun is shining on my face, the next I'm nose deep in mud, struggling to breathe with something or someone holding me down. That was how it started anyway, now it's much worse.

"Now, I am the one doing terrible things, but I have no control. It's like I'm possessed. My body moves without my say so. I dream of pulling people's nails and slicing heads off; of stabbing someone in the chest and then burning their body. I dream of rape. It's like in my dreams, I become a monster. And I can't wake up until it's over. No matter how hard I try."

"That sounds like our dad," I say.

"What do you mean? Does he do those things in real life?"

"Both. Sometimes just in people's heads, so they wake up scared, other times he provides a different dream as a distraction and then harms them in real life. They don't even scream." Kyle explains. Marcus' face turns white.

"But why? Why would he do that to me? I don't know him!"

"That's what we need to figure out. He clearly knows who you are, and he doesn't usually do anything without an ulterior motive."

"Do you mind if we stay here tonight, to see if it happens again?" asks Kyle. I elbow him. I don't want to stay; I need to get back to Ella. Especially after what he said. I should never have left her with Jeremy. I can't leave them alone all night!

"Err," says Marcus, "I don't have a spare room."

"If you say no, we'll just wait outside in the car," Kyle replies stubbornly.

"Fine. You can have the couch. Just don't touch anything." He surveys the room. I don't know what he thinks we might like to pinch around here. Dusty lampshades, crinkled up paperbacks that have seen better days, maybe the random turtle ornament?

111

He shuffles off to bed and we make ourselves comfortable in the dimly lit lounge. There's so much dust, I don't believe he usually sits in here himself, never mind lies on the couch. Just moving a cushion releases a puff of dust and I hold my nose trying not to sneeze.

Kyle seems pleased with himself.

"This is a lead, right? Dad is playing with his brother's dreams. He must have known that we'd track him down, he's giving us a clue, right?"

"Or he's just playing us, again." Forcing me to leave Ella with Jeremy.

"Did you ever figure out what he was using Charmaine Krunk to blackmail her husband about?" he asks me.

"I thought you were looking into that!"

"Nah, I've got bigger things to worry about. I bet it's about Jeremy though, don't you?"

"Maybe."

"Perhaps the Minister doesn't want word getting out confirming what Jeremy is. His only son, a weird P.I.N.S. or whatever you called it. That sounds like something Dad would use to his advantage."

"Can we not talk about Jeremy anymore?" I ask sternly.

"Why? Are you worried about what he might be getting up to all alone with Ella? With all that nervous tension of not knowing when you're coming back, or if someone else might barge in to capture her. I bet it's pretty stifling in that room right now, don't you?"

I throw a cushion at him which he punches towards the ceiling and coughs as more dust is released.

"You asked me to come here with you! Do you even need me?"

"I thought you'd want to meet our uncle. And besides, I thought Dad might be here, hiding out."

"He could be nearby, now you mention it. To be doing those dreams, he might have something of Marcus' and therefore be miles away. Or he could be hiding out in the shed at the bottom of the garden," I suggest.

Kyle goes to the kitchen window and peers into the darkness.

"How do you even know there is a shed out there?"

"Of course there's a shed. There's always a shed."

"Do you think we should check it out?" he asks, clearly less than keen on the idea. It's very dark out there. In the middle of nowhere there are no streetlights, so when it's dark, it's dark. You can even see the stars here, on a clear night. But it's not a clear night. It's a heavy cloud, dark and oppressive night. The last thing I want to do is go tiptoeing down to the shed at the bottom of the garden. A shed that will be full of spiders in the best-case scenario, and full of our dad in the worst. Goosebumps cover my forearms.

"I think we should, but I don't want to." I answer honestly.

"Same," he returns to his seat. "Shall we just play dumb?"

"If he's out there, we can't go to sleep. Even to watch Marcus' dreams. We'll be vulnerable too – physically, not just in our heads. He might storm in here and do something!"

"He's not going to kill us, we're his kids," says Kyle.

"Are you sure about that? He has spares now. Damian, Maria... Maybe he could get rid of us." But I still don't want to go down to that shed.

"Well, we could take turns. One of us stays awake and on guard?" suggests Kyle.

"One of us doesn't stand a chance if he bursts in here, you know that. We need to find out. We need to know exactly what the situation is." Fuck. "I'm sure he's not in there. He's probably miles away. It's too small and boring, he wouldn't hide out there. Right?" We both look at each other and swallow.

113

"Are we really doing this?" he asks me, and I wonder when my brave brother stopped being so headstrong. He sounds as nervous as I am.

"We are."

We find a spade and a trowel outside the front door and take them as weapons; better than nothing, but not good enough. We'll need very fast reactions if he is down there.

I can barely see a thing. We stay close together and it feels like we're kids again, going down to the toilets in the middle of night on a camping holiday. I have that giggly urge because it's so quiet and everyone else is asleep. Nervous excitement, I guess. I'm petrified. We reach the door of the shed.

It stands there, dark and sturdy. Wooden but covered in flaky paint. It's too dark to tell what shade it is painted. There's no padlock. That's a bad sign. I want to back away, but I have to be strong. We said we'd take our dad down; I can't be a wimp now. Kyle reaches out to open the door, slowly pressing down on the lever.

A scream makes us jump out of our skins.

Not from the shed, from inside the cottage.

We hesitate only for a second before running back inside and looking for Marcus. We find him sat bolt upright in his bed, scratching his eyes.

"It burns! It burns!" he wails at us.

"Shh, it's okay, you're okay now, it was only a dream," I reassure him like a child and rub his back. "Would you like that drink now?" he nods. Kyle goes down to the kitchen whilst I sit with our uncle and try to console him. He's very shaken.

"He, he, he, oh it was so bad, so bad, and then he poured acid into my eyes! The burn! The blood!" He won't leave his eyes alone, scratching them and his cheeks. I try to restrain him to prevent serious damage. When he catches

114

his breath again, he turns to look at me with his sore red eyes. "Did you see? Were you watching?"

Kyle returns with a hot cup of tea, allowing me a moment to delay my response. Before I can say anything, Kyle quietly mumbles, "the shed door is open."

Fuck.

So he was in there, and we fell for the distraction. We almost had him! Goddammit! We almost had him!

"You didn't see, did you? You lied to me, you left me here to be tortured. You don't want to help me. Did you steal my good china? Did you take my couch? What's left in there now?" Marcus rambles.

"We think our dad was hiding in your shed." I tell him.

"That's preposterous! Why would anyone stay in there?"

"Our dad is… complicated. Look, we think he's gone now, so you should be okay. You should be able to sleep properly again. But we'll check on you again."

"You're leaving?" His red eyes open wide.

"We need to catch him." I confirm.

"But I didn't tell you everything about the dreams. I didn't tell you all the details. Maybe you should stay a while longer, just in case. He might come back! I can tell you about the victims; whatever you want to know. Please don't leave me here. He'll kill me. He'll kill me!" His voice gets louder and more rushed with each word.

"I don't think you serve any purpose other than as a distraction. Believe us, he's on to the next stage of his plan now. He must have wanted to get us out of the way for something. We need to head back to the city."

We walk away, leaving the old man in bed, sipping his tea.

Outside, Kyle shouts, "shit!" at the top of his lungs. Our car has gone and, in its place, a note, secured under a stone.

"Thanks for the ride boys, see you soon," he reads aloud.

The road is still and quiet. How the fuck are we going to hitch a ride around here?

Jenny (1992)

My eyes are sore but still the dream-memories continue. Younger Me won't stop reminding me of my mistakes.

No, not again! Gerome looks into my eyes.

"I need you to take her, Jenny. Look after her. Raise her to be great." His bags are packed by the door. "They're coming for me. I have to go."

"But what will I do? Where will I go? I don't have any money!"

"Here, take this," he hands me a wad of notes. "And when you run out, you know what to do. You've seen me do it. So, practice. Or find another man to look after you. I don't mind. You have my blessing. Go anywhere you want to my love and look after my daughter. I will find you one day, when the time is right for us. Just don't admit to anyone that you know me or tell anyone who that baby's real father is. Okay?"

"Okay." I answer quietly.

He kisses me softly on the lips, then kisses the wriggling toddler in my arms, bends to lift his bags, and leaves.

28 December

Ella

"Hi honey, I'm home!" I shout and slam the apartment door behind me. I take in the beautiful sunset beaming through the floor to ceiling windows.

"Mummy!" A small blonde child accosts me carrying a bucket and spade. The spade scrapes against my bare legs. I put my arms around her and kiss the top of her head.

"Daddy said we can go down to the beach and build sandcastles, but only for a little while. Is it true? Can we?" she asks, eagerly.

"Of course we can sweetheart, just let me get changed out of my work clothes and then we can go." She runs away and I head to the bedroom. Jeremy is sat on the bed, topless.

"I hope that's okay, I told her it wouldn't be for long. She just really loves the sand," he tells me, getting up and wrapping me in his arms. "Mmm, you smell amazing."

I push him away.

"Well that may be so, but somebody is waiting to go to the beach," I tilt my head purposefully. "Are you coming with us?" I open my chest of drawers and look for something suitable to change into.

119

"Of course I am, I can't let the two most important women in my life go down to the beach alone, can I? What about the sea monsters?" he jokes. The little girl comes bursting through our bedroom door,

"Sea monsters!" she squeals, charging at Jeremy with her spade held out like a sword. He growls at her and starts waving his arms around and saying he's going to destroy the sandcastles. She screams happily and battering him with her spade until he 'captures' her and holds her upside down by her ankles.

"Now, now, everyone. Let's calm down before somebody gets hurt." My parental tone sounds natural and surprises me.

The little girl's legs are lowered to the ground, and she crawls to collect her spade. She stands up straight by the door like she's ready for action.

"Okay, I ready now Mummy. Let's go!"

*

I can't believe I dreamt about Jeremy again. What is going on? It must be all of his 'you won't dream about me unless you want to' lines getting to me. I don't really want to dream about him. I want Adam.

I don't know where I am, but I'm tied to a chair. Jeremy is also tied up next to me, so at least he's not dead. I'd rather people didn't die trying to protect me, I could do without that on my conscience.

I remember Adam's dad arriving and acting like a movie-criminal, I remember keeping my eyes open for as long as possible, but the next thing I remember, I was walking a tightrope connecting two skyscrapers, my toes cramped with the fear of falling and trying to clasp the rope with my toes. It was a dream, obviously. And it must have been closely followed by the one about Jeremy.

120

I'm sure Gerome gave me the first one, to get me here. But did he stick around and watch the second one? Did he make that happen too? Jeremy might not be able to influence my dreams, but Gerome definitely can, and I wouldn't put it past him to try to get me moved on away from his sons.

I wonder where he's gone. Are we his leverage? His bargaining chip? Is this part of his revenge on the Minister perhaps?

There's a whimper from elsewhere in the room, I twist my neck to see.

On the far side of the room there's a woman, late twenties/early thirties with lovely dark red hair tied to another chair. She's also gagged, so we can't speak. I wonder who she is and what her connection is to Gerome Clarke.

It's dark in here, with only a tiny bit of light shining in from somewhere out of sight. It illuminates the woman's hair, but that's about it. My eyes feel heavy, perhaps I was drugged. Jeremy appears unconscious, despite his upright position. He hasn't moved, but he is breathing; I can see his chest rise and fall. I decide to let my eyes rest for a minute.

"Hello? Can you hear me?" a voice asks. I frown and look around the space. I'm in a field on a bright summer's day. There are daisies scattered amongst the grass, and bees buzzing between branches of a lavender bush. One flies near my ear, and I flinch.

"Who said that? Show yourself!"

"I'm not very good at this, I don't know how to," the voice answers me.

"Who are you?" I ask.

"I'm Maria. I'm the one tied up at the back of the room with you. I'm apparently the psychopath's long-lost daughter."

121

"Huh. Why would he tie up his own daughter? Is this a trick? Is this him now, pretending to be you? I'm not falling for this. Whoever you are, leave me alone. Someone will find me soon enough, I'm not succumbing to his mind games." I continue to look around the lovely field I've found myself in.

"I've been down here for two days, I think. I've lost track. People won't find you until he wants them to. You should do as he asks. He's not invincible, he makes mistakes. If you do as he asks, you might just get out alive."

"And why should I trust you? Have you not already tried that, Miss High and Mighty? Why won't Daddy set you free?" I sneer. I don't know what's come over me, but I'm not taking any chances. This could be Gerome messing with me, I'm not going to play nice. I'm being sensible, it's the only way to survive. These people are big on manipulation, so my guard is up, and it's not coming down.

"He said he'd hoped I'd be like him, cruel and powerful, but I'm not. I'm weak and nice and I don't care about Dream-Walkers. I wish I was human. I'm a vet, I love looking after animals. I couldn't care less about his crazy plans. I don't know what's so hard for him to understand, he didn't raise me so why would I be like him? But clearly, I'm the kind of disappointment you leave tied up in the basement until they change their mind. Or rot."

"So that's where we are then? A basement?"

"Yep, as far as I can tell. Anyway, what's so special about you? What does he want you to do? Unless he's your dad too."

"I don't know what he wants. I'm definitely not his daughter, but I didn't give him a chance to ask me for anything yet. Maybe he wants to lure the Minister here, since the other guy in here is his son," I say, keeping my personal 'skill' to myself.

"Ah, I thought I recognised him."

The voice goes quiet as I sit down in the field, enjoying this brief reprise from the dark basement at the very least. It's warmer and smells a lot nicer in this dream.

"What's that smell, by the way? In the basement?" I think out loud.

"Me. I haven't moved since I got here, whenever that was."

So it's shit, literally. Wee and poo. And she's what, sitting in it? No way! It wasn't that bad, was it? Maybe she's managed not to poo yet. It is like that carpark stairwell wee stink, I suppose. Gross.

I'm torn from the dream as a bright light goes on in the basement, making my eyes sting. I quickly glance at Maria before watching the bottom of the stairs for Gerome's arrival. He addresses me,

"I see you've woken up and met my disappointing daughter. Have you had a chance to consider my offer? You help me, I help you?"

I nod. He reaches forward and pulls at the tape around my mouth, tearing it away, not mindful of taking any skin with it. I guess I don't need to worry about growing a female moustache any time soon.

"What do you want me to do?" I ask quietly.

He grins. I can't help seeing the similarity between him and Adam and Kyle. He is absolutely the older version of them, they must be the spitting image of his younger self. All he has are some extra lines on his face, and that incorrigible evil glint in his eye. He's like an aged movie star. A real George Clooney better-with-age type. Good looking. It's a shame he's pure evil.

"I want you to help me get at least one of my boys back on my side. Either one. Preferably Kyle, because Adam's got a bit too much Dorothy about him, a bit too much of a conscience. Then I'll tell you where your real parents are,

123

and I'll let you go. I'm a reasonable man. I can hold up my side of a bargain," he assures me.

He's very convincing, but I know he's a master manipulator. I can't trust a word he says. He'll double cross me without a second's thought. What am I to him? A playing piece. Besides, Jeremy told me my parents are dead. How stupid does he think I am?

"How am I supposed to do that?" I ask.

"My boys are chasing me, as you know. They want to see me caught again. But more than that, they want to see you safe. I can lure them here, but after they 'save' you, you must convince one of them to join me. Tell them whatever you want. Tell them I've changed or that they should try to trick me once I think they're on my side. It won't be true, of course, I know them too well, but I need one of them for the next phase of my plan."

"But why? Why do you need anyone? Aren't you like super-powerful?" I ask. Flattery never hurt.

"Oh, I don't need anyone, you're quite right. But I do have a bit of a flair for the dramatic, I'm a creative soul and I want to create a masterpiece. For that, I need my replicas. I'm working on Damian, but he's a bit of a square, and I need another one for this to work. Of course, if you'd rather keep Jeremy, I'll happily take them both."

"No!" I respond quickly. "I want Adam!"

"As I thought. So, do we have a deal?" He clasps his hands together.

"What are you going to do with Jeremy?" I ask.

"Now, now, Ella, one matter at a time. I'm not here to tell you all my secrets over tea and biscuits, I'm not your gal pal. Do we have a deal?"

"But are you going to hurt him?" I can't help worrying about his safety. He's been seemingly knocked out ever since the hotel room.

"Look I gave you a choice, and you chose Adam. Whatever happens to Jeremy isn't any of your business. Okay?" He glares at me.

"Fine, I'll do it. Help them find me and I'll convince Kyle to join you. But I can't guarantee he'll stay, he's not stupid."

He smiles again.

"Of course he's not, he's my son. Unlike this freakish piece of crap," he says, pushing Jeremy's chair over. His body doesn't react as it hits the ground. What has he done to him?

"And I want to take her with me," I say, pointing at Maria.

"Nope. No more negotiating, you agreed. Wait there whilst I go set the wheels in motion. I don't think they'll be far behind, although I did hear they were having some car trouble."

He laughs menacingly as he retreats back up the stairs. He forgot to put the tape back over my mouth but accompanied by an unconscious Jeremy and a gagged woman called Maria, I have little else to say.

Jenny (1993)

I'm done with all this dreaming, I want to wake up. I don't understand why this is happening to me. I'm bored of seeing this all back, of hearing my past thoughts. I don't want to watch my visual diary anymore. I get it, I'm a bad person. I never deserved to do so well in life. I should have helped Beth. I shouldn't have abandoned Jeremy. I should have told someone, probably everyone. But it's done, right? You can't change the past. So why do I have to keep rewatching it? How long has it been now? Shouldn't I be dead? I am not eating, not drinking... All I am doing is dreaming, and it is most uncomfortable. If only I could get this blooming mask off my eyes, perhaps I'd stand a chance.

Although, it's not like Gerome is controlling this dream session. This narration isn't from him. This is me, my younger self. My guilty conscience.

Did he know this is what would happen if he left me here to dream?

He couldn't have, could he?

My self-disgust doesn't help him. It doesn't help anyone. All it does is make me feel like rubbish.

Ah.

So maybe there is a point.

*

"You don't have to do this, you know," I tell him, looking up from the marriage register, a tear glistening on my cheek. He smiles and takes both of my hands in his, causing the pen to drop out of my hand, and gently nudges my engagement ring. We haven't got our specially engraved wedding bands back yet, but we couldn't wait.

"Yes, yes, I do, Jenny. I want us to be a family. You, me, Maria and whatever future children we have. I love you." I sign the register and quickly wipe my face to prevent tears from landing on the important page.

Rob is quite possibly the best man I have ever met. The most honest, the most trusting, the most caring. He has the most beautiful soul and now not only is he my second husband, but he's also Maria's adopted father. But that stays between us. To everyone else he is her father. We moved to a place where nobody knew us, and they accepted us as what we appear to be: a happy little family.

That previous time of my life is behind me, it has to be. Gerome lied to me, I saw his wedding announcement in the paper. He didn't get taken, he got married! To some country bumpkin called Dorothy who probably had no idea what she was letting herself in for. It hurt, reading that he left me for another woman. It hurt even more when I heard he'd had twins with her.

But I had to put that life behind me, for Maria's sake. My final connection to him. I promised him I would look after her, and I am doing that. She is flourishing under Rob's influence. I can't imagine it's what Gerome would have wanted, but I'm not sure I care about that anymore. She's mine now, he gave up his rights to her the moment he left. Perhaps even the moment he conceived her. I realise *now that I was a fool to believe it was Al'. Of course it was Gerome – Al' wanted out. Blaming him was just Gerome's way of punishing him, and he fooled me into helping.*

Well, no more. I'm a changed woman. I won't be complicit in anything like that ever again. Rob and I are quiet members of the Dream-Walker community, we live in an area dominated by regular humans, and we blend in. Maria will grow up to be a kind young woman, nothing like her real father.

I haven't told Rob about Gerome. I told him that Maria's dad was dead. I didn't even admit I'm not her biological mother. I've had a baby, so it was plausible, why complicate things? Perhaps I should have, perhaps one day I will, but I can't help thinking that it's safer this way.

Sometimes, when I look at that red mane around Maria's face, I think of Beth and the time we shared together. It feels like a lifetime ago, especially those good days at the start, those innocent days when we thought we were lucky to be chosen by Gerome to be with him and spread his ideas. Before he broke my heart and raped her.

I do feel bad that she doesn't get to know her child, but it's not like she ever wanted her anyway. I know that she would look at her and see Gerome because I do, too. She'd recognise his brown eyes and the shape of his nose and chin. It's all there, beside her red hair.

The resemblance doesn't stir hate within me, like it should. I'm glad she looks like him. She's like a comfort blanket for when I want to reminisce about those times silently, in my head. It wasn't all bad, was it?

Kyle

"We need to find a car," says Adam, staring longingly up the dark road.

"No shit Sherlock," I scoff, "let's start walking that way." I take the lead on the narrow pavement. It's so dark that it's hard to see where we're walking, and we keep nearly tripping up. Absolutely no cars pass us the entire 45 minutes it takes for us to get to the slightly bigger road. We pause at the top and survey the roads below from our vantage point, now overlooking some routes back towards the city. It's going to take a miracle to find a car.

Adam is clearly shitting himself over what Dad might be up to, extra worried because he left Ella behind. It reminds me of how I felt when Philip took Izzy; how I was so far away and completely unable to come to her rescue. We begin to walk along the top road, keeping our thoughts to ourselves.

Like some kind of mirage, about four hours after we left Marcus' cottage, a light comes from behind us. I spin around and begin waiving my arms frantically. Please stop, please!

The headlights appear to slow down as they get closer, and the car finally grinds to a halt. I rush to the window and it's only then that I see the face inside.

"You have got to be kidding me," I mutter.

The passenger door window is opened and Damian leans over from the driver's side,

"Alright brothers, do you need a lift?"

I can't fucking believe it. Damian. It's obvious who sent our raised in captivity triplet out here to collect us, Dad. I look at Adam to gage his reaction and decide how to play this. He steps forwards,

"He's got Ella, hasn't he?" he asks Damian.

"How would I know?"

"Don't play dumb. He told you to come and get us, didn't he? After he fucking stole our car earlier."

I've not seen Adam be like this before, so protective and aggressive. I want to hold him back, but I'm kind of proud.

"What makes you think that was him?" asks Damian.

Adam and I frown at one another.

"Did you see him?"

No.

"He left a note," says Adam. Damian laughs condescendingly.

"Oh gosh I can really see why he's disappointed in you now. You're not the smartest chips off the old block, are you?" His tone is aggravating me.

"And you are?" I snap.

"Well I'm the one with a car, aren't I? Now do you want a lift, or do you want me to leave you to your night-time stroll?" We hesitate. Adam speaks first.

"Where are you going to take us?"

"Where I'm told to," he replies in a childish singsong voice.

"Do you always do as you're told?" I butt in. Damian has been a pain in our backsides from the moment we found out he existed. Which admittedly wasn't that long ago in the grand scheme of things, but doesn't make him any less of a pain.

"When it's the right thing to do." He flashes a toothy smile.

"Now who's the stupid one?" snaps Adam. Helping our dad is never the right thing to do, by anyone's standards, not The Resistance's and definitely not the HJD's.

"Look, I'm not going to wait here all bloody night. Do you want a lift or not? You're letting the cold air in!"

"Fine." I answer for the both of us. Might as well discover what our dad has planned sooner rather than later. I hope Ella's okay, she might be with him by now. Probably is, given that we seem to have acted exactly according to his plans so far and I doubt Jeremy would have put up much of a fight. I notice Adam's knuckles are white from the pressure of squeezing his fists.

It's only a short journey before we pull up outside a large, detached farmhouse, and for a moment I can't help but remember the dream I shared with Ella all those months ago, almost a year now, when I saved her from a zombie apocalypse and brought her to a farmhouse just like this, on horseback. We snuggled by the fire, skin to skin.

Adam nudges me and I fear I've somehow shared that thought with him, but he's just trying to point out that the car we drove to Marcus' cottage is parked at the side of the property under a car port. Phew. It's a pain when I get those flashbacks. Those steamy dream-memories are so inappropriate and make me feel like the absolute shittiest brother ever. Especially now that Adam gets fake dream scenes of me and Ella together when he has sex with her. I don't need to provide him with real ones.

But I can't help how I feel about her. The lines got well and truly blurred over this past year, and it's not like I can just grab a pencil and ruler and make them clear. I caught

131

feelings. Feelings I hadn't had since Izzy. Not quite as deep, but still, feelings. I know they're wrong and completely inappropriate and uncool, but I couldn't help myself.

And it's not like I can even distract myself with Tasha on my crew, because she is so clearly into Max – and of course, now that I know her sister is actually my half-sister, that all just took on a whole other level of confusion and wrongness. I suppose there's always Frankie…

"Wait here," instructs Damian, exiting the car and locking us in.

"Oh for God's sake," says Adam. "Now we're sitting ducks!"

"Calm down," I reassure him. "I'm sure Dad hasn't had us brought here to kill us, let's just play it cool and see what happens."

"That's easy for you to say, he doesn't have your girlfriend tied up somewhere. Or worse."

"Hey! You don't know that! She might still be with Jeremy."

"Oh sure, Jeremy the blonde male model who has the same bizarre issue she does but is otherwise just a boarding school educated poser? Sure, he'll have been able to stand up to our dad. He'd probably faint at the sight of him; tosser."

Jealousy really is ugly, it would seem.

"You're probably right. Besides, they might have been distracted having sex and testing his theory when Dad turned up. It's hard to fight when you're balls deep." I can't resist winding him up.

"Shut up," he grunts. "We need a plan."

"I don't think we're really in a position to make one right now, do you?"

"Well we need to do something before he comes back! What if Ella's in there and Dad's going to try to get us to

132

join him in exchange for releasing Ella? What do we do then?"

"We join him and release Ella," I answer.

"Obviously, but can I trust you to protect her? If something happens to me, or we get double-crossed or whatever Dad's grand plan ends up being – are we both agreed that no matter what, we protect Ella?" He's practically begging.

"Of course."

"Okay, good."

The only person I'd save over Ella is Izzy. And she's been dead three years.

Jenny (1994)

Younger me is starting to feel more like older me now as I find myself in hospital.

As I look down at the latest bundle of joy in my arms, I feel conflicted. Here I hold my second born child, a little girl who will be raised as Maria's little sister despite them having no biological connection. Her half-brother is now about eight years old, and he probably thinks I'm dead. At the very least, he hates me. I abandoned him. He has a wealthy and well-respected father whom I'm sure will see to it that he gets a good education, but a child needs more than that. A child needs a mother.

How can I ever call myself a good mother to Maria or little baby Tasha, when I abandoned my firstborn child? When I treated him like a job, like an obligation I could cut out of my life, rather than a young boy with feelings. This little girl looks a lot like he did as a baby. I can already tell that she has inherited my blonde hair, and it looks like she will have blue eyes too, though they say all babies do to start with.

My heart breaks when I look at her because all I can think of is how I left Jeremy. Why should she get to live with me when I abandoned him? I'm a terrible person. I don't

134

deserve to have children, yet somehow that's all I seem to be capable of – having children and looking after other people's children.

I help at a playgroup now because thanks to my time in The Resistance, I never got any qualifications. I dropped out of school just before I should have taken my O levels. The owner did a brief check on me and then agreed to let me help out, just so long as I'm never left unsupervised. It's better than sitting at home all day, and it means Maria gets to attend for free, not that we need to save money.

Maria is starting school next September; I wonder what type of school Jeremy has been sent to. Despite Rob's healthy income, Maria is going to the local primary school. Something tells me Jeremy is more than likely already away at a boarding school by now, allowing Francis to focus on his work.

I want to write to him, to explain myself, to tell him that if I could go back and do it all again, I would never leave him. But that would be a lie. I would always have done whatever Gerome asked me to. I would probably have killed him if he'd asked.

Tasha opens her mouth and stretches her tiny fingers, wriggling slightly before going back to sleep. My baby girl. Will I ever tell you about your half-brother? Will you ever meet him? I could make that happen, but I'm scared.

I'm scared of telling Rob the truth about my past, I'm scared of Gerome finding me in the future and destroying the new life I've created. He told me to never tell anyone about Jeremy, to completely erase that part of my life. It never happened. I'm not supposed to have any connection to the Minister or the HJD, or even Gerome. When he left me that day, his instructions were clear. Until he returns, none of this ever happened. But we never agreed what happens when he returns.

Those instructions left me with a large gap of time to fill with made-up stories. Rob often asks me about my late teen years and tries to find similarities between what we both got up to, he's nostalgic like that. He talks of pub nights and movies and what definitely didn't happen behind the bike sheds... How can I ever tell him that I spent those years with Gerome Clarke, the most dangerous known Dream-Walker, and that I loved him, despite his crimes?

I can go days, weeks, even the occasional month without thinking about the time I spent with Gerome, but when something reminds me of him – it could be the smell of a particular brand of cigarette, or even the sound of a beer being opened – I crumble. There's a lump in my throat and I feel sick and it's like I can't go on anymore. I miss him like crazy when that happens. I know it's irrational, but I do.

I usually tell Rob it's PMS. The last nine months I've blamed pregnancy hormones. He believes me, too. Because he's never had a reason not to.

But if I told him the truth, would he accept it? Would he believe that I am truly happy with him in our new life? Or would he remember those random emotional outbursts? Would he leave me because I'm still not over my ex? My ex that was never even mine. Not really. He was a fantasy, a powerful crush. An addiction.

Have I really been pondering this since 1994?

Jenny

I hear a key in the lock of the front door and I open my eyes to look at the darkness inside the eye mask, determined not to fall back to sleep.

"Well, that was a dead end, huh? I hope your mum can shed some more light on things," says a male voice.

"Yeah, Al' was even less use than your psycho aunt!" says another voice, I think it might be Tasha.

"Hey!" Screeches another, playfully.

"Mum?" Tasha's voice calls.

I let out a sigh of relief, realising I was holding my breath.

"In here!" I shout. I hear multiple footsteps entering the room, Tasha must still be with her group from yesterday. She rushes over to me and removes the eye mask. I open my eyes and blink to recover from the sudden injection of light. She's with a couple of the people she was with last time, but there's no sign of Gerome's son or one of the other men. There's three of them, Tasha, the beefcake, and the redhead with the attitude.

"What happened?" Tasha asks, struggling with the ties. "Shit," she pauses to check a nail she has just broken. "Can

137

you do it?" she asks her male friend. He kneels down beside me and gets to work undoing Gerome's knots.

"It was Gerome. I didn't know he was here but as soon as you left, he came downstairs and tied me up."

"Oh my God! I'm so sorry. And you've been tied up ever since? You must be starving!" She kneels down with concern in her eyes. "But, why would he do that? I thought you were a team, even if you didn't admit that to us."

"I don't know! Maybe he didn't want me to tell you he was here?" I answer, flustered.

"But why bother? He had already been to the vets for Maria, why was he here? Mum, what aren't you telling us?"

"Maria? Is Maria okay?" I ask, ignoring her question. I had forgotten he went after Maria. That feels like so long ago now. I truly am a terrible mother figure.

The man finishes untying me and I stand up, motioning that we should all take a seat on the couch. The cushions feel so much nicer than our hardwood flooring. Tasha rushes to get me a glass of water.

"I don't know what you want me to say, love. I used to know him, so maybe he sees me as a threat."

"But you did everything he asked you to. It doesn't make any sense for him to come here. Not for any negative reason, anyway." Tasha has always been sceptical, but never of me. Her eyes are so full of doubt and anger, it physically pains me.

"Maybe he just wanted to see me," I shrug. I wish. I wrote to him for years and he never responded. I have a very vague idea what he was looking for upstairs, but I need to check if it's gone before I'll admit it. There's no use admitting to something irrelevant.

"Mum, we're all in danger now that Gerome is out and clearly, he has plans for Maria. I need you to tell us everything. And you need to tell Dad, too. He's on his way home now. Luckily, he was out visiting a farm when

138

Gerome ransacked the vets and took Maria, he ended up staying there overnight as there were some complications with the cows giving birth. He went straight from there back to the vets this morning, so he doesn't know what's going on. All he knows is that the vet clinic was broken into. You need to tell him the truth. It's not safe for him not to know anymore. It was never safe, for any of us."

She is so serious, and so right. How did I raise such an intelligent and strong individual? She knows right from wrong so much better than I ever did. I suppose that's Rob's influence. I cannot take credit.

"I know. I'm sorry. But I told you everything earlier. I used to be with him, and then I looked after Maria, and that's it." I look up at my beautiful baby girl. Those blue eyes have never looked so distrusting of me before. The man caresses her arm, and the other woman with fiery red hair glares at me.

"Can I ask who you are?" I address the woman. She rolls her eyes at me.

"Sure, I'm Frankie. I'm Beth's niece. You stole my cousin from me."

"I thought I recognised that red hair and attitude," I smile at her.

"It's strawberry blonde," she snaps. I'll admit, she's done a good job styling it, but there's no denying she's a redhead. And she shouldn't be ashamed of that either, it looks good. It matches her attitude. She and Beth would have got along well.

I catch myself just before I tell her that, realising that the reason she doesn't have much of a relationship with her aunt (I imagine) is because I helped to have her committed, because she didn't want Gerome's baby. She's another reminder of what a terrible person I am.

I excuse myself to the toilet, informing them that we may as well wait until Rob is back before I say anything else, because he's going to need to hear it all from the beginning. I stand in front of the sink and stare at my reflection. My blue eyes seem less bright today, they're red and puffy from crying. My once-blonde hair glistens with strands of grey against my blotchy unwashed face. Frown lines cross my forehead, and my skin itself is so much looser than it was in youth. Perhaps Gerome didn't like what he saw. Perhaps I haven't aged to his liking. I have put on some weight. With the lines and the greys, perhaps I am no longer his type.

Perhaps I never was.

But I still felt that connection when I saw him, even when he did what he did. He must have felt it too. We're electric; we're meant to be. Perhaps it's just a game, or a test. Perhaps he is watching to see how easily I will confess his secrets.

But what do I have left to confess? Aside from Rob, they know the basics now, and they know the biggest secret: Maria. If I tell them about Jeremy, is that not my secret to tell? Gerome told me to do it, but ultimately, it's my secret, it's my shame. I'm the one who did it. It has nothing to do with him. Surely, he wouldn't care about that secret getting out.

My final idea seems silly and highly unlikely. I think I should keep it to myself. One last secret. I'm probably wrong, but when I get a moment alone, I'll check if it's gone.

"Mum, we need you to come out here please."

It's Tasha, sounding very authoritative. She got like that when she joined The Resistance. Or rather, The Resistance '2.0' as I like to think of it, since I was in the original Resistance, and this lot are a poor imitation at best. It's like everything, I suppose. Gone are the days of rioting and rallies, of really fighting for what you believe in, of taking action. These days they have petitions, they argue in courtrooms, but they don't physically do anything.

Since Gerome got locked up, nothing has changed for Dream-Walkers. Not really. Several are still raised in cages, several are still tested like lab rats, and those of us who live relatively freely, are still observed and required to live within the lines. I have no problem living within the lines established by the Human Justice Department, I just don't believe that we should have to. Just because we can do more than other humans, doesn't mean that we should be regulated. So what if we have an 'advantage' which enables us to trick people sometimes? Other people can do that too, they just have to go about it in a different way. It's not like we're the only ones committing fraud or tricking people into falling in love with them.

Oh Rob, will he think I tricked him? There's no denying our lives would have turned out quite differently if he hadn't taken Maria and I under his wing. He has always been so caring and supportive.

"Mum, come out, now," Tasha orders. I sigh and unlock the bathroom door.

I reach the living room just as Rob comes through the front door. His grin falters as he looks at Tasha, her man, and Beth's niece.

"What's going on? Has something happened?" He rushes over to me and wraps me in his arms before I can say a word.

"Mum has something to tell you," Tasha informs him, squeezing the hand of the man. I wonder if he is her boyfriend, we still haven't been introduced. Rob looks at me, concerned.

"Is this about what happened at the vets?"

I ignore his question and start at the beginning.

"Darling, I… When I told you about my past, I skipped over a few details, and I fluffed some of the facts."

141

"Okay," he smiles reassuringly, with only a slight frown.

"It's," I swallow my nerves and try again. "It's a long story. Please, sit down."

We sit together on our smaller two-seater couch, Rob holds my hand and strokes it comfortingly, like he always has.

"When I was eighteen, I joined a group called The Resistance, led by Gerome Clarke. You've heard about him, right?" He nods.

"He's a piece of work, that's for sure. He's the one who's been causing all this madness, isn't he? At least that's what people are saying."

"Apparently," I nod. "I worked with him, trying to fight for our cause, equality for Dream-Walkers everywhere and, um, after a few years or so, he asked me to do something for him. Something big." I look over at Tasha and her pals, I didn't mention this part earlier.

"He asked me to go and have a baby with the future Minister of the Human Justice Department, Francis Krunk."

All eyes are on me.

"So Maria wasn't your first child, you'd had one already?" Rob asks. I nod slowly and bite my lip.

"I had a little boy, blonde hair, blue eyes, adorable little thing. And then I left him, because Gerome told me to."

"What? You're telling me I have a brother out there?" Tasha interrupts.

"Yes, your brother is called Jeremy, he's the Minister's son."

"But why didn't you tell me about that? If Gerome made you do it, and he can make anyone do anything, why didn't you tell me?" asks Rob.

"Because I was scared, I wasn't meant to tell anyone. And, anyway, there's more."

Rob frowns.

"Maria isn't my child, I adopted her. I didn't have a choice. I was sworn to secrecy. Her real parents are Gerome Clarke and Beth Parker."

"But why didn't you tell me? I would have understood. Why lie, Jenny?" Rob still looks at me with love. Where is the hate that should be filling his eyes right now? I lied to him. He should be angry.

"I couldn't tell you. That was an even bigger secret."

I start to cry, and he pulls me into him.

"Darling, I love you. I always knew there were things you weren't telling me about your past, but I figured they didn't matter because they were in the past. We've built a life together, Jenny." He looks up at the others. "What danger are we in now that Gerome's free?"

"Well, we think he's taken Maria, and he tied Mum up as he passed through." Tasha responds, matter-of-factly.

"He what? He's been here?" His eyes open wide in alarm. "Tell me, what should we do?"

"You don't need to do anything, Dad. Just maybe go away for a while, stay somewhere safe. I can't believe you aren't mad that Mum never told you the truth. She's been lying to you for as long as you've known her!"

It's like a switch has been flicked inside her, she's furious. Rob didn't give her the response she needed; he didn't have a go at me and now she needs to vent. Luckily, Rob is still calm.

"I love her, Tasha. Your Mum and I-"

"-You built a life on lies!" she interrupts again.

My baby girl hates me. I suppose it makes sense, given that she believes Gerome is the ultimate bad guy. She doesn't know him like I do, or thought I did. But I can hardly tell her that, she'd never understand.

I watch as her possible boyfriend whispers into her ear and tries to comfort her. I don't know what I can do or say to make any of this better.

143

"Is there anything else?" She practically spits the words out.

I shake my head,

"No, I think that's everything."

"You think?" She raises her eyebrows. "Well you said you told us everything the first time, too. So how about you think a little bit harder, hey?" She tilts her head; I can't believe she's being so aggressive.

I can't back down now. I can't admit there is one small thing that may or may not still be upstairs and may or may not be the key to one of Gerome's special skills. I might be wrong, and, what if this is a test like I thought? What if Gerome is waiting to see if I tell them? I can't. I have to keep this one thing secret. It's the only secret I have left. I can do that.

"Tasha, if your mum says that's everything, then that's everything." Rob comes to my defence. I feel so guilty.

"I think I can fill in the gaps, if you'd like," offers Frankie, Beth's niece. I frown at her. What does she think she knows?

"I went to see my aunt recently, and she shed some light on your time together, on the dynamics of the group, if you get what I mean." I do get what she means, and I don't want her to say it. What am I going to do? This is a detail they don't need to know. It's only going to make them hate me more.

"Um…" I try to take the spotlight, but words fail me. Tasha gives Frankie an irritated glare, clearly aggravated that she's been holding back information.

"Go on," says Frankie, smiling.

"I, err…" I clear my throat. "Okay, well, back in the day, you know, a long time ago when I was naïve and I didn't know any better, I sort of, maybe, perhaps, had a bit of a thing for Gerome Clarke."

Frankie laughs,

144

"That's putting it mildly from what I hear."

I look at Rob and he shrugs. He doesn't mind because he knows it's in the past, like he said. Besides, I'm probably not his first love either. How did I get so lucky?

"Mum!" shouts Tasha, bursting my bubble and clapping rudely in my face. "Did you or did you not love Gerome Clarke?"

"Excuse me? You're my daughter, how dare you speak to me like that! Who I loved before you were born is none of your business!"

"So, you did?" she retorts. I stand in frustration.

"Yes, okay? I did. I admit it. I fell for the 'bad guy', the guy with all the power and promise. I'm so sorry to disappoint you!" I shout, losing control.

"Did you help him today? Before we arrived, before he tied you up, did you help him find Maria?"

"No! Of course not!"

"But you loved him! You would do anything for those you love, wouldn't you, Mum? That's what you've always told us. Do you still love him? Did he break your heart?" I can see she's shaking, and her possible boyfriend is trying to calm her down. I hate how much I'm distressing her.

"It's not what you think. It's all in the past, okay? It's all in the past. I did what I did back then partly because I loved him, but he left me, and I moved on. Okay? I looked after Maria, and I looked after you, and we built a nice life here, didn't we?"

"I don't know, should I be glad you didn't abandon me like you did my brother, or should I be angry that you have been lying to me for my entire life?"

"Tasha, please, calm down. You know your mum only lied to keep you safe. To keep us all safe. She couldn't tell us." Rob tells her reasonably.

She turns and cries into her possible boyfriend's chest, who strokes her back awkwardly. I may have misjudged

145

their relationship. But he seems kind, I hope they explore their connection. Frankie is tapping on her phone, probably reporting everything they've just found out to somebody who is going to make this all so much worse.

"I want to meet my brother," Tasha says between sniffs.

"I'd quite like to see him too." I admit.

Rob squeezes my hand,

"Me too."

"Oh well isn't this going to be one happy family reunion?" Says Frankie. "Unfortunately, Maria and Jeremy are currently with Gerome, rumour has it, so unless you want to confront him too…"

I feel as if a hand is holding my heart and squeezing. Gerome. We need to talk. I need to see him, on a level playing field.

"Do you know where he has them?" I ask the fiery woman with an evil glint in her eye.

"I can find out," she grins and returns to tapping on her phone.

Ella

"Jeremy, can you hear me?" I whisper at his motionless body. Surely, he's going to wake up soon. I watch for movement. He's still on the floor, attached to the chair, like he has been since Gerome knocked the chair over.

"Maria, if he's unconscious, can you get in his head? Is he dreaming?" I squint into the darkness at the back of the room and just about decipher a shake of the head.

I hope he's not going to die. He's the only person I've met who's like me, who understands that mixed emotion when you release and ride the wave of orgasm only to have it ruined moments later as you study your partner's face and they are definitely not in a state of 'bliss.'

There's so much more I'd like to talk to him about. Even if we don't test out his theory, we could still take notes, figure out similarities and differences between our P.I.N.S. abilities. I would also love to see him reconnect with his dad, the Minister. As much as he's after me, for leaving the MIU and for being one of these weirdos, he always seemed like a kind man. I think he would like to get to know his son again, and not just as a test subject.

Or maybe I'm just naïve and have completely misinterpreted him. Jeremy obviously doesn't see him that way.

I can hear movement in the room above us, footsteps of more than one person. Pacing. Muffled voices I can't quite make out. Maybe this is it, already. Adam and Kyle have come to save me.

Speaking of which, I can't believe I'm waiting to be saved again. What kind of misogynistic bullshit is this? I think I should make a vow to myself that this will never happen again. I'm going to learn that thing, oh, what's it called? That martial arts thing that women often do? Krav Maga, that's it. I'm going to learn to kick butt and I'm going to get super fit. I'll find some kind of gadget or medicine that stops you closing your eyes or sleeping, and I'll become un-kidnappable. Uncatchable. Un-arrestable.

Although, if any such gadget or medicine exists, I'd like to think that the right people already know about it, that they're using it against Gerome. Surely there has to be something. Dream-Walkers have been around for centuries, haven't they? Surely not every human who has known about them has been walking around with crossed fingers every day, hoping they don't blink at the wrong moment.

The Minister himself is human, he can't possibly be taking that risk day in day out. He must have something. That would be a top priority, surely. A necessary defence. You can't work with creatures more dangerous than you without some kind of defence plan.

Without one, he'd be insane. There's no way he'd have lasted this long. He can't trust them. Surely, he doesn't trust them. He's not stupid.

The basement door opens and I'm dragged away from my internal monologue, keen to see who is coming down to see us this time.

Adam? Kyle? Or Gerome again? A man makes his way down the steps, but I hear the door close and lock behind him. Legs. Middle. Head.

But which one of them is it? It's dark, it could be any of them.

"Adam? Is that you?" I ask as he reaches for the light and blinds me.

*

Once I'm able to see again, I realise it is indeed Adam, or at least one of the three brothers who share that face. He looks pained as he rushes to my side and begins untying me. He doesn't pay any attention to the other two hostages, despite stepping over Jeremy's body. It seems almost too heartless to be Adam, but then again, I've seen how icy he can turn when he's hurt. Like when he first learnt what Kyle did for us.

"Is it over? Did you do what he asked? Is Kyle with your dad now?" I ask him.

"Yep," he replies, struggling with the tie around my right wrist.

"Adam, are you okay? Talk to me."

"I've got your mother's address and we're going to go meet her there now," he says with zero emotion. I know that's not true because my mother is dead, and Adam knows that too. So, who is this? Damian? Kyle? Please let it be Kyle. Damian was not a nice guy the last time we met. I look around at Maria.

"Don't you want to meet your half-sister at least?" I ask, playing along. I'm sure the real Adam would want to.

"Nope."

He doesn't even look up. Once my arms are both free, I grab his forearms to make him stop and look at me,

"Adam, please!"

149

"I'm not in the mood, Ella," he says with a warning tone.

"What happened?"

"You really want to know?"

I nod.

"*He* is what happened." He points at Jeremy. "I heard about your little smooch session with him just before my dad got there. How could you Ella? After everything, how could you do that to me?"

"But I didn't! We didn't! I swear, he's lying to you. We didn't do anything!"

"But you wanted to."

He plays the role of 'Angry Adam' very well. Could Jeremy's information have been wrong? Could my mother be alive?

"No, I didn't! I just... I just wanted to know." I feel tears building up, threatening to spill. I don't want him to be mad at me. I miss him.

"I.e., you wanted to fuck him."

"No!"

He yanks me by the arm to pull me up.

"Come on, let's go find your mum, see if she's a slut too."

"Adam, stop it! Why are you being like this? Let go of me!" I struggle.

Jealousy can make a man do terrible things, perhaps even team up with their evil father and manhandle their girlfriend. It's possible I have broken him. Oh, Adam!

"How do I even know it's you?" I ask, wiping my eyes. "After what happened last time in the MIU with Damian, how do I even know it's really you and not another trick?"

He huffs at me.

"Seriously?"

"Yes. I'm not going with you if you might not be who you say you are. Perhaps there's a whole army of men who look like you!"

He tilts his head and raises his eyebrows, mocking me. He taps his foot as he thinks.

"Alright then, how's this for proof?" He pulls me into him, my breasts press against his chest, and then he kisses me. Lightly at first, then with more and more pressure until I feel like my legs have turned to jelly and I desperately want to rip his clothes off. I pull away to catch my breath.

"Wow," I say.

"I missed you," he shrugs.

I am so confused. Yes, that was a good kiss. But was it with Adam? Or was it just another distraction, something to stop me from questioning who this man really is? Would Angry Adam really kiss me like that? There was something different about that kiss, something different about the taste of his mouth, but I can't quite put my finger on it. I roll my tongue around my mouth as I consider it. Perhaps it's just my breath. I haven't done my teeth in a while.

"Are you ready then?" he asks.

"Okay."

It's not like I could beat him in a fight anyway, whoever he is.

Adam

"Look! Over there!" I point as a door opens at the side of the property. Two figures walk out towards the car we took to Uncle Marcus' cottage. One of them looks distinctively like us, and the other is smaller and feminine. Ella?

"What the fuck is he playing at?" exclaims Kyle, reaching over and punching the centre of the steering wheel. The horn has been disabled so nothing happens.

I press up against the glass window and try to get her attention by banging and shouting, but we're too far away. They get into the car and drive away without even glancing in our direction.

"Do you think she realises that's not me?" I ask Kyle.

"Of course she does. She's not stupid."

"But why is he moving her? If they had her secured here, why bring us here to see her be taken elsewhere? What is Dad up to?"

"As if I know! We need to follow them!"

"Great plan, when did you learn how to hotwire a car?" I ask him, already knowing the answer.

"I didn't."

So we're stuck, waiting outside a farmhouse which no longer contains my girlfriend, until our dad decides to reveal whatever the hell he's up to.

"Hey, do you think Jeremy is in there?" I ask him.

"How would I know? But yeah, if I was going to bet, I'd say so. And maybe some other people Dad's taken along the way, people who might be useful either for their skills or as bargaining chips."

"Ooh, maybe our half-sister is in there!"

He nods slowly. I wonder if it's occurred to him that he might have actually slept with our half-sister, before we found out she existed. We know he did with her cousin, repeatedly, and don't they say that sort of thing can happen when siblings don't know about each other? There's a peculiar attraction to something similar but different; that feels familiar for seemingly no reason. Plus, if she has red hair, he clearly likes that on Frankie, so it stands to reason there are probably a few red-haired notches on his bedpost, as it were.

Although, Izzy was a blonde, I think. I only met her a couple of times. She's the only girl my brother has ever truly loved. Unless you count Ella, which doesn't bear thinking about.

There's a tap on the glass and we both turn to see our dad stood there, smiling at us. Where did he come from? He presses the button on his key to unlock the doors.

"Where is he taking her? What do you want from us?" Kyle's questions pour out before I can think of anything clever to say to the man who created us.

"She's fine, for now. I'm just getting her out of the way, so you don't get any ideas. She thinks she's with Adam."

"Are you sure about that?" I give him a sideways glance.

"Well judging by their reunion kiss, I would say so." He pouts and starts making kissing noises.

153

Oh for fuck's sake, another man taking a go on my girl. The jealousy ripples through me.

"What do you want 'Dad'?" asks Kyle.

"Oh, it feels so good to hear you call me that Kylie-boy!" he chuckles, "I need your help."

"You never need anyone's help," Kyle replies.

"Alright, you've got me. I want your help. Damian's a bit too… boring. He's got the thirst, but he hasn't got the passion. He doesn't care about anything or anyone. Whereas you two, you care too much which means you can get the sympathy vote. People will believe you because you can cry like bitches and tug on their heart strings. Believe me, I tried to get Damian to cry once, and ice came out."

"You brought us here to cry?"

He laughs.

"I brought you here to help 'fix' my reputation."

Kyle and I exchange a look.

"I have no intention of actually changing, obviously, but there are a couple of things I'd like to do properly, and one of them requires me to be elected as the new Minister. I need people to vote me in. As you know, votes are cast with eyes open, and the voters are kept isolated for two weeks prior, so there is no way I can influence their final decision. Plus, that's just a whole lot of effort, and I don't want Francis Krunk to accuse me of cheating. I want his people to turn on him truly and completely with no doubts. They are going to choose me over him, and you're going to help make that happen."

"The people are scared of you; it's going to take more than the sympathy vote for that to work." I inform him.

"Well it looks like you've got your work cut out for you then, but I know you'll pull something out of the bag, if you ever want to see Ella again."

"There it is," mutters Kyle.

"Sorry?" says Dad.

154

"I said 'there it is.' The standard blackmail. Help me or I'll dot dot dot. Honestly Dad, it's getting boring already and you only just got out."

"Can't help if it works," he shrugs, "and look how easy you made it for me by both caring for the same girl!"

He begins to give us ideas of little publicity stunts he wants to do, that paint him in a 'good' light and suggest his power could be harnessed for good, but I can't concentrate, my mind is elsewhere.

Where is Damian taking Ella, and does she really not know that I'm not him? Does she think she's safe? Is he going to pretend to be me, to all extents of the term 'boyfriend'? He'd better fucking not. I'll kill him. And what about Jeremy? He was supposed to be looking after her. Whatever his intentions, I'm pretty sure he wouldn't have let this happen lightly. Is he hurt? Did Dad kill him? Is that also part of his plan to destroy the Minister? Although, if so, he clearly didn't get the memo about him testing Jeremy as a kid and their complete lack of unity as adults.

"So, what do you think? Will you be ready for the rally tomorrow?" asks Dad.

I look up, no clue what the end decision was. Kyle seems to be on board, so I agree too. The sooner we destroy the world and help our dad become Minister, the sooner we can save Ella from whatever she's going through. But of course, there's no way we're actually going to help him become Minister, we're just going to have to figure out another plan whilst looking like we're doing as we're told. He's not the only one who can bluff.

The closer we can get to him, the easier it will be to work out his real end game and everything else he has going on. I just have to be patient. And hope that Ella isn't fooled by Damian. Fuck.

Ella

There is no way my mother either lives or ever lived here. The person who lives here is not a prostitute and didn't get killed in a freak supermarket accident. No. Way. A prostitute does not live in a house like this, in any century. Well, unless it's a live-in position, I suppose. Ring the bell if you need me… Yuck.

It's a great big house, very dated, with marble pillars and an actual roundabout for a turning space. The grounds are huge so far as I can tell; it looks like the kind of place that has its own stables. The kind of place you might find in a Jane Austen novel, a place one might hope to live if only they can gain the affection of the home's most eligible bachelor.

Despite that, I'm not getting romantic feelings as I look at the property. I'm noticing the darker details, the gargoyles and moss-covered statues. A broken window on the first floor. The darkness within.

This house is not a home. There's no warm glow coming from inside. There will be no jolly governess to greet us. It's empty, I can feel it. I look at Adam, still undecided if it's really him. He could believe that Jeremy's information was wrong and believe my mother lives here. But I doubt it.

"Come on then," he says, marching me towards the grand front door.

"Are you sure this is the place?" I ask him nervously.

"This is the address I was given. Why? Are you scared?" he asks me, but I don't hear any real concern in his voice. He doesn't care if I'm scared. It's not him. It can't be. Adam would care, no matter how angry and hurt he was, he'd care. Wouldn't he?

"Of course I'm bloody scared! But that's not why I asked. Don't you think this feels like a set up? A trap? Can we really trust your dad? Shouldn't we get back in the car and watch the place for a while?"

"Ella, it's fine. We gave him what he wanted, didn't we? So he gave us your mum's address. It's a business transaction."

"But what if she doesn't like me? What if she doesn't want to meet me?" I pull back, staring again at the empty house. I'm growing ever more certain this is a trap, and I don't want to cross the threshold.

"Who wouldn't want to meet you? You're amazing," he smiles at me.

"But she gave me up, she didn't want me. Why would she want to see me now? I know I wanted answers, but maybe she won't give them to me. Maybe I don't need to hear what she has to say about who or what I am. I think maybe this was a dumb idea. I want to go. Home. Anywhere. Away from here. Please, Adam. Don't make me go in there," I beg.

His jaw tightens, I can tell he's annoyed but trying not to show it.

"Don't be silly, we came all this way. We won't outstay our welcome, but you may as well meet the woman!" He reaches for my hand to pull me along, but I slap it away.

"No! I don't want to. Please!" I look back at the car. "Let's go get a coffee, think this through before we trample over her peaceful life."

"I'm sure she has coffee inside, Ella. Come on, you're being silly."

I start walking back towards the car.

"Ella, come back here! This is your childhood dream, is it not? To finally meet your birth mother, the woman who carried you inside herself for nine months. You can't back away now, you need to see this through." He storms towards me.

"Please Adam, don't make me go in there." I beg him again.

"I'm doing this for you, Ella. I drove you out here so you could meet her, so you could finally meet someone who shares your flesh and blood; who understands what you are. She might have some tips for us, Ella. For how to cope with your condition. Please, I really think we should go inside."

"She doesn't have any tips, Adam. Whatever you're hoping to find out isn't going to happen. She's in there alone, remember. If she had any tips, she would have stayed with my dad."

"She may have learnt more since back then." He tries to reason with me.

"Hardly. This P.I.N.S. stuff seems to have been kept very quiet. So, unless you're trying to tell me you think she's a scientist, or- Oh crap, you don't think the Minister is my dad too, do you? How incestuous is this Dream-Walker community? Is Jeremy my half-brother? Oh my God…"

"Look, we're never going to get any answers if we stand out here kicking stones in her driveway. We're going in." He grabs my bicep and pulls me back towards the front door.

158

"But what if she's not even in?" I ask as I struggle unsuccessfully to free my arm.

"Then it'll be a very short visit, won't it?"

He knows she's in. Or that whoever is really behind that door is, anyway. I pull away again.

"Please, Adam. Can't we think about this, come back later or something?"

"We're here now, and we're going in," he says, straining to pull me along.

"Adam, you're hurting me!"

He pushes me to the front step and hammers on the door. Hardly the polite way you might knock when you're about to meet your girlfriend's birth mother for the first time.

"Adam," I hiss.

As the door starts to open, I feel a sudden sharp prod in the back of my neck and I start to feel woozy.

"Adam?" I say again, as my legs give way, and he holds me under my armpits and drags me inside. He sits me on a chaise longue, but I feel dizzy, I can't sit up straight. I sway until I fall to one side. "Adam?"

He squats down to my level.

"Stop calling me Adam. I'm Damian and you knew that the moment you set eyes on me. The act is over, okay? We can stop pretending. Thanks for the kiss though, do you think you have room for another Clarke brother in that heart of yours?" He chuckles.

Oh no, I was right. This is a trap. The room is still spinning though, and I can't get a focus on the person who let us in. Is it a woman? Is it my mother? It's like I'm on a merry-go-round and I can't quite catch them. Each rotation I try to get a look, but the ride is going too fast. He/she is just a blur. I'm not sure.

I close my eyes briefly and breathe in the musty air. There is no way this is anybody's current residence. It's

159

also really cold. What kind of heating did they have back in Austen times? Was it just fireplaces? I shiver.

Have I been brought here to die?

If we're not meeting my mum, then why did Gerome send me here? What more could he possibly want from me? If Damian is here, that means Gerome has probably got both Adam and Kyle, so I'm of no further use. Right?

What is this place?

I can't think, and the spinning is starting to make me queasy. I realise Damian is talking to someone, but I can't even comprehend the words. They're distorted, like when FM radio plays up on a hot day; you're trying to listen to a song but you get French news playing over the top. Is he on the phone? Or is he talking to someone here, in this room?

My eyes are starting to feel heavy now, I'm struggling to keep them open. That's never a good thing these days. Once my eyes are closed, anything could happen. It'll be like Damian's big 'distraction' plan all over again.

Oh please no, if he puts me on a Dream-Walker rollercoaster again I think I might actually spew this time. I try to keep my eyes open as the world goes round me by spotting things as they go past.

A vase.

A pair of wellington boots.

Laughter.

Where is that coming from?

This room, or my head?

Where have I heard that laugh before?

It feels familiar, and yet I can't quite grasp it. Another rotation and I think I can see a second figure with Damian, a woman.

Is it my mum?

Surely not, she's dead.

It must be someone else under Gerome's control, helping him to trap an innocent woman. I can only catch glimpses of black. A long dress or something like that. But wait, is that red hair?

The world goes dark as my eyes close and all I can hear is that strangely familiar laughter as I sink deeper and deeper into sleep.

Adam

"Back in the eighties, I held rallies and protest marches and the people loved me. But that was before the 'me too' movement and Instagram and all that other stuff that I don't understand. It was before people saw me as a monster. But you guys understand all that, you can make them love me again. I know you can." Dad delivers his pep talk with a completely straight face.

"You realise the 'me too' movement is women speaking out about historic sexual abuse, right? Speaking out about people like you?" I query.

"Hey, they wanted to be with me, some of them just needed a bit of dream-world convincing."

"Oh, so Beth the lesbian wanted to be with you, did she? She wanted to carry your baby for nine months and then have you lock her up like a crazy lady? Are you sure about that?"

"Who told you that? Besides, Beth was different, I thought I was doing her a favour. How could she ever know what she was missing out on when she spent all her time lusting over Madonna and that woman from Crossroads? She needed to feel the warmth of a man inside her." I scoff,

162

"Sure Dad, I'm sure she was really glad you gave her that experience. That's why she tried to kill the baby, it had nothing to do with not wanting to have her rapist's child." I hope Frankie's information is accurate.

"Oh shut up! I was young, I don't do that anymore. You need to tell everyone, I am a changed man." He puffs out his chest.

"I feel like you're trying to make us sell devil worship to Christians. I don't think they're going to buy it."

"Well okay, maybe I'm not changed, I was just misunderstood. All those stories were nonsense. I was never like that. How does that sound?"

"It sounds like bullshit," says Kyle, finally joining in the conversation from his position at the edge of the room. We're in an abandoned office building trying to come up with a marketing plan before we begin our 'work' to make Dad popular enough to win the vote against the Minister.

"How about we dig up some dirt on Francis, make him seem like the bad guy instead?" I suggest. Perhaps if we can get close to the Minister, under the guise of digging for dirt, we can secretly formulate a side-plan with him to have Dad captured.

"Alright, I'm listening, what are you thinking?" Dad finishes his beer and burps. "Child molestation? Necrophilia?" I tilt my head at him.

"I think it's best to avoid things you've been accused of, or you might get some bounce back. You don't want to be jogging any memories. For those who were children I mean, not dead bodies. Did you ever? I always wondered about that rumour," I pause in thought.

"Did I ever fuck a dead body? Well, Adam, yes. If you're being technical. She was alive when I started though."

"Right." I look at Kyle. How on earth are we ever going to convince people he is a good man? This is a bloody joke.

We're screwed. We really need to set a trap before this gets out of hand.

We have three hours to come up with a speech and a plan to make Dad 'popular.' He has a list of venues he wants us to attend over the next couple of weeks so that we're seen by enough of the voters before they start their isolation. He has 'negotiated' with hosts of Dream-Walker only events to take over their planned events and influence their Dream-Walker audience. It's amazing what people will agree to when they're afraid, even when it's going to lose them a lot of money.

Dad's plan also means that the HJD are unlikely to get in the way because these events have been prearranged and preauthorised and have guest lists that are Dream-Walker only. They will only find out after it's too late, and when they do, they will have nothing to clean up. The Minister might not like Gerome having a chance to influence the voters who will ultimately determine the next elected Minister but, aside from already being an escapee, he isn't doing anything wrong.

Our objective is to sell Dad as a father, as a good man, as somebody who wants to see Dream-Walkers flourish (rather than someone who wants to take over the world). Someone who wants Dream-Walkers and humans to live side by side, someone accepting.

The world today does not approve of the division he loves, of people putting themselves above one another. Nowadays we are all equal. No matter the colour of our skin, our religion, our gender or sexual orientation, even our 'species' as the old-timers like to refer to it. Are we not also human? The lines are blurred.

There's no avoiding this first speech, no matter what. We need to think of something positive to say. I look at Kyle and he's just sitting there, staring blankly.

"Come on, you used to worship him, you must have something positive to say." He looks at me,

"I don't even remember what I liked about him now, it was probably all fiction. I loved him because I didn't know him, because he wasn't around. I loved him because all little boys love their dads. Except you, I suppose. You were always a mummy's boy."

"You say that like it's a bad thing."

"No, I'm jealous. I wish I had seen through him the way you did. You noticed more than me, like the way Mum was when he was around. I couldn't see it." I frown.

"I don't think I did either back then."

"But you were always by her side whenever he came home in a mood. It was as if you knew what he was going to do to her."

"I didn't."

"Huh. I always figured you did. You two were so close."

"We were only close because I didn't have any friends. She pitied me."

"Well, either way, I think that's why I admired Dad. I thought you had Mum, so I had Dad. But I didn't have Dad, not really. Nobody had Dad. He doesn't have feelings like normal people. He had no trouble leaving us, and no desire to keep in touch once he was caught. He didn't care about us then, and he doesn't care about us now. He's just using us, like he's used everybody else in his life. I wish his brother had turned out more useful. I was desperate for there to be someone else who could put him in his place."

Look at Kyle, opening up to me! Maybe soon he'll tell me what really went down with Izzy, his fiancée who was murdered. I know that's the real reason he wanted to break Dad out in the first place: to use the user for revenge, aim and fire. It was a good plan, except Dad doesn't help anybody other than himself, and there was nothing in it for him.

165

"Fuck, Ad', what are we going to say?" Kyle asks me.

"Not the truth, obviously. We'll tell them what Dad wants them to hear, I suppose. We'll give them their dream leader, or describe him as that, anyway. Make the whole thing up and just hope they believe us. Or that Dad thinks they believe us. It's all we can do, isn't it?"

"Or we could make a run for it," he suggests.

"How? Where? He's only in the next room, he's probably listening right now. And he has Damian and whoever else he wants on his side."

"Yeah, I know, but there has to be something we can do, we can't go out there and sing his praises like he wants us to, we just can't. We'd be hurting the entire community. If people trust him, the world will go to pot. There'll be nothing left once he's done with it. Right now, people know that he's dangerous. We need to keep it that way. Okay?"

"You're talking a great talk, but I still don't see any other choice. Come on Kyle-with-the-plan, pull something out of nowhere!" I encourage.

He stands and starts pacing.

We're stuck. There's no way he's going to come up with a plan other than doing what Dad wants us to. Unfortunately, that's just how the world works when Gerome Clarke's around. There's no point fighting, it gets you nowhere.

All of a sudden, Kyle spins around and claps his hands, making me jump.

"I've got it!"

"Seriously?"

"Yep. It's not perfect, but it might work. Dad is on his own out there at the moment, right?" I nod. "Great."

Kyle

Kyle-with-the-plan. I've done it again, I've pulled an impossible plan out of thin air because that's what I do, I'm Kyle, the one with the plan. And thin air is precisely what we work in as Dream-Walkers, isn't it? We're in that space inside your head. Not actually air, obviously, but what I mean is our domain is invisible. Dad wants us to convince people in the real world that he's a great guy, worthy of power and authority. He doesn't want us messing with dreams and such, because he wants them convinced deep down, long term, so it doesn't fade when they're in isolation. That means, he's going to be paying a lot of attention to what we're saying, and not to what they're dreaming about.

How many people can honestly say that they listen to long speeches without zoning out? Without thinking about what they need to pick up at the shop later, or whether they remembered to take the washing out of the machine, and was so and so still up for drinks on Friday? Exactly. We can't help it. The mind wanders. And that's exactly what's going to happen when Adam begins to regale a long speech about fatherhood and brotherhood and Dream-Walkers and humans walking hand in hand into the future. Whatever

167

bullshit fairy tale nonsense he can come up with. And whilst he's doing that, as he's building this amazing picture of Dad, and Dad's lapping it up, smiling and patting himself on the back for a job well done, *that* is when I'm going to undermine it all by getting into the head of every zoned-out Dream-Walker in attendance.

It's hard to deliberately affect multiple people at once, you can't be so attuned to the intricacies of their mind. It's not like when I dream-dated Ella. If there are multiple people, it's best to stick to images, flashes of scenes that will pop into their mind like memories or thoughts to guide their minds to wander down those paths instead of the other ones they've started down about the shops and the washing etc. But I will show them the truth, whilst Adam spouts the fairy tale, and at the end of it all, they'll clap. But they won't have believed a word he's said.

When they get home and think about it later, they won't think Dad's a good guy because they'll remember the violent images I showed them, the truth of what he's like. Those images will eat away at any progress Adam has made on his behalf and hopefully, Dad will be oblivious. He'll think it's all gone according to plan.

The only problem is, I can't tell Adam my plan because Dad might hear. I can't tell him in his dreams either, because Dad may also watch for that too, until he's distracted by the speech. Dad doesn't trust anyone, least of all people he thinks he has control over. That's his key to staying powerful, never trust anyone.

Adam will take the lead on the speech, which is good because he's the 'good' son and has the image Dad wants. Sure, there was the scandal with Ella, but that got straightened out near enough. The community as a whole doesn't care if the Minister still wants her trapped, so long as she keeps our secret, and they seem to trust her now.

Especially now there's another rumour spreading about her being a P.I.N.S., she might as well be one of us.

I'm hardly a respectable image. Yes, I fight with The Resistance, but that's about it. And The Resistance doesn't always see eye to eye with the community as a whole. Some people view our tactics as unnecessarily violent, even though we do what we do to keep our people safe and to stop certain people from getting out of control. People like our dad. He never did understand that if he had only toned things down, he could have stayed a free man. Just a little moderation. The volume on 12 not 20. But no, Gerome Clarke is an ear-splitting volume of a man with a heavy bass, he cannot and will not turn it down.

*

We head out onto the stage as instructed by Dad, and I put my arms behind my back and stand beside Adam. As agreed, he takes the lead.

It's a good job he likes writing, because he's building castles in the sky with this speech. He's completely rewriting our childhood and I don't understand how anyone could possibly buy it, knowing the facts, and yet, they seem to be. I wait for my moment.

I decide to focus my attention on one of the suckers in the front row. Someone whom I believe in the past, Dad would have easily won over with his swagger and sex appeal. A horny mother of three who has little life beyond waiting at the school gates and PTA meetings and watching Loose Women. Not to stereotype her, but it's written all over her face. She looks at the poster of my dad like she would a topless picture of Channing Tatum. Hungry. But even someone so ridiculously easy to manipulate can lose attention when Adam starts talking about vegetables.

Come on, vegetables? I frown at him. I don't think five-a-day is the way to make these people vote for Dad. Even this mother of three would rather shove those vegetables somewhere other than her children's plates, it's all over her dreamscape. Seriously. And they let her raise children!

The guy standing next to her checks his phone. Another woman has started muttering to the person next to her about Adam's socks being on show. This is my moment. They are no longer interested in the speech; they couldn't care less if our dad's a good guy or not. They just want to get home and get on with their lives. They're probably all annoyed Dad has hijacked whatever show they thought they were coming to see today, especially the voters, with limited time left before their two-week enforced isolation.

I start with an image they should almost recognise. It's fictional, but plausible. My mum, crouched on the floor, covered in bruises. She weeps, and her face is turned so they see her nose is broken and one of her teeth. Blood spills down her chin. It's a scene which never really happened, only in her head, in her dreams. But it still hurt her, and these people know who she is. Was. Everyone knows 'poor Dorothy.' To really drum it in, I now show them my dad, Gerome Clarke, standing in a doorway, watching her. His fists are bloody, and he is smiling. He is proud of what he's done.

Adam has now moved on to talking about Dad's plans for the community, regurgitating some of what Dad told us he used to say in his heyday, but updated and tweaked for modern society. Vote for Gerome and he will fight for equality, reduced use of MIUs and less hiding from humans. We are more powerful than they are, so why should we be the ones hiding?

Gerome will make the world a happier and more accepting place, starting with England and moving outwards. He will make the world a place of understanding

170

and wellness. There will be no fear of being captured for just trying to figure out who you are and what you can do. Everyone will be free to experiment away from the watchful eye of the HJD. Inter-species marriages will be authorised. There will be a ban on reproduction cages.

He's making good arguments, if only they were true. I show those whose minds have wandered another series of images. It's a dream Frankie confessed to Ella, which has shocked me ever since I heard about it. At a children's party, they play musical chairs, skipping around joyfully until the music stops and Gerome is already sat on the final chair. He pulls the closest child onto his lap and penetrates them. It happens too fast to fully comprehend, only the look on the child's face will stick in their minds. Shock. Pain. Confusion. Fear.

Gerome Clarke is not a family man.

I study the crowd's faces, wondering how many have seen my glimpses and how many have still only heard Adam's false claims. I need to do more, just in case. Then hopefully, their own gossiping as they leave will fill in the remaining gaps. But what should I show them to make them remember he is a bad man, that he would be an irresponsible and selfish leader who would cause chaos and laugh? I don't know.

As Adam describes the future, another sunny day in paradise, it hits me. I show the bored audience members a beach, people lying there sunbathing, hats over their faces to cover their eyes from the sun. Then I show them what Gerome Clarke would do to that situation, a situation which offers itself up for disaster as easily as a young child with an ice cream. Like a child will get ice cream around his or her face and probably down their top, these innocent sunbathers will die. It's kill or be killed with Gerome in charge.

171

I show them all sit up like they aren't in control of their own bodies, rigid and automated like robots. One woman places a book down by her side and reaches into her picnic basket. She pulls out a knife and stabs her partner. Further down the beach, a man stands up and walks straight into the sea until his head disappears, never to be seen again. There's a series of gunshots and ten young girls who were headed to the sea's edge fall to the sand. Slowly the scene grows, each character I have planted doing something completely horrific. It's repulsive and hard to watch, even as I'm making them see it. No one wants to look at that stuff.

Adam rounds off his speech by asking everyone to remember that people can change and that Gerome Clarke is the man who can make our society blossom into something beautiful. He assures them that a vote for Gerome, is a vote for the future. He bows and slowly an applause starts, but it's not the uproarious applause Dad will have been expecting, it's half-hearted at best. Perhaps I tried too hard, they are already having doubts. This is not going to go down well.

Adam

"What did you do?" Dad demands. I feel like I'm five years old again.

"N-n-n-n nothing," I stutter, looking fearfully from him to Kyle. I did exactly what he asked me to, I stood on that platform and lied. I made him sound amazing. Was it my fault they didn't all believe me? That the nation is sceptical after the last time? No. I stand my ground, determined. "I did everything you asked me to."

"And you? What did you do?" he growls at Kyle like he's ready to rip his throat out, literally.

"Nothing. I stood there and nodded and that's about it."

"Oh really?" he snarls sarcastically. "Now why don't I believe you?"

"Hey your trust issues aren't my problem," replies Kyle.

"No, but my undermining sons are," he reaches forwards and knocks Kyle on the head, causing him to blink. He stumbles backwards clasping his stomach like he's been stabbed.

"Dad, stop it!" I step forwards.

"Which one of you did it?"

I look at Kyle and think of all the times he's stood up for me over the years and protected me, especially after that

173

sleepover. I blamed him, I accused him, but despite all that, he was always there when I needed him. When I was being ganged up on and called names. This is my chance to repay him. But, against Dad?

I'd be a fool to do that.

A real sucker.

A glutton for punishment.

A hero?

Ooh, now, I like the sound of that. Yes. I could be a hero. A proper one, without Kyle's help for a change.

Kyle winces again, presumably from another dream-inflicted wound.

"It was me," I say quietly. Neither of them acknowledges me, staring each other down and each daring the other to blink. I raise my voice. "I said, it was me." Kyle shoots me a warning with his eyes, and Dad frowns. "Leave him alone!" I shout.

"Excuse me if I don't believe you," says Dad, mockingly. "This has Kyle written all over it."

"You don't know me; you don't know either of us! You abandoned us and never looked back!"

"Oh boo-hoo, go cry me a river, Adam. That's about all you're good for anyway." He rolls his eyes at me and looks down as if I'm not even worthy of his horrible comments. Like I'm a piece of shit on the bottom of his shoe. Well, you know what they say, you can't polish a turd, but you can throw one.

I launch myself at Dad, closing my eyes in readiness. He's so surprised he can't help blinking so I do what I've longed to do for years, what huge numbers of the population have been waiting to do. I do it for everyone who has ever been wronged by Gerome Clarke. Those who've been tortured, raped, killed (in their dreams), I do it for everyone, but most of all I do it for my mum. She would be so proud of me.

174

Wouldn't she?

In reality, I smash his head into the ground, forcing his eyes to remain closed for longer. I rip my t-shirt off like some kind of super strong hero, releasing my inner beast, and I tie it around his head. In his head…

Gerome is bound and gagged and sat on a tall platform. His eyes are free to observe the crowds before him carrying signs and shouting for justice. These are his victims. I don't know everyone he has harmed, but I have inserted those I do, and the rest are just random creations from my imagination. A young version of my mum climbs on to the stage. The crowds cheer. She has a small instrument in her hand, and it's unclear what it is until she pounces gracefully onto Gerome and squashes and tears his right index finger off in one smooth move. Blood spurts out and he tries to spout unholy words, but they can't be heard through the gag.

Mum dances around like a beautiful ballerina, before leaping in again, and taking another finger. She throws it into the crowd. Next, I bring up the young Beth Parker in all her 80's glory – legwarmers and permed red hair. I'm not sure if that's an accurate depiction, but I'm in charge, so…

She is holding a hacksaw and laughing. It's a manic, hysterical kind of laugh. She approaches his chair at the centre of the stage and points it at his midsection. She turns to seek approval from the audience, and they cheer again, egging her on. Dad wiggles in his chair, attempting yet unable to move.

"Do it, do it, do it," the crowd chants.

She undoes his trousers and yanks them down to his knees. His pathetic knob sits there, surrounded by grey pubes, powerless. She picks it up with her left hand, pinching the skin like it's a specimen. She pulls a disgusted

175

*face, and the crowd laughs. Then she raises her right hand
and lines up the saw.*

*Dad's verbal abuse is coming out at full speed now, but
nobody can hear a word. He is furious and terrified.*

*She makes a small cut around the base and watches as
the first bit of blood starts to seep out. Then she goes back
and does it again, deeper. And again, and again. Soon it's
only holding on by a small piece of skin. She's covered in
his blood splatters and laughing. Dad is no longer hurling
abuse. He looks like he's going to be sick.*

"Adam, stop!" Kyle pushes me off him. "You're killing
him! You're actually killing him!"

I open my eyes and see Dad is lying on his back,
choking on his own vomit. I help Kyle turn him onto his
side.

Fuck.

Maybe Mum wouldn't be proud of me. I'm a monster,
like him. Like all my friends told me all those years ago. I
leave the room.

Moments later, Kyle comes to find me.

"What the fuck was that?" he asks me. I'm shaking.

"I don't know, I just thought, well, he wouldn't expect
that. And I wanted to be the hero for a change."

"By killing him? Dude, you're not a murderer. Don't
lower yourself to his level. He doesn't deserve that. You
know who would be proud if you'd done that? Him. You'd
be taking on his bloody legacy. Ad', promise me you won't
do that again."

"I didn't realise he was, you know, actually dying."

"It doesn't matter. The fact is you lost control. You can
never lose control Ad', you must always be aware of your
surroundings. Didn't I teach you anything?"

"I just wanted to scare him. To show him what it feels
like," I mumble.

176

"Well bro, mission accomplished. And he's not come out here to reap revenge yet, so I'd say you did a pretty good job. Now then, shall we go track down Ella?"

I nod.

"Come on then, he's not going to give us too much of a head start. Let's go see if there's still a car outside we can take." He puts his arm around my shoulders and leads me from the room.

I can't believe I did that. I can't believe I got so carried away. I had no idea I might kill him in real life. I really believed I was just giving him a show, like he does to everyone else. Our power is scary, it's dangerous. I wish I was normal.

I wish I hadn't been inflicted with this skill. I never bothered to train myself properly either, which is probably why that just happened. What was I thinking? I'm such an idiot. I'm not a hero. I'll never be a hero. I'm just Kyle's useless goody-two-shoes brother. I was a fool to think I could destroy our dad. And yet...

"Kyle, if you hadn't stopped me, this would all be over. He'd be dead."

"And you would have a murder on your conscience for the rest of your life. I'm sorry bro, but he isn't worth that."

Huh.

That's perhaps the nicest thing Kyle has ever done or said to me.

"I love you," I tell him.

"Did you hit your head too?" he jokes, shoving me. "I love you too bro." He winks and leads me to the car.

Adam

Through the window of the car, we watch as Dad paces around the abandoned office punching walls and kicking chairs. All we can gather from the snippets that he shouts particularly loudly is that wherever Damian took Ella, it's not where he was supposed to.

So where is she? And whose side is Damian on?

Kyle is going to reach out to his team, to see if they have heard anything, or made any other progress whilst we've been preoccupied. He drives us to a layby, gets out, and jogs over to a phone box. I can't remember the last time I even saw a phone box. I've never used one. Where are we, the 1980s?

He gets back in and restarts the engine.

"Okay. I don't know where she is, but I think Frankie might be with her."

"Why?"

"Because she was helping my team, but she vanished. It can't be a coincidence, especially after the revelations about her aunt and cousin. Crap, I keep forgetting about our half-sister. I wonder if she's back at that farmhouse. Are we awful brothers? Should we go back and check? I think I can probably find it again," Kyle rambles. It's my turn to reassure him.

"Nah, we're great brothers, to each other. We don't know her. We don't owe her anything. We should focus on finding Ella," I reply. I don't want any distractions. Although… "What about Jeremy? We should have checked if he was there too!"

That's someone's whereabouts that I do care about because if he is out there playing the hero and snuggling up to my girl and trying to win her over, I'll… I'll… I don't know, but it makes me feel very angry. It makes me feel like I could be like dad if I was presented with the right motive.

No, not a sadistic power-hungry rapist, but a Dream-Walker who has no problem using their skills to inflict pain for personal revenge. I suspect I've got a thirst for it now. Something has awakened inside me, and it scares me. Good Adam feels tainted. The ink is spreading. My blood is turning black.

How long until I turn into him? Until I lose all self-control and honourability? Was I always doomed to turn out like him? Were we both? Because Kyle hasn't changed. I thought he was the one who took after Dad, but I'm the one spinning out and acting crazy. He's still so level-headed, so calm, like Mum.

I never saw that twist coming. Was my angelic façade just that – a façade? Am I not the good brother after all?

Shit.

"Are you okay?" Kyle asks.

"Yeah, why?"

"You look like you're having a bit of a moment in your head. Don't overthink it, Ad', you did what you had to. So what if you got a bit carried away, it's in your genes. I stopped you from taking it too far. You're okay, it's over now. You just need to focus on Ella."

179

"But what if I'm dangerous? What if that was just the start? I couldn't control myself. And, I enjoyed it."

"Adam, I don't know anyone with more self-control than you. How long did you date Ella before you slept together? Months! And you were completely obsessed with her before you even met. Does that sound like someone without self-control?"

"No, but what if I've awakened something inside me now, a thirst for violence and cruelty like Dad? Maybe we shouldn't go after Ella, maybe we should stay away."

"And leave her to suffer whatever Damian has planned for her?"

"I don't want to hurt her."

"You won't."

"How do you know?"

"Because you're Adam! You love her, the only person you would ever hurt is our dad, because he is a bad man. You would never hurt Ella. Now tell me: do you want to go back and see if we can work out what happened to Jeremy, or do you want to follow my theory and hopefully find Ella?"

"Find Ella, obviously. What's your theory?"

Whilst I was mentally spinning out, calling myself names and fearing for my future, Kyle-with-the-plan was of course, coming up with a plan. He was thinking over everything he knew about Frankie and trying to put it all together in a way that made sense.

He knew that she had a thing for him, and thereby assumed she could easily have fallen for Damian. So, working on the theory they might be working together, if they have stolen Ella from our dad, they most likely tricked Dad and told him they were taking her to one place, then actually took her somewhere else. But Damian doesn't know places, he spent his life in a cage or MIU lab. So, if

180

they have a location, it must be linked to Frankie. And Kyle and Frankie go way back.

Kyle had thought through every place they had ever been together including family lunches and birthday parties, and Halloween parties up at her 'haunted' Victorian mansion in Cristleton Forest. The perfect place to hide someone. The only problem is, he's not entirely sure where it is, and he's pretty confident it's not labelled on Google Maps. It's possibly not even called Cristleton Forest.

He has a vague idea of the approximate location, and he gives me some landmarks to look out for which he remembers from previous visits. Several hours later, we enter a wooded area which Kyle is confident is the right forest.

There's something about the woods that always freaks me out. It's those twigs randomly snapping and making you think there's someone watching. The scuttling of the wildlife and insects. The feeling of trespassing. Because isn't that what we're doing when we walk through the woods? Trespassing? It's not our home, it's theirs. But we plod through anyway, with our children and dogs, we drop litter, dogs poo wherever they want, and we just carry on, like it's not someone's home we are destroying.

I'm getting carried away. We're following a single-track road through the forest but I can't see the house yet, I can't see any buildings at all. I think we might be lost.

I hope we're going the right way, I just want to grab Ella and run. I want to go abroad, somewhere warm and far, far away from here. From him. I know nothing would stop Dad following us, but he has plans here so, I think he'd leave us alone for a while. And hopefully someone would capture him before he had a chance to come after us. I reckon the Minister would let us go. He doesn't tend to get involved with Dream-Walker activity overseas. Us leaving is the only hope I have. We have.

This wasn't meant to be our story.

We were meant to fall in love and live happily ever after. That's what happens in those movies Ella loves so much, those movies that Mum enjoyed too. Why can't I just give her that? I never meant to ruin her life. I bet she wishes she never met me now. That 'I' had stayed in her dreams.

Bloody Kyle.

"Shit! Shit, shit, shit, shit, shit!" The car slows to a stop as Kyle takes his frustration out on the steering wheel.

"Kyle?"

"Yes, brother?" he answers whilst squeezing his eyes shut and massaging his temples.

"What's wrong with the car?" He takes a deep breath before answering.

"Well Adam, cars need fuel to drive. I thought we had enough to get here. If you hadn't made me miss that turn and have to double back on ourselves for forty miles, perhaps we would have made it."

I look outside at the forest looming over us. Should we get out and walk the rest of the way on foot? Or should we retreat back to the main road and nearest fuel station, fill a jerry can and come back again to continue in the car?

If she's there, we're going to need a car. If she's not, we'll need one to go look elsewhere. But last time we left a car, it disappeared.

"You don't think Dad is behind this, do you?" I ask Kyle.

"Oh yeah, like he knew the exact amount of fuel that would leave us stranded in a forest. No Adam, I don't think Dad is behind this. Damian, maybe."

Ella

"Donna?" I say, my eyes focusing on the long red hair of a woman with her back to me.

I am no longer in the hallway by the door, I have been moved to some kind of living space. It could be a bedroom or a lounge but I'm not quite sure. This room possesses a meagre fireplace with a modest fire which is barely doing anything to warm up the room. It certainly isn't giving me those warm winter vibes that it ordinarily would. 'Cute and cosy' I'd normally call it, but it's not the same when you're tied up and uncomfortable.

The woman turns around and my guess is proved correct, though it makes absolutely no sense. Why is she here? What does she have to do with my mother, or Gerome? Besides wanting him locked up, of course.

"Aw, you remember me!" She grins. "But I should probably tell you my real name now, since you'll hear it soon enough. I'm Frankie-Lou Parker. I believe you've met my cousin?"

Clearly, I'm out of the loop. I struggle with the ties around my wrists.

"That girl back at Gerome's place, she's my cousin. She's also Adam and Kyle's half-sister. How exciting is

183

that? I suppose that makes us family, kind of." She pulls up a dining chair and sits opposite me.

"What are you doing here Donna? Sorry, Frankie?" I ask.

"Saving you of course!"

I tilt my head, my neck aches. She continues,

"You didn't actually believe Gerome was going to tell you where your parents are, did you?"

I shrug, not bothering to explain that I already know my parents are dead.

"Believe me, you don't want to know where he was going to move you. You're lucky Damian and I hit it off so well." Damian appears in the doorway. "Isn't that right, sweetheart?"

She stands up and sashays over to him. I remember that about her, she never could behave normally around men. Always swaying and sensual, always trying to attract them. She made me feel so irrationally jealous that first night I met her when she was all over Kyle – even though I was with Adam – because she's just so bloody full on with it. Syrupy sweet. Artificial.

"What is this place? Why did you bring me here?"

"It's an old family place, dating back to er, I don't know, the eighteen hundreds maybe? History was never my strong suit. The National Trust have been on about turning it into a heritage site, but so far my grandparents and parents have yet to give in. Oh, and the paranormal investigators want to do an investigation here, to see if there are any ghosts. Do you believe in ghosts, Ella?"

"Stick to the point, why did you bring me here?" I ask again, trying not to think about ghosts.

"Well there's no need to be snappy, we're just catching up! I thought you might want to know the history of your new home."

"I don't want a new home. I want to leave."

"Well that's not a very nice thing to say to your rescuers, is it? Besides, if we let you leave, Gerome will only capture you again. And next time, you won't escape."

It doesn't feel like I've escaped anyway, I'm still tied up, I've just got new captors and a new view. A haunted house. How lucky am I?

"So you brought me here to live? That's it?" I ask.

They exchange a look as if deciding who gets to tell me the news. Come on, spit it out, I think to myself.

"Not exactly. We have a theory we'd like to test out, but it requires a special somebody, like you. A P.I.N.S.," she says.

"Oh great, so you're no better than the Minister! You just want to experiment on me!"

"But it's for the greater good."

"That's what he'd say!"

Frankie frowns.

"Ella, we want you to seduce my father," Damian takes over, "or we can use drugs if necessary."

"Excuse me?" I am stunned.

"We think his fears and nightmares would destroy him if he was forced to confront them by someone like you."

"You want me to sleep with my boyfriend's dad? How sick are you? Not only is he ancient, but he's also known for raping women. Shit, you want him to rape me, don't you? Oh my God." I stare at them both. A pair of sick, vindictive, I-don't-know-whatsits. "Since when were you on the same side anyway? I thought Frankie wanted Gerome locked up, but Damian was the one who helped him escape. And I thought Damian was still locked up in an MIU! What happened? What changed?"

"Our paths aligned," answers Frankie with a smile. I still keep wanting to call her Donna. Holding Damian's hand, she approaches me again. "I do want Gerome locked up, and he will be. Damian no longer wants Gerome to be free because he has realised how selfish he is, that he was just using him and doesn't want to team up with him; he's a lone wolf and he has no interest in his long-lost son. Damian wants to help us destroy his father, so that he can take his place as the most powerful Dream-Walker. And I know what you're thinking, how is the next generation any better than the first one? Well, Gerome didn't have someone like me by his side, did he? I will help Damian to control himself, stop him from getting carried away. We make a great team."

I can't believe she could be so stupid. I knew she was callous, so suggesting I get raped seems relatively on par for her, but thinking that she can control Damian? That he won't be exactly the same as his father?

"Who are you trying to convince?" I ask. "You don't seriously believe that he's going to be any different to his dad, do you? Power makes people crazy. He's already strong, I know that, so what makes you think he isn't already planning to double-cross you when the time comes? He's not going to listen to you when people are fearing him all over the country, when the strength and power goes to his head. You can't control people like that. The power hungry."

"He loves me," she says, a line creasing down her forehead. The smug look has gone from her face. Perhaps I hit a nerve.

"You're a fool if you believe that. How many times did Kyle use your feelings for him to his own advantage before kicking you to the kerb? I thought you said you were past all that. How can you not see that you're making the same mistake all over again? With a man who is a mirror image of Kyle, who should serve as a constant visual reminder of what happened in the past?"

She nods slowly.

"Don't listen to her babe," Damian warns. "She doesn't know what she's talking about."

"You only met him, what, a few weeks ago? He's a creepy lab rat with a daddy complex. Donna, sorry, Frankie, please, don't do this. Don't become one of them. Don't make me endure rape just to test a theory, which let's face it, won't help anybody even if it does work. Even if Gerome crumbles, if Damian takes his place, it will be for nothing. Please, let me go."

Frankie looks at Damian as if her whole world has just imploded. Did she really need me to spell it out like that for her to realise what was going on?

"Damian, do you love me? Or is she right?"

"Of course I love you," he asserts.

"I don't think we should do this. She doesn't deserve this. She just wants a normal life. Can't we give her that?"

"Babe, you agreed."

"Yes, but I forgot how it feels to be so vulnerable, so weak against a powerful Dream-Walker like your dad. If we let Gerome rape her, she'll be destroyed. I'm not sure she deserves that."

"She'll be fine. Perhaps a little scarred. She'll get over it. People get over things like that all the time."

"But hasn't she been through enough?" I watch this scene play out in front of me as if I'm invisible. "My aunt was one of Gerome's first sexual victims, the first to bear a child that we know of. She ended up in a mental hospital. If we do this, what's to say Ella won't end up in one too?"

"Since when did you give a shit what happens to her? You were completely fine about this yesterday. What the fuck has got into you?" Damian finally snaps.

"Was I fine, or was I seeing things the way you wanted me to? Have you been in my head Damian? Convincing me that you love me? Have you? Was nothing you told me back in that MIU true? Was I only ever a step in your plan?" She looks as if she's about to cry.

"I'm not listening to this nonsense." He walks away and locks the door behind him.

"Shit," I say, looking at Frankie. The least she can do now is untie me now that we're both stuck in here, but she seems preoccupied with trying to work out how she really feels about Damian.

Finally, she snaps back into motion and begins to untie me, ignoring the tears running down her cheeks.

"I first met Damian when you were in that MIU during the trial. He was so sweet. I could tell he had a kind heart, but he was stuck working for the HJD because of a deal his dad made before he, Adam and Kyle were even born. After Gerome's escape, I went to visit him, and he convinced me to help him escape too. You know how well I got on with the guards there," she sniffs.

"A couple of days ago when he asked me to join Kyle's team, I should have known he was just using me to keep an eye on them. I should have seen past that beautiful face because it's what Clarkes do, isn't it? They use people. I need a tissue." She leaves me with one arm restrained as she searches for a tissue. I start to untie myself with my free hand as she proceeds to fill tissue after tissue with snot.

"I'm such an idiot! I should have known better. I'm so sorry, Ella. I'm so sorry. I thought he loved me. I thought we were going to rule the Dream-Walkers together, like king and queen. We were going to harness his power for good. We were going to make a difference." Her shoulders bounce as she smears mascara-stained tears across her face.

Once my second arm is free, I do the most natural thing in that moment. I hug her and let her cry onto my shoulder, big, shuddering weeps. It doesn't matter what she did, what matters is that she realised before it was too late. Now she is on my side, I have a Dream-Walker on my side. We can fight. We have a chance. It's more than I had before.

29 December

Jenny

I'm not convinced that Beth's niece has our best interests at heart, but it looks like she gave us the correct address before she left us. I just hope it's not a trap. I'm surprised she didn't want to stick around and meet her cousin; I wonder what else could have come up. What motivates a woman like her? She's very different to how I was at that age.

The property is a detached farmhouse, Gerome's favourite style for keeping a low profile, but least favourite for playing around with neighbour's dreams. We used to vary the type of properties we stayed in as we moved across the country according to his mood at the time.

"Well come on then, what are you waiting for?" Tasha marches towards the entrance, closely followed by the man apparently named Max (possibly her boyfriend, but I still haven't dared clarify their relationship). Every time she looks at me, she glares. Rob reaches for my hand. I still don't know what I've done to deserve his kindness.

"Shouldn't we be careful? What if Gerome's here?" Max asks Tasha.

"Nah, he's not here. Adam and Kyle have been chasing him around the countryside. That's what Kyle said, anyway."

"Well we are kind of in the countryside…" Max points out.

"Don't worry, I have a good feeling about this," she tells him, then turns around. "Who's ready for a big family reunion?"

She pushes the door open, finding it unlocked, and we walk inside. It has all the basics, but it doesn't feel very lived in. Almost like one of those rental houses by the sea, out of season. There's a couch, but the cushions don't look like they've been leant on in a very long time. I imagine the cloud of dust that would be released if I should dare take a seat.

"Hello? Is anyone here?" Tasha starts repeating as she moves around. Rob is still holding my hand and looks at me comfortingly. I feel so nervous to see Jeremy again, I can't even consider that Gerome might have hurt him or Maria. I'm just focused on seeing them, on having all my children together at last. Especially for Jeremy to meet Tasha, and vice versa. I'm sure they will get along well, even if they both hate me. It's good to have things in common.

But what about Maria? How will she feel about me now, knowing that I'm not really her mother?

Max finds a door which leads down to a basement. He reaches up and pulls a cord, illuminating the stairwell with eery yellow light. We follow him down.

The first thing I notice is the smell. Before I can assess the room or the condition of the people inside it, if there even are people inside it, I have to cover my nose. I squeeze my nostrils tightly together and before we can find another light, I fall over something in my path.

"Ow!" I exclaim from the floor. "What was that?"

Rob locates a light switch which turns on dimly at first and then kicks into full brightness.

"Oh my God!" says Tasha, completely ignoring me and reaching for the man whose feet I tripped over. "Is this him? Is this Jeremy? My half-brother?"

A weird, muffled sound comes from the back of the room, and we look up and spot Maria. Rob rushes over to untie her. I remain on the floor, staring at Jeremy.

"Is he okay? Why isn't he talking? What has Gerome done to him?" Tasha asks, looking to Max for help. Jeremy is tied to a chair that has been knocked over, so they carefully push him back up the right way round, before working on untying him.

"He's been like that ever since he got here. I don't know what's wrong with him," says Maria, attempting to stand up for the first time since she got here. Rob stands close, ready to support her.

"Is he alive?" I ask. Tasha nods.

"He's breathing. Do you think maybe he's dreaming? Like he's stuck in some sort of dream torture that Gerome has subjected him to?"

"Try opening his eyes," says Max. Tasha lifts his eyelids but they quickly close back down. "Hmm." He crouches down in front of Jeremy's chair at eye level and then slaps him hard around the face, nearly sending him tumbling down on his side again. Luckily Tasha is there to bounce the chair back in place.

It doesn't work, but something clicks in the back of my mind. This was the skill Gerome was working on all those years ago, a way to trap a person in their dreams, a way to make them completely alone and unable to be influenced by other Dream-Walkers. A prison cell of the mind.

Violence, slapping, throwing buckets of water are the usual harsh methods employed to wake a person up, but Gerome was working on something that would be harder to crack, more awkward. Like a fairy tale 'true love's kiss' for Snow White type situation. He called it 'the padlock.' And if Jeremy's in the padlock, that means Gerome found my diary. That's what I worried he might have found back at home.

My old diary is the only way Gerome could have locked Jeremy in that state. It's a special 'gifted' diary, with a special 'gifted' padlock that served a much greater purpose than locking away my teenage woes. I bought it from a handmade goods stand at a car boot or a craft fayre, I can't remember exactly, but Gerome repurposed it. Not by himself, of course. He asked a woman who owed him a favour, and he was thrilled by the results.

At least he was, until he realised how boring it was trapping people in places even he couldn't reach. I guess he changed his mind.

Now I have to figure out what Gerome would have set as the answer to waking Jeremy up. Could it be me? Would he have expected me to come here? Could it be so simple as a mother's touch? A mother's love? A mother's kiss? I have to try.

I stand slowly and hesitate in front of my son's beaten-up body. I'm so sorry this has happened to him. I feel so guilty for not being there for him over the years. The others are watching me, and I feel foolish. What if this doesn't work?

I reach for his head and place one hand over each of his ears. I lean forwards, so I am only inches away from his beautiful but battered face.

"My son, Jeremy. I am so sorry I left you. I love you. Please wake up." A tear escapes as I close the gap and kiss him softly on his forehead. Then I step back and watch with the rest of them.

It takes a moment but then finally, my gorgeous boy's blue eyes open. It worked! And he looks so grown up. So rugged. So handsome. Did I really create that?

"Hello? Jeremy? Can you hear me?" asks Tasha, taking charge again. "You can explain to us how you did that later," she says pointing at me.

Jeremy frowns and squints at us all.

"Who are you?"

"I'm your half-sister, Tasha. This is my boyfriend, Max," Max looks at her with shock and she shrugs, so I take that as the answer I was looking for about their situation: it's a new relationship. "That's my dad, Rob," she points, and he waves, "and that, is our mother. The one who abandoned you. Sorry if you thought she was dead."

I smile at him meekly.

"What happened?" he asks quietly.

"Oh shit, sorry, I forgot to say, that's Maria," continues Tasha, pointing. "She's been down here with you for some time. I thought she was my sister, but it turns out she's not. Anyway, you've been down here with her for a couple of days or so. Gerome Clarke put you down here, we think. Is that right?" She looks at Maria for confirmation.

"Yeah, that's about right. We were taken at different times, from different places. But yeah. You arrived with another girl, but they took her away."

He continues to sit there quietly. I imagine this is a lot of information to take in.

"Where did they take her? The girl?"

"Dunno. The deal she was offered involved finding out who her real parents are, so maybe she went to meet them?" Maria answers. Jeremy leans on his arms and attempts to stand up, grunting in pain.

"I need to speak to my father."

195

"Wait, don't you want to get to know me? I'm your sister! And she's your mother. Don't you want to talk first?" Tasha asks.

"No offence, but I don't know who you are. And she," he looks at me, "let me think she was dead for most of my life, so excuse me if I'm not in the mood for a joyous reunion. I want to get out of this pit and go see my father. Ella is in danger."

"Is she your girlfriend?" I ask.

"No, she's… Look, it doesn't matter. I was meant to be looking after her when we were taken, and I need to check she's okay. I made a promise, and I don't break my promises." He starts to hobble towards the stairs.

"Did he beat you up?" I ask, concerned.

"Do you think I walk like this normally?" he responds sarcastically. I suppose we won't be making up anytime soon then.

Rob helps Jeremy up the stairs, and I follow with Maria; Tasha and Max skip up behind us.

"Who has a car?" Jeremy asks as soon as we're all at the top and he's caught his breath.

"Um, I don't think you should be driving in your condition," I say. I can't help myself. It's my motherly instinct, even if I am a useless mother. He rolls his eyes at me.

"Who can take me to my father?"

"I'll drive," offers Rob, "but we all came here together, and I don't think anyone is going to want to stick around, so I suggest we all come with you. It'll be a bit of a squeeze."

We all agree.

I love my family, but boy do I wish we'd all paused to take a round of showers before we squeezed into that five-seater. Jeremy and Maria stink, and that's putting it politely.

196

Jenny

We fill Jeremy in on the way over to Francis' house. Well, I say 'we,' but I mostly just agree with the accusations being made about me. They are all true, but it doesn't make it any easier.

Yes, I am your mother. Yes, you were only made because Gerome told me to. Yes, I abandoned you also because he told me to. There's no nice way to say any of that. Jeremy looks at me like I'm scum, like I'm worse than scum. Like I am that little niggly bit of limescale around a bath tap that annoys you when you see it, but after several attempts of scrubbing, refuses to go away, so you just ignore it and pretend it's not there.

Maria remains quiet, she hasn't said anything about me not really being her mother. Does she understand? Does she forgive me? I hope we can talk once things have calmed down.

We park outside a modern residential building, and Jeremy turns to address the group from the passenger seat.

"I think it's best if the rest of you wait here. I need to speak to my father about some important information and I don't want him to be distracted. Okay?" He's looking mostly at me. I'm a bit relieved. As much as I feel like I

197

need to see Francis, and I really want to find out how much he knew about our situation all those years ago, I can't deny that I was dreading it.

"Can I come with you?" asks Tasha. "Just me. As your half-sister, and as a representative of The Resistance. We're all on the same side at the moment anyway, the HJD and The Resistance. We all want Gerome Clarke caught. I think I should be there to hear whatever it is you need to discuss."

"I don't think that's necessary. What I need to discuss is not about Gerome Clarke. It's about Ella-Rose Thompson, and me. About what we are, and who her parents are. It's really not the business of The Resistance."

"About what you are?" I start to say but Tasha cuts me off.

"Do you think I'm stupid, brother?"

"No?" He smiles.

"Then don't dare to assume that I don't already know exactly who Ella-Rose Thompson is, and her connection to Gerome Clarke."

"Okay, fine." He holds his hands up. "But this is not about her connection to Gerome Clarke. This is about who she is, biologically."

Tasha twists around to look at me, she's sat on Max's lap to my right.

"She's not related to us too, is she?"

"No!" I deny. "Jeremy darling, you said it's about what you are, so, what are you? Are you not a Dream-Walker? All those years ago, I wondered why Gerome wanted me to have you, and I feared that you would become a Dream-Walker and be your father's private experiment, but I never heard. I assumed you must just be a regular human. I was relieved."

He laughs at me.

"Mother, Jennifer Carmichael, whatever you would like me to call you, I am a well-educated fuck boy. But it's not my fault and I know am too old to behave as I do. It's not a choice, it's a condition. When you created me, you didn't create a Dream-Walker, but you didn't create a human, either. You made something my father calls a 'Personal Instigator of Negative Stimuli.' A P.I.N.S.

"The reason I am an eternal bachelor is because when women have sex with me, be they human or Dream-Walker, they see their worst nightmare at the moment of climax." He pauses for dramatic effect. "If you were worried about me becoming my father's private experiment, you wouldn't have left me there, so you can stop pretending to care. I believe that Gerome and my father knew that something might happen, that something would be different about me, but they didn't know what. My father put me through rounds of experimentation all throughout my childhood, but I never showed any signs. Then, as a late teenager away at a very expensive boarding school, I finally figured it out. It wasn't easy, it's not like I could just ask the school nurse about it. But I worked it out in the end, and Ella is the same."

"In that case, I need to come inside with you. I need to speak to him. I need to know what his agreement was with Gerome back then." I tell him.

He huffs and steps out of the car. I push Maria towards the door next to her so I can climb out too, and Tasha tumbles after us.

"Wait!" I beg.

"If you want answers, why didn't you ask questions back then?" He shouts at me. I shrug.

"I was young and stupid. I was in love. I didn't think of the repercussions. Can you honestly say you have never made a mistake?"

"Oh, I've made a lot of mistakes, mother. It's what happens when you don't have a strong mother figure in your life. Or any mother figure. You might have noticed that my stepmother Charmaine didn't enter our lives until I was an adult. My father was distraught when you left us. He cared for you. Yes, maybe he hoped you might together make a new species, but you meant more to him than that." He shakes his head. "He wanted someone to love. Did you never bother to get to know him? He might be flawed, but aren't we all? He never wanted anything more from you than a happy marriage. He was bad with women, that's all. He was awkward and geeky, and Gerome told him he could get him a girl who would love him. All he asked for in return was a head start. He could tell my father was in line to become Minister someday, so all he wanted in return was for him not to come after him straight away. To throw a few red herrings about. To allow him some freedom before he was captured. Gerome always knew he would be captured, but he bartered for extra time. Time to spread his seed, I suppose, given what you've told me today."

"He just wanted someone to love?" I repeat softly.

"Yes. My father is a good man, if you hadn't realised. Even I can see that, and I was one of his experiments! Did he ever hurt you? No. He loved you, despite what you were, and you broke his heart."

"I, I…" I don't know what to say. I'd come to believe that even though he was nice to me, he must have been in on it. He must have known it wasn't 'real.' Nobody gets married and has a baby that quickly, unless they are in love. Did he really love me?

I broke his heart, and Gerome broke mine. And I'm standing here now, probably breaking another man's heart too. I look at Rob, but he doesn't meet my eye.

"I need to come in with you. Please. I need to apologise."

"Apologise?" He raises his eyebrows at me. "That man spent at least fifteen years pining over you, hoping you would come back, not knowing what had happened, not understanding what had gone wrong. He told his son you were dead! Do you really think he wants to see you now? To learn it was all a scam?"

"It wasn't a scam, it was a job!"

"A job?" He mocks me. "Well done! You broke a man's heart and left a little boy motherless. What's your current position? Oh right, yes, you decided to actually stay with your next baby daddy. How nice."

"Please, you don't understand." I beg.

"No, I don't understand, and I never will. Now, if you could just wait here, you have already delayed me enough." He starts to make his way to the front door, and I hurry after him.

"Please, let me come in with you. Let's all go. The three of us, we can sort everything out. We can find out what you need, and we can clear the air. It will be good for us."

"Mum, if he doesn't want you to come in, he doesn't want you to come in. Can you blame him? I don't even want to see you right now, and I grew up with you." Tasha's words cut deep.

"I didn't say you could come in either," Jeremy tells her. "But fine, whatever. Just let me do the talking and get what I need first, alright? Don't make it all about you. It is very important that I get the details I need before it's too late."

"Care to shed some light on those details, brother?" asks Tasha.

"No," he smiles sweetly back at her.

My heart lifts. I think they will get along just fine, one day.

The three of us head inside.

*

"Jeremy! How nice of you to join me today. It has been too long! Come in, tell your old pa what you've been up to.

201

You look quite a state, would you like to use the bathroom before dinner?" says Francis, the Minister, not bothering to get up from his position at a desk in the centre of a large and airy study.

"Actually, I was hoping we could talk about Ella-Rose Thompson."

Francis scratches his head, still unaware of mine and Tasha's presence behind Jeremy, just out of sight.

"That girl who was mixed up with the Clarke brothers? Why do you want to talk about her? My teams will soon have her back under our protection."

"I know what she is."

"Oh." He puts his pen down, rests his elbows on the desk, and clasps his fingers together. "And what do you suppose that is?"

"A P.I.N.S." He carefully enunciates each letter.

"Where did you hear that term?"

"In your files. You didn't really think that I wouldn't look, did you? I knew you would have a name for what I am, and what she is. I was curious."

"Well if you have all the answers, what do you need me for?"

"I want to make sure that the details I found in Ella's file are accurate. Her biological parents, I need names and addresses. I know you like to plant false information in case of leaks, so I need you to confirm the accuracy."

"It's all correct, I haven't planted any lies about them. Elaine Robertson and David Watt – a prostitute and a greengrocer if I'm not mistaken. But why do you need to know?"

"Gerome Clarke has offered to introduce Ella to them."

He shakes his head, concerned.

"That's impossible! They're dead."

"That's what I read," nods Jeremy, looking concerned.

Before they can ponder this any further, I get an unstoppable urge to sneeze. Tasha whips her head round at me in outrage.

"Is someone with you?" Francis asks Jeremy, standing up.

"Well, I suppose now's as good a time as any. Come in!" He stretches his arm towards us, and we take small steps inside the room. "This is Tasha, my half-sister, and I think you remember Jennifer."

Francis falls back down to his chair. His face contorts in confusion and sadness, and I don't know what else. He pushes his glasses back up to the top of his nose.

"Jenny? Is that really you?" He looks from me to Jeremy and back again as if he can't believe his eyes. "And you know her?"

"Look, we can explain it all later. Right now, I need your help. If Gerome planned to introduce Ella to her birth parents, that means there are two imposters out there pretending to be them. We need to figure out who they are and what they're up to. Ella might be in danger."

Francis nods with understanding then clears his throat as if clearing his emotions. He grabs hold of a handkerchief and stands up again.

"Right. Follow me."

Ella

Donna, sorry, Frankie, is sat on the floor meditating. Her eyes are closed, legs crossed in Sukhasana with her hands in Gyan mudra, index fingers and thumbs connected, resting on her knees. From her mouth comes a quiet hum, like a bumblebee. I can't remember what that's called. It's been a while since I did a yoga class, it's something beginning with 'b' I think. Brama? Ba… No, I don't know.

Anyway, she's doing that, and has been for a while now. She said she's trying to reach inside Damian's head. The only problem is, we don't know where he is, and they haven't been together long, so her connection is weak. Plus, he probably lied to her the entire time, so it's not like she knows him all that well. And he'd need to be asleep for that to work anyway.

Eventually, she opens her eyes and huffs.

"Well that was a waste of time," she says, standing up.

"Where are we? Should we focus on breaking out instead?" I ask.

"This property is on ten acres of private land, most of which is forest, if you recall your journey. We'd never get out before he caught us. Even if he's gone, he'll have taken precautions. He's just like his father: a paranoid psychopath."

"Okay, so if we can't leave, what do you suggest?"

"I don't know. That's why I was trying to reach him, to figure out what he really wants, why we need to be locked up here. If he's trying to take over from Gerome, I can't see what use we are to anybody. It's not like Gerome will stand down in order to save us, we're basically ants to him. Or worse, woodlouse!"

"I am not a woodlouse!" I exclaim.

"Oh I'm sorry, what insect would you rather be called?" She snaps back at me.

"A butterfly."

"Oh nice, pretty. And you started out as a caterpillar. Ha, I get it!" She laughs. In other circumstances I'm sure we could have been friends. "But either way, we are insignificant to Gerome, so I don't know why Damian feels the need to lock us up. I can't believe I fell for it again. The Clarke brothers, my kryptonite. You heard about my aunt too, right? So it's like a generational disease. Clarke-itus, trying to destroy Parkers everywhere!"

"He wants me to have sex with Gerome, doesn't he?" I say, quietly reminding myself of the fear eating the back of my skull. I don't want to think about it. It's not going to happen. I'd rather die, and I might die, if it happens.

"As if Gerome would have sex with a woodlouse. Sorry, butterfly. He'll never fall for it. Damian will have to think again."

"I wish I shared your confidence." I tell her earnestly.

"Don't worry, Ell', I've got your back. And you of all people should know, it's actually quite hard to get a Clarke to have sex with you. They have all sorts of pretentions. You know how long it took for you to break down Adam's barriers, and you were giving it to him on a plate. Gerome doesn't take what's handed to him, he takes what he wants.

205

And that isn't woodlice. Sorry, butterflies. He'll be on the prowl for a lion, or perhaps a deer. Or what are those ones on the nature channel? Is it buffalos?"

"Are we seriously equating ourselves and other women to various insects and wild animals?"

"Do you have something better to do?" She asks.

"No."

"Well then, what do you think I am? If not an ant or woodlouse?" She asks keenly. I feel like I'm at a ten-year-old's sleepover, but I can't deny, it's kind of a relief to talk complete nonsense and not think about what's going on outside this place. What's happening to Adam and Kyle, what they might be being forced to do.

"A snake," I suggest.

"Ouch, you think I'm venomous?" I shrug.

"I don't know, you've always seemed kind of conniving to me, but I suppose I'm seeing a softer side now. Perhaps you ate a few too many bunnies and now they're softening you up from the inside." I laugh and she shoves me playfully.

Yeah, we definitely could have been friends in other circumstances.

Jenny

"As I said, Gerome Clarke offered Ella a deal which involved introducing her to her birth parents." Jeremy explains to his father. "We know that they're dead, but it seems that Gerome doesn't, or didn't. Unless he's part of the ruse. But I don't see how that would help him in any way, so I think that's unlikely."

"I agree." Francis takes a seat behind a computer. "What else do you know?"

Jeremy looks at Tasha who takes the lead.

"There's this woman, Frankie. She knew where to find Jeremy and Maria, and she's pretty close with Kyle Clarke, but she went off somewhere instead of coming with us to find them."

"You think she might be in cahoots with Gerome?" He raises an eyebrow. 'Cahoots' is such a Francis thing to say.

"Not necessarily, but I think she knows more than she lets on. She seems to have her fingers stuck in a lot of pies."

Jeremy pulls a face and I laugh.

"Sorry, that was a bit of a gross image." Tasha smiles. Francis purses his lips and types something into his computer.

"I believe I know the one. Long red hair and full of confidence?" he asks. Tasha and I nod. "Yes, she's quite popular with the guards in a lot of my MIUs, unfortunately." He rolls his eyes. "Here we are, Francesca Louise Parker," he clicks.

We move around him so we can all see the screen. There's a lot of information about her and her family.

"I'll get someone to keep an eye on her and let you know if anything interesting pops up." He says, typing a message and then pushing his chair back. "Do you have any other ideas?" He talks directly to Jeremy and Tasha, avoiding looking my way at all.

"Do you know of any recent escapees who might be impersonating the deceased? Or any criminals in general that you're trying to capture? Anyone who could use a new identity?" Jeremy suggests.

"Son, as you know, my facilities are usually secure. Gerome Clarke's escape was not commonplace, you cannot easily escape an MIU. I do not have a list of escapees! I do however have a list of dangerous criminals we would like to capture, but I don't know their individual motives so I don't know that we could ever narrow it down without further information."

"So that's it, we just wait? And hope this Frankie woman leads us to something important?" asks Jeremy, clearly aggravated. I want to rub his back, calm him down. I want to tell him it will be okay. I want to be his mum.

"Why do you care so much anyway?" asks Tasha. "She's with Adam Clarke, I'm sure he and Kyle will keep her safe, or rescue her, if she needs it."

"I was supposed to be keeping her safe. She was with me and then Gerome took us and then I don't know where she was taken next. She might be in danger. Adam trusted me to keep her safe."

"And that's it?" She smiles at him knowingly. I love watching my children interact like this. This is how it should have been a long time ago, siblings teasing each other. It's sweet.

"Yes, that's it." Jeremy says before breaking eye contact.

"If you say so…" Tasha teases.

I accidentally make eye contact with Francis and note he is smiling too. He quickly looks away.

It's hard to imagine we were once a married couple raising Jeremy. This could have been our life if we had stayed together and had another child, if I hadn't been so completely obsessed with Gerome Clarke.

Ella

Outside the room, Frankie and I hear movement. Damian is back, if he ever went away. He's talking on the phone and from his tone, I'd guess he's denying knowing where I am. The conversation sounds heated. But if it's Gerome, doesn't he want to tell him where I am, so he can attempt to enforce his plan? Who else would be calling and arguing with him? Adam and Kyle don't even have phones that I know of, possibly burners, but they definitely don't have his number if they do. I hate feeling this useless.

Frankie has given herself a French plait and is now studying her toenails.

"I would love a pedicure right now," she says. "I don't suppose you have any nail varnish in your pocket?"

"I don't even have pockets."

She looks up at me and narrows her eyes.

"Oh right, of course. I forgot you were taken in your jim-jams. Lucky you were wearing some." She laughs at me and I cover the Disney Princess on my top. They were cheaper than the adult ones, a definite benefit of being petite in a 'growing' world. The kid's clothes go up to sizes I will never reach. I'm wearing age 12.

At least Gerome put shoes on me before moving me. I don't remember him doing it, but I'm wearing ankle boots. It's a great look with cut off pyjamas, but I prefer it to the alternative. Plus, I also need a pedicure. Things have been pretty hectic since we started running from the HJD at the start of December, and I haven't exactly had a chance to pamper myself. My poor toes have suffered.

Damian is still talking aggressively on the phone. Whoever he's talking to is winding him up. I really hope he doesn't come in here and take it out on us.

Not that he needs to physically come in here to do that. I keep forgetting what these people are like. I think of them like normal criminals, but they're so much more. Supervillains. Is that a thing? I've never been into all those comic-based movies, but that sounds about right.

When I was stuck in that MIU last year, I used to try to contact Adam and Kyle in my head. I used to lie there, waiting for something to happen, for one of them to invade my dreams. I knew it wasn't safe, I knew several people around me could do it, and I knew I couldn't trust anything that happened in there, but I still hoped. And it never got me anywhere.

Apparently, aside from when Kyle was dream-dating me, they don't tend to do that from afar; to wait for opportunities to enter your dreams. There's no alert to say, 'Ella's got her eyes closed, do it now', so I have no idea how he did it so smoothly back then. Perhaps some of the dreams were just me. That, or he was even more of a stalker than Adam was. Either way, I have no false hopes this time. I know that they aren't going to be jumping into my dreams any time soon. Partly because they promised they wouldn't, and also because they don't know when to try, but mainly because they're busy doing whatever it is they're doing. Chasing their father and whatever that entails.

Christmas feels like so long ago already, I miss the three of us being together. I miss the banter and the feeling of safety. There is real love there between those brothers, no matter how much they wind each other up. They're good men, and they would both do anything to protect me. But they're not here. Now, it's just me and Frankie, and the least trustable triplet, Damian, on the other side of the door.

I don't think Frankie is used to being trapped, of not getting her own way. I've experienced this before, so I know what to expect. She's like a wasp trapped in a glass, confused and bashing her head.

Everything has gone quiet on the other side of the door now, so I wonder if he's left again. I'm getting hungry, we've been here for hours.

"Do you think he's going to feed us?" I ask her.

"No idea."

"Well were you planning to feed me? As per the original plan?"

She looks at me,

"Of course I was! What do you think I am? I was going to feed you some of my new recipes!" I raise my eyebrows.

"You can cook?"

She puffs air through her lips.

"I'm learning French cuisine," she says smugly.

Now I'm glad she's stuck in here with me. She was probably going to serve me snails, or frog's legs. Those are not top of my 'want to eat' list. In fact, they fall below mushrooms, which is saying something.

I hear a noise outside. The stones on the driveway are being trampled, a vehicle is coming this way. I hurry to the window even though I know it's useless – the window in here faces an inner courtyard; if somebody is driving up the driveway, we won't be able to see. I press my ear to the glass, to see if that helps me hear. It's cold.

There's a squeak of breaks, I think, and then I hear one, no, two, doors bang closed. Adam and Kyle? Please, say it's you!

We feel the escape of air as the large main door is opened on the other side of our room. We look to one another and back away from the door, just in case.

There are still no voices. Why are there no voices?

I don't know how long we stand there, waiting, on edge. Knowing that something is about to happen, but clueless as to what. My ears strain to hear every little sound, but there's very little to hear. It's as if whoever it was, has vanished. Or perhaps they went the wrong way.

"Should we shout?" I whisper. Frankie shakes her head.

She's right. We don't want to draw attention to ourselves in case it's not Adam and Kyle. But won't they find us anyway, whoever it is? Aren't they just going to go door to door until they do?

The minutes tick by and still nothing. I'm beginning to wonder if we imagined it. Or perhaps it was just Damian, messing with us. We both sit back down. Frankie lies on her back with her knees bent in a restorative resting pose. Her knees fall to one side as she starts to fall asleep.

I feel like I should stay awake whilst she sleeps, to stand guard in case anything happens. Not that I'll be much use if it does. But I feel tired too, my eyes are heavy and keep closing involuntarily. My head falls and I jolt awake again.

I suppose I could lie down too, get slightly more comfortable. It feels like bedtime. The room has finally warmed up just enough and there's a hint of lavender, like my old pillow mist. Mmm, the old days, when I used to hurry to bed to dream about the most perfect man I'd ever met. In my head. My dream man. Damn, what I'd give to go back to that right now. For it to all be a dream. To wake up and find I haven't quit my job with Kristina, to pick her up on a rainy day and drive her to work. To have not gone on that date with Jeremy either. To just be me and my ridiculous fantasies. Life was so much easier when they were ridiculous fantasies.

When dreams become reality, you know you're screwed. Because dreams are never as good in real life.

I don't mean Adam and Kyle don't live up to my dreams, what I mean is that dreams are always going to be better. They have the edge, every time. The sparkle and magic. Real life is never so shiny, never so polished. Dreams are whatever you make them, life just isn't.

Believe the spiel if you want, but there's only so far you can go in life. You can build a decent life, but it'll be firmly superglued in reality. Perhaps you will get lucky and move in next to a hunk of a neighbour, some guy who likes to do gardening or carpentry or something else manly and sexy topless in full view of you, and for a few months you might imagine you're living in a rom com and he's really going to fall for you (the girl next door). But it won't last. Maybe you'll get a shot at it. Maybe you'll even get with him. But the problem with real life is, even if it goes 'perfectly' it still won't be as good as a dream. He'll have B.O. or a psycho ex-girlfriend, or other current girlfriends, or he'll fart in his sleep; big monstrous protein farts which wake you up and make you heave.

In dreams, you can have all the good stuff and none of the horrible reality.

What would I be dreaming about now, I wonder, if none of this had happened? If Kyle had never walked into my dreams and Adam had never introduced himself? If I didn't know about Dream-Walkers?

If I let myself fall asleep now, I know I'll dream of Adam. Because even though he won't dream-walk into my head, he's stuck there. Or Kyle is. He's a habit at this point. The other man in our relationship. The one who doesn't suffer the side-effects of my P.I.N.S.; the one who doesn't look at me like I just cheated on him every time we do it; the one I don't hurt with every tilt of my hips. The one who wants me and doesn't hold back.

Dreams are always better than reality.

"Frankie," I whisper. I want to ask her if she really did have a serious relationship with Kyle way back, or if it was always this complicated user relationship they seem to have. She doesn't stir.

I'd love to know what made Kyle turn out the way he is. He's so different to Adam and yet, it's like he doesn't want to be. Is it purely the Gerome-effect? A result of having *that* as a father figure. Or is it more? I know he is still affected by what happened to his fiancée.

It's funny to think that Kyle spent so long pretending to be Adam, that he effectively created a mashup of both of their personalities in my mind. He made me fall in love with both of them and neither of them at the same time.

My dream man was smooth, chatty, but a good listener. He was sexy, he was gentle, but also voracious. He made me feel things no man had ever made me feel before, and it was all in my head. He'd take me for walks on the beach, our feet barefoot on the sand, sinking and leaving footprints; our hands interlocked as the wind blew through my hair – making it look tousled, not knotty. Slightly wavey. We'd watch the sunset, perched on a rock, my legs across his lap. He'd smile at me, and my heart would melt. He'd pull me towards him, and my eyes would close as I'd breathe in his scent. And then he'd kiss me, and it was electric. Like I'd been plugged into the mains after a lifetime of extension cords. Like I was finally seen. He lit me up. He made me complete. I never wanted to let him go. I would wrap my arms around him and squeal as he carried me in circles, stumbling in the sand. He'd pretend to drop me into the sea just so that I'd kick my legs and hold him tighter. He was so strong, so warm, so funny and just so... dreamy.

Adam

"I can't believe I let you talk me into going into that bar last night, Kyle. We've lost an entire day!"

"Hey, I only wanted to go in to find out where the nearest fuel station was. You're the one who wanted to have a drink and put your feet up!" He slams the car door as we hurry to the entrance of the mansion. It's an impressive building, but I don't have time to take it in.

"One drink! One! Not shots!"

"I don't recall forcing them down your throat!"

"You peer pressured me! I couldn't say no!" I hate when people do that to me. I become that shy ten-year-old who would've done anything to make a friend. Eat a worm? Hold a spider? Take ten shots of flaming Sambuca? Guilty.

"Alright, whatever you say bro. It did you good to relax for a while. We're here now, we can save Ella and you two can ride off into the sunset. Come on!" We enter and I am immediately stumped as to where to begin. This place is huge.

"Where is she?" I shout, storming around the mansion with Kyle at my heels.

"I don't know! Ella! Can you hear me?" He shouts.

We pace around the entire building, throwing doors open and shouting. She's not here. He was wrong.

"Ella! Ella!" I shout repeatedly as we move from room to room. Then we hear music coming from another side of the building. We follow the sound. It's a piano, playing something classical. I thought we had checked every room, but clearly, we missed this one. I charge at the door and burst in.

"Frankie?" Says Kyle, addressing the long copper red plait snaking down the undressed spine at the piano. She whirls her head around and stops playing.

"Oh, thank goodness!"

"Where's Ella?" I snap, completely ignoring her lack of clothing.

She rolls her eyes, irritated.

"Did nobody come to save me?"

"I'm pretty sure you brought yourself here, Frank. Besides, you're not even tied up. It looks like you could leave anytime you want." States Kyle.

"I'll have you know I was locked in with her actually, Damian used me." She flutters her eyelashes.

"Well where is Ella now? Did he take her somewhere? What is he up to?"

"No, it wasn't Damian that took her. I imagine he's going to be royally pissed off when he realises she's gone."

"Spit it out then!" I snap.

"Alright, alright, calm down." She grins. Fucking bitch. "Some silver-haired fox took her not long ago. Handsome guy, around your dad's age. One of us. He was wearing a suit and he walked with confidence, like he owned the place. I've never seen him before."

Kyle and I share a joint look of 'what the fuck?' Ella doesn't know any other Dream-Walkers. Who could have taken her?

218

"Did it seem like he might be working with our dad?" I ask.

She shakes her head.

"No, I don't think so. He seemed too 'proper.' Your dad has that 'Del Boy' kind of vibe, a grown up 'Oliver Twist', a bit rough and ready, you know? This man seemed like he was, I don't know, royalty. Like he has a reputation to look after, and a shit tonne of money."

"And he wasn't interested in taking you with him too?" I smirk, amused that Frankie got left behind.

"Oh no, he was only after her. Didn't let her see him though, he carried her out whilst she was sleeping."

"And you didn't think to stop him? Or wake her up?" Kyle jumps in, sharing my annoyance.

"Why would I? I don't care what happens to her. Besides, she has you two running around after her, it's not like she'll be wherever she is long before someone comes to her rescue."

"Jealousy is an ugly trait, Frankie," he says, narrowing his eyes at her.

"Is it though?" She tilts her head at him, still half-naked.

I try to remove myself from the bizarre sexual chemistry going on between the two of them to focus on the problem at hand. Who could have taken Ella, if not the Minister, not my dad, and not Damian?

"And it definitely wasn't someone from the HJD?" I ask, to rule out the Minister and his workforce.

"I doubt it. Like I said, he carried himself differently. And he was definitely a Dream-Walker."

"Any ideas?" I ask them both.

"Nope," says Frankie instantly.

Kyle fishes out the photo he has of Uncle Marcus.

"For the sake of ruling him out, it wasn't him, was it?"

Frankie looks at the photo and laughs.

219

"Whoa! Did Gerome let himself go?" She bursts into hysterics. "That's the funniest thing I've seen all day!"

"So I'll take that as a 'no' then?" he asks, putting the photo back in his pocket.

"Yes, take that as a no. I don't think that man is capable of carrying a cup of tea without spilling it, never mind a young woman!"

"Well I'm glad this is all so hilarious for you," I tell her, "but if you're not going to help, we'll be off now." I eye Kyle and head for the door.

"But what about bringing down your dad? He needs to be stopped!"

"One thing at a time, Frank."

"But-"

"No buts, Dad could destroy the planet and I wouldn't care so long as Ella was safe."

"Well that's a bit extreme, what if-"

"-Bye, Frankie."

Kyle picks up her bra that was dangling over a chair and pings it at her like a slingshot as we head out to the main hallway.

"Wait!" she pleads from the doorway. We look at each other and keep walking. No, not this time Frankie.

30 December

Ella

"Everything's going to be okay, I'm here now," I tell the man lying on a low camp bed on the floor. I carefully remove his buttoned uniform to separate it from the wound. The blood is sticky, and the wound looks painful. I grab a gauze with antiseptic and begin dabbing. He gasps.

"I'm sorry, I just have to clean it," I explain. The man opens his eyes and I realise the battered and bruised man before me is a dishevelled and unshaven Jeremy. His blue eyes look deep into my soul.

"Kiss me to take the pain away?" he whispers with a smile. Before I even know what I'm doing, I've leant over him and kissed him lightly on the lips. He makes a low growling sound. "More."

I kiss him again, careful not to lean any weight on his hurt body.

"More," he asks again as I try to pull away. I giggle and look around.

All the people that were rushing around before have now disappeared, we are alone. I carefully straddle him, my knees against the metal edges of the bed. It's uncomfortable, but nowhere near the pain he must be feeling. I lean towards his mouth again, still not putting any

222

weight on him, and he surprises me by slipping his hands underneath my shirt. Perhaps he's not so injured after all.

Ella

When I wake, embarrassed and confused that I dreamt of Jeremy again, I'm surprised to find myself lying on a sofa in a lounge I don't recognise, that definitely doesn't feel like part of the old-fashioned mansion I fell asleep in. Somebody has kidnapped me in my sleep!

There is an older man wearing a cashmere jumper and formal trousers sat reading a newspaper across from me. He looks up as I rub my eyes.

"Where am I?" I ask.

"Home," he answers, folding the paper and placing it by his side. I push myself up to a sitting position.

"No, I'm not," I reply bluntly.

"You are where you belong. You'll be safe here. I have a lot to tell you, but first, would you like a drink?"

I nod and he clicks his fingers causing a woman to appear in the doorway. She smiles at me politely and asks me what I'd like. I ask for water because I'm too distracted to ask for anything else. She disappears and reappears quickly, placing the glass on a coaster on a table she positions in front of me. I take a large gulp and wait for the man to continue.

"I am your father, your biological father. My name is David Watt. David, not Dave, and I am a Dream-Walker."

"What?" I ask, incredulous. Jeremy said my father was dead and was potentially murdered. This can't be him. My real father had an autopsy!

"Do you need me to repeat?" He frowns at me. There is no way this upper-class Mr Fancy Pants is my father. No. Way. And how dare he look at me like I'm slow. Just because I'm sat here in three-day-old pyjamas.

"I understand what you said, I just don't believe you." I clarify for him.

"And that is completely understandable. It's a lot to take in, but I assure you, it's the truth. I am your father, and your mother is here too. I'll introduce you to her a bit later as she might get emotional, and I don't want to make you uncomfortable. I know what a shock this must be."

I decide to play along, ignoring the fact that my father is meant to be dead. Perhaps the Minister got it wrong, or perhaps, this man has no idea who his child is and mistakenly believes it's me. It's probably hard to keep track of your offspring when you give them away so soon after birth.

"But why now? You've had plenty of time to introduce yourselves over the years, why now? Why bring me here during all this chaos?"

"Because you weren't safe."

"I wasn't safe a few weeks ago either, or were you okay with me being locked up like a criminal?"

"We were confident that Adam and Kyle would get you out, one way or another. We didn't need to get involved."

225

"You know about Adam and Kyle? What else do you know about me?"

"Of course we know about them, we've kept an eye on you ever since we left you."

"Do you know what I am?"

He sighs,

"Yes. We had hoped you wouldn't inherit your mother's affliction."

"Affliction? That's what you call it?"

"Yes, it's unfortunate."

"Unfortunate? Do you know what it's been like for me, having every man I ever loved or started to fall for run away without explaining why?" I glare at him. "No, you don't! So where is she? I want to see my mother! Only she might understand!"

He stands and brushes his trousers down, shaking his head as if I'm behaving most ungraciously, as if he hasn't just abducted me in my sleep to tell me he's my father with absolutely no evidence.

"Fine, follow me." He leads me out of the room and up a central staircase, then takes the branch to the left. He keeps walking until we reach a bedroom, where he opens the door wide enough for me to step past him and enter.

It's massive, bigger than my flat. There's a four-poster bed, a sofa, a large dressing table and an ensuite bathroom with corner tub and just as I'm opening the wardrobe to have a nosey in there too, the bedroom door is closed and locked behind me.

Oh for crying out loud!

I bang on the door,

"Hey, *Dave*! Let me out! What's going on?"

He replies calmly from the other side,

"There is no need to panic, I am going to bring your mother to you."

"And why do I need to be locked in?"

"Just a precaution."

"Why?" I shout. The sound of him retreating back down the stairs is my only answer. I suppose even expensive stairs can creak.

Ella

"Hi sweetie. It's so nice to finally meet you," a woman says as she enters the room. Her brownish grey hair is tied back in a bun, and she has a round stomach, covered by an apron. She looks like she belongs in the kitchen rather than being an equal to the man claiming to be my father. She certainly doesn't look like his wife. And she looks nothing like the photo Jeremy showed me either.

Could she really be my mother? Could she be a retired prostitute, or was none of what Jeremy told me correct?

I thought I'd feel it when I met them; I thought I would instinctively recognise my DNA. There would be something, some obvious similarity. Perhaps in a smile, a laugh, perhaps in the shape of a thumb. I thought I'd know.

I don't feel any connection to this chubby woman, nothing at all. Even less than I did with the self-righteous man downstairs.

"Yes, well, the delay was all down to you," I comment. What more is there to say?

"I know, I'm so sorry about that. We really did believe it was the right thing to do. For you, as well as for us." I can't help rolling my eyes.

"What a great decision. Thanks Mum."

"Hey! I'm sorry. Let me start again. Do you want to know why we gave you up?"

"Not particularly. I figured it must be because of what you are, you probably couldn't bear to be together so thought it best to get rid of me and have me grow up not knowing who or what I really am, so that when I reached sexual maturity and began scaring the men I loved, I would be alone and depressed and not understand why nobody stuck around. It was a great plan, Mum. Really. Wonderful." I walk away from her and sit on the sofa. "I do have one question though."

"You can ask me anything," she smiles sweetly.

"Why are you here now? Why are you together? If you couldn't stay together because of what we are, I get it. It puts quite a downer on a relationship. But why are you together now? If you made it work, you could have kept me. Why send me away?" Okay, maybe I have more than one question.

"We didn't make it work. Not romantically, anyway. I live here with David because I have nowhere else to go. It's a long story."

"But if you live together, why couldn't you have raised me?"

"I wasn't meant to live here. We weren't meant to get together at all. It was all a terrible, terrible mistake."

"Oh, jeez, way to make a girl feel wanted. So I was an accident. Is that why you gave me up?"

"No! It's complicated."

"Well, I'm not going anywhere, you might as well start at the beginning. You can make up for all those bedtime stories you never read me. Or all those nights you could have comforted me when yet another boyfriend stopped returning my messages. Do you know what it's like to go through that, and not know what you're doing wrong? To wonder if you have a messed-up vagina?"

229

"Yes, I do."

"So why would you let me go through that on my own?"

"We didn't know if you would inherit my condition. We didn't know anyone else like me. We hoped you'd be normal."

"But when you realised that I wasn't, and I know you realised because David told me you both watched me grow up and meet Adam and Kyle, so I'm sure you knew about my affliction long before I did; why didn't you step in then? You could have said 'oh hey, I'm your birth mother' and explained what was happening to me at any time. I didn't have a great relationship with my adoptive mum, as I'm sure you are also aware. There was nothing stopping you from stepping into that role. Nothing at all. But you didn't."

"Ella, I-"

"-You what? You're sorry? No. Sorry isn't going to cut it."

"Ella, please. Let me explain what happened. I want us to get along."

"Fine, off you go. Storytime. It'd better be good." I plonk myself down on the bed and stretch out. It's comfy. She joins me, perching herself on the far side of the bed and placing her hands in her lap.

"Once upon a time there was a man called David, though he liked to go by 'Dave' back then. He was a great Dream-Walker and his family's status in society meant that he was unhindered by the calls of the MIU. He was trusted and left to develop and establish himself. I don't know if you're aware, but even the Dream-Walkers who don't grow up in cages still have to visit MIUs for compulsory routine check-ups and evaluations. It's the Human Justice Department's way of keeping an eye on them and their abilities. Of making sure there are no unwelcome surprises. But the Goldsmiths are one of very few families who have earnt their freedom. Decades or centuries of paying off the

Human Justice Department has enabled them to live a free life.

"Anyway, back to Dave. Everyone thought he was headed for greatness. He had it all, the money, the power, the status, the looks, and the charm. But no matter how many women threw themselves at him, he wasn't interested. They were not what he was looking for."

I interrupt,

"Can I ask why he used to go by 'Dave' instead of 'David'? He doesn't strike me as a 'Dave', you know, with his fancy rich upbringing. David, maybe. Richard, perhaps. Or William. Edgar," I suggest. If I'm supposed to believe what I'm being told, I'm going to ask questions. The woman smiles,

"His father's name was David. As was his father, and his father's father and so on. I think it was a form of rebellion. He started calling himself 'David' again once he stopped seeing his family."

"Ah! Posh boy rebellion. I get it. Carry on." I hope this is going to be a good story, even if it is a pack of lies.

"Dave was bored and lonely, those women fluttering around him didn't remotely excite him. They were dull, ordinary, and desperate. He wanted something different. His family pressured him to marry, but he would not. And you don't pressure anybody with his abilities to do anything they don't want to do.

"One Sunday, after a particularly irritating roast dinner with his parents and smugly married brother, he decided it was time to find a wife. But he wasn't going to look within his circle. He already knew all the so-called 'suitable' women, and each one of them was dull in her own unenlightened way. He decided to rebel. To do the one thing he'd never done, that his mother would surely smack him round the head for. He decided to visit the laundrette.

231

"Now I know that probably doesn't sound shocking to you, but to Dave's mother, the laundrette was a place of disrepute. A place for poor people, a place where dodgy dealings took place amongst the 'dirtiest' people of London. It was not somewhere David Watt should ever have been seen.

"He arrived at the laundrette completely ill-prepared, without dirty washing and looking very much like a duck out of water. He was instantly noticed and chose to stand awkwardly beside a machine that dispensed fabric softener as he surveyed the women in attendance. He started to believe perhaps his mother was right, this was no place for a man of his stature, but just as he opened the door to leave, he collided with the most beautiful woman he'd ever seen."

She blushes.

"You'll have to excuse me talking about myself in the third person. It's just easier to explain it the way he saw it. Now, she was no upper-class lady, she had smudged black eyeliner under her eyes and her perm was most certainly an at-home job, but her eyes and her smile instantly intrigued him. She did not shy away from him and appeared confident in her own skin. When he offered to help her, she merely laughed and continued on her mission.

"But Dave wouldn't leave. He followed her to a washing machine and attempted to make conversation. She was not interested. She wouldn't even tell him her name, not her real name, anyway. She told him to call her 'Nightmare', which only heightened his curiosity.

"What has led this woman to be so self-depreciating that she calls herself a nightmare? He wondered. This beautiful woman looked nothing like a nightmare, her only darkness being that of her eyeliner. He couldn't stop looking at her despite knowing that other women were whispering to each other and watching them.

232

"He continued to attempt to make conversation with her whilst she waited for her washing to finish, with very little success. She was unwilling to give him a chance. He considered that perhaps whereas he was willing to take a chance on a woman from another position in society, she was suspicious of his motives. He wondered how he could convince her that he was not looking at her beauty like that of a future mistress, but that of a future bride."

"There was only one way he could think of, he had to show her what he wanted from her, the best way he knew how. But he couldn't do that there, with an audience of unknowing humans. He needed to convince her to go somewhere private with him, without fearing rape or murder.

"When her washing was finally clean and dried, his back was aching from standing up for so long, and he had a new appreciation for the luxuries he had grown up with. Nightmare also appeared tired and, after hours of listening to Dave talk at her, her determination to ignore him was weakening. When he offered to help carry her washing back home, she accepted.

"This was a breakthrough! Dave tried to restrict his grin as he picked up the bag of washing and followed Nightmare to the door. As they walked, a lot further than he had anticipated, Nightmare finally started to open up to him. But she still wouldn't tell him her real name, and she ignored any words of flattery. He learnt that she was an only child and that her parents had died about five years earlier, leaving her a small home she now lived in with her cat, Charlie. She was much happier to discuss how she had found Charlie and his hunting habits and misdemeanours, than she was discussing herself.

"This did nothing to deter Dave, despite him being more of a dog person. He was captivated by her. When they reached her doorstep, he did what he had to do. They shared an awkward moment of eye contact and then he leaned in for a kiss, hoping against all hope that she would close her eyes to participate. She did.

"He showed her glimpses of a possible future together living in a big house with several children running around. He showed them holding hands, kissing each other, and appearing blissfully happy. He showed her everything he believed a woman wanted to see in her future.

"Unfortunately, he had miscalculated. Nightmare stepped back and stared at him accusingly. She asked him what he was and how he had done that before swiftly unlocking her front door and slamming it shut behind her. Dave couldn't believe she wasn't interested in him, that she hadn't gone instantly weak at the knees for the future he could provide her. He wasn't used to women saying no.

"He refused to give up and determined that one day they would get married, this was only a minor setback."

"Okay, so then he came back and wooed you and then what?" I try to shorten the story. It's a lot longer than I anticipated.

"I expected it to be a one off, like it always was. I gave the name 'Nightmare' because I was used to it. I considered myself to be a man's worst nightmare. They never wanted more, and I was certain this posh boy would be no different. What I didn't count on was falling pregnant.

"After we had sex, he was surprised, like they always were, and I took that as my cue to leave. I didn't see him for weeks after that, even though he turned up at my house. I hid. I didn't want anything to do with him and his creepy visions. I couldn't believe any of the things he had shown me would really happen in my future. I thought he was some kind of wizard. I hunkered down with my cat, Charlie, and waited for him to lose interest.

"Then I realised I'd missed my period and, at first, I thought perhaps that was due to the stress of this whole bizarre situation. But it wasn't, so I had to tell him the truth. I didn't know what else to do. I had no one to turn to for advice. As a wealthy man, I thought he'd send me somewhere to have it 'taken care of' or give me something to take to make it all go away.

"Instead, he proposed. To me. A nobody from a much lower class who couldn't do whatever it was he could do with the visions he was able to put in my head. I had no idea what he was back then, and I turned him down. I wasn't interested in a loveless marriage. A sexless marriage. I tried to lose you in a scalding hot bath, but I guess it wasn't hot enough. Eventually, I went back to him and told him that I couldn't marry him, but I would have the baby; but only if he would look after it."

I've come over tired suddenly, so I don't bother to ask how they chose my adoptive parents, and instead ask one final simple question.

"What is your name then, if not Nightmare?" I wonder if this will tally with what Jeremy told me.

"Elaine Robertson. Laine, to the girls; Nightmare, to my exes."

I nod slowly and try not to raise my eyebrows. I fully expected her to give the wrong name. That whole story sounded rehearsed, but that is my mother's name, if Jeremy's information was correct. So, who is lying? Are my parents alive, or are these people impersonating them? Did they kill them? My dad was meant to be a greengrocer, not a rich guy. If they went to the effort to find out their names and my mum's backstory, why didn't they bother with my dad's? Something just doesn't add up here. And if they are pretending to be my parents, why? Why would anyone want to be my parents? Not even my adoptive parents enjoyed the position.

Since they know all about Adam and Kyle, are they hoping to use me as bait to capture Gerome or get him to do a favour for them? Do they not realise that Gerome doesn't care about me, only his sons do? He's not going to come rescue me from this luxurious cell. If he's heard where I've ended up, I'd bet he finds it hilarious.

The woman notices me stifling a yawn and excuses herself, telling me to rest and that she'll be back in the morning if I want to continue our chat. As if I have any choice in the matter, or anything better to do.

Kyle

Feeling the urgent need to make it up to Adam, I've picked up a burner phone and am about to contact everyone I know whilst Adam takes a turn at driving. I don't regret delaying our arrival at the mansion, even if we did only just miss Ella. Adam needed to unwind after everything that had happened. We'll catch up with her soon enough. He'll forgive me.

Connecting to the internet reveals quite how busy Dad's been. There are bizarre reports of 'Murder Planes' and 'Massages Gone Wrong' that have Gerome Clarke written all over them. I suppose it's only natural for him to cause chaos because he wants to appear to be the solution when he takes over from the Minister, if he takes over from the Minister. Never mind that he's the one causing the chaos in the first place, the people don't need to know that.

I wonder how his plan is going after I tried to derail it. Perhaps this is Plan B, to make himself the only option by terrifying all humans who know nothing about us. They must be worried there's a lunacy virus spreading with all of these so-called accidents going on. I'm surprised they're even leaving their houses.

"Where to now?" asks Adam.

"I don't know. We don't even know who has her. I'm not sure where to start." I reply honestly.

"But we can't give up!"

"I know, I didn't say that. I suppose we could go back to Dad again, make sure he hasn't got her back?"

It's worth a shot, though neither of us are keen on seeing him again, or taking the risk of being forced to help him again. Although, considering how carried away Adam got last time, perhaps Dad will be slightly less confident when we return.

"I'll find out where he is."

Jenny

I'm so relieved that Jeremy is letting me be a part of this. He got a call from Francis with information on the pair pretending to be Ella-Rose Thompson's parents. Whoever she is. We're going back to his apartment now to take a look. I'm hoping they will let me be the one to share this information with Gerome. I want to speak to him, properly, and this is my way in.

We pull up outside and Jeremy wastes no time in jumping out and heading inside. He has barely spoken to me since he picked me up, so he clearly hasn't forgiven me. But it's okay, I understand. I wouldn't forgive me either.

The apartment is different to the last time we were there, it's noisier and there are other people talking and rushing around. Jeremy leads the way to the room with the computer in that we went to previously and we find Francis wearing his white lab coat and talking in serious tones to a group of people who are lapping up his every word. He looks up as we enter.

"Jeremy, how lovely to see you. I see you brought Jenny." I smile awkwardly as people turn to look at me.

"She thought she might be able to help," Jeremy explains. Francis looks over the top of his glasses and nods.

He asks the group around him to give us some space. We head over and take their place.

"Alright, this is what we've found. Francesca Louise Parker seems to have been working with Damian Clarke and allowed him to use one of her family's residences as the next holding place for Ella. I have spoken with Damian, and he has admitted he had other nefarious plans for Ella, but that she was stolen from him before he could progress his plan any further. He was out when it happened, but he had set up a camera guarding the door of the room she was locked in, so he got a good shot of the person that took her."

Wow, this is a lot of information. Jeremy seems to be taking it all in. I'm lost already. Who is Damian?

"In exchange for a few more days of freedom, Damian has provided a photograph and we have run it through our database and every other system we have access to, looking for a facial match. There are none. But, all is not lost. Remember, I have a list of criminals we wish to capture. On that list is one such man I believe may be capable of this. His name is David Goldsmith, and he's a Collector, with a capital C."

"What does that mean?" I ask.

"He's building a collection of species, rather like a zoo. I imagine he wants to capture Gerome, as a particularly significant Dream-Walker, and Ella, as a P.I.N.S. I should also warn you that he is a specific kind of Dream-Walker, in some ways he is stronger than Gerome. He has some abilities even I am unaware of because he is unmonitored. I can't get in to the 'hows' and 'whys' right now, but you should bear that in mind if you plan to approach him." He looks at Jeremy with concern. "He also has a sidekick, a woman who has been spotted with him on multiple occasions. Michelle Symonds, 'Shelly.' She's known for her potions. A modern-day witch."

"Right, where can I find them? Where do they have Ella?" asks Jeremy.

"I have a better idea," says Francis.

"You do?" Jeremy frowns.

"Yes, since your mother wants to make amends, why don't you let her deliver this information to her ex-lover, Gerome, and then when he and his boys go to rescue Ella, perhaps this David Goldsmith fellow will capture Gerome for us. Two problems solved for the price of one."

He wants me to talk to Gerome. I can't believe it. This is what I wanted, a chance to clear the air, to talk properly. So why don't I feel happier? Why do I feel so nervous?

"Wait!" says Jeremy, "I want a back-up plan. If those fools can't get to her, I still want Ella to know that those people are dangerous. We need to get someone on the inside."

"I commend your passion, Jeremy, but I'll admit I'm not entirely following. What are you suggesting? How can we get someone on the inside?" Francis asks.

I'm too preoccupied with the thought of finally getting to talk to Gerome to listen properly, but I gather they're going to get Ella's human friend involved. What a foolish idea, tangling a human up in all this mess. And that's coming from me.

31 December

Ella

There's a knock on the door and I push myself upright. That bed was surprisingly comfortable, I didn't expect to sleep so well in such a strange place. It smells like flowers in here, making me wrinkle my nose. I don't remember them being there before, but I spot the culprit now, a beautiful arrangement containing those pink lilies which are always so fragrant. There is no TV in here, but there is a bookcase and an antiquated rocking chair. It's a little creepy but thankfully there's no old-fashioned doll sat on it, rocking slowly.

Someone knocks on the door again.

"Come in!" I say, before noticing the bell on the bedside table. I ring it gently.

A head peers around the door slowly before entering. It's my self-proclaimed mother.

"How are you feeling?"

"Wonderful! I'm a prisoner, aren't I?"

"No! Not at all. You're home. Remember?" she says calmly.

"I remember. But I didn't ask to come here, and you're not letting me leave. You've explained what led you to give me up when I was born, but I want to know more about

243

what I'm doing here right now. I think that's reasonable, isn't it?"

"Of course sweetie, I'll explain as much as I can. But first, don't you want some breakfast? And then there's that surprise I mentioned…" Oh yes, she did say something about a surprise last night just as she was leaving, but I was so tired, I wasn't really paying attention.

"What breakfast is on offer?" I ask. I can't remember the last time I had a proper meal. Christmas?

"Whatever you want. Fruit, eggs, bacon… What do you fancy?" My stomach growls and I cover it with my hand, embarrassed.

"Um, poached eggs on toast, with bacon, and a coffee and fruit juice." I say, then reconsider. "Do you have baked beans?"

"Yes."

"Throw some of those on there too. What about cereal?"

"We can get anything you want." She smiles.

"Golden Nuggets. No, Cheerios. No, Frosted Shreddies. Oh I don't know, surprise me, but nothing too healthy." She gives me a knowing look,

"When did you last eat?"

I shrug.

*

She returns with my food about half an hour later and I almost feel guilty for making her go to so much effort and no doubt have to run to a shop, but then I remember that I'm a prisoner and she's most likely an imposter and I shake it off.

The food is good, so good. It's not until I'm scraping up the last of the bean sauce that I consider it might have been poisoned. These are murder suspects, after all. They may be responsible for the deaths of my biological parents.

244

I sit back and straighten out my full stomach. If it was poisoned, it's a good way to go. Those poached eggs with runny yolks were delicious. They went perfectly with the smoked bacon, and the toast which I forgot to even ask for. The juice was a mixed fruit combination rather than just orange or apple. I'm not sure what was exactly, but I detected some grapefruit in there, and possibly mango. The only thing that wasn't quite up to scratch was the coffee. And by not up to scratch, I mean grim. It tasted the way I imagine it would out of those polystyrene cups at a fayre, or in a dingy police station when you're being questioned for murder. I guess she's not a coffee person. Or maybe she's used to police station coffee; she might be a murderer after all. Perhaps she's a repeat offender.

Whoever she is, she takes away my various crockery and my almost-full cup of coffee, and then returns to the room for another fake mother-daughter day. I'm going to need some kind of evidence before I accept her as my biological mother. For the meantime, I'm going to assume she's an imposter, either deliberately or accidentally. Mistakes can happen, it could be a mix-up. But given how my life seems to go these days, if I was betting money, I'd bet on the deliberate imposter. If only I could figure out why she would want to impersonate my mum…

"So, what do you want to talk about next? I think we have a little time, but then you'll want to shower and get ready for your surprise." I try not to let her further reminder about 'the surprise' bother me and get straight to the point.

"You can start by telling me what you know about yourself, about what we are and what we do. I've only recently learnt that we have a name. We're P.I.N.S., but I assume you already knew that."

I wonder what story they've concocted to answer this question.

"A what? Pin?" She scrunches her nose.

245

"P.I.N.S. Personal Instigator of Negative Stimuli, or something like that. It's the scientific term for people like us. We have a label now."

"You mean there are more like us?" she asks, I nod.

"I know of at least one other, yeah. And he's a bloke too, so it's not just women."

"Wow. I always thought it was just me." I can't decide if that's the truth or just a rubbish lie that she and David decided on together.

"Hmm. Well, it's not, so if you don't have anything useful to add on that topic, let's move onto why you both brought me here, since you're so keen for me to go and get ready for my surprise." I fail to hide my sarcasm.

"You're here because we needed to protect you from what's going on out there. Gerome Clarke is destroying the country, and it's not safe."

"I'm well aware of that."

"Well your father is also powerful and he has the benefit of not being under the watchful eye of the HJD. He's able to move under the radar, so to speak. They have no records about him, so Gerome doesn't know what risk he poses." I frown. No records? David Watt had a formal autopsy; he was definitely on the record. Who is this imposter? This secret Dream-Walker?

"What risk? What's he going to do? Gerome is strong, that's why he was locked up before. My dad can't just go out there and destroy him, it's not that simple."

"He knows it won't be easy, but he wants to protect you. You've become dangerously involved with that family, and your father is going to make things right. We should never have abandoned you, but we're here now. I'm useless, but he can really help you. And he will help you." She's quite convincing. She really sounds like she cares for my wellbeing.

"What's he going to do?"

246

"Oh, I can't even pretend to understand what he's going to do. How do you even explain how they do what they do? He has some technology he's been working on ever since you started dating Adam; when he thought perhaps Adam was going to be a threat."

"What so instead of introducing yourselves, Daddy made a gadget?"

"We couldn't introduce ourselves after so many years. We'd been watching you, and we made sure you were comfortable, that Audrey and Ian looked after you. It was a shame when they had their own daughter, and we honestly did consider stepping in then, but we were hardly in a position to play happy families." Gosh, they really have done their research. I lose myself in the moment, exploring the possibility that they really could be my parents.

"Why not? Once they had Viva, they stopped caring about me. I was just the other child. The one who wasn't really theirs. The pain in their backside. The other one to drag along. You could have taken me and taught me who I really am." I feel bad saying this after how nice Dad was the other day, but I want this woman to feel guilty, even if she is only playing a character. She wrings her hands.

"We couldn't. We weren't together. We lived together, I let him look after me. But we weren't together, we couldn't be. Not with what I am. It's not possible to live like that, putting the worst nightmares into your lover every night."

"But weren't you able to do anything, to dull the effect? Perhaps he could share a dream with you which in turn also distracts him from seeing his nightmares... There are meant to be ways to make it less painful, aren't there?"

"If that's what they told you, then they lied. We never found anything that helped. We didn't try very hard, but over the years we did try a few things, and nothing ever made a difference. Sweetie, you and Adam are never going to live happily ever after. Not if you want to have a sexual

247

relationship, anyway. He probably just isn't ready to move on yet. He cares for you, like your father cares for me. But it's not fulfilling for either of us. I don't want that life for you."

Can I trust this woman? Even if she's not who she says she is, is what she's telling me true? Are we doomed? Or does she just want me to forget about Adam?

"But maybe there's a cure? If we allow them to do tests on us, there might be a way to stop it happening. Jeremy, the man who is like us, he wondered if perhaps we could fix ourselves by having sex with each other, like one big explosion. Or at least, we'd know if it still happens when both participants are the same."

"That sounds like he just wants to have sex with you, but maybe. I don't know. There's no cure for dream-walking, I don't see why there'd be a cure for us. We have to find comfort in other things."

"What, like vibrators?" I laugh. I'd never say that to her if I actually saw her as my mum. As she's most likely an imposter, there are no boundaries.

She laughs.

"Yep, vibrators and dildos. Anything that puts a smile on your face that isn't a man with a dangly thing between his legs." She cackles. "Oh, but in case you're thinking of trying lesbianism, that doesn't work either. So long as you are an active participant working towards the climax, the nightmare effect happens. There's no correlation between penis insertion or whatever."

I blush,

"Mother!" As an older woman, whoever she is, I did not expect her to be that upfront. She shrugs,

"Well, you know what it's like. The men didn't come back, so I tried women!"

"Wait a minute, you said 'active participant' – does it not happen if someone rapes us?" I'm thinking about

Damian's idea to have Gerome rape me, and that guy who tried to rape me outside the club last spring.

"Oh, sorry! I don't know. I just meant if you're having sex, with or without the insertion of a penis in any orifice, it happens. I can't say I've ever been raped, or then asked the rapist if they saw anything, and I don't recommend you try it either."

"No, no. Of course not." So she knows nothing helpful at all, but she does sound more believable today. She's answering my questions more casually rather than reeling off what sounded like prepared lines like she was yesterday. That story was definitely rehearsed, the vocab was from David downstairs, not this 'Laine' person. Whoever she really is. "How long do I have to stay here?" I ask, ready to change the subject.

"As long as you want to, but at least until Gerome Clarke is locked up again. Or dead."

"And where exactly are we?"

"I can't tell you.," she answers solemnly. That's it for the casual answers then, she's back on script.

"Can you let Adam and Kyle know I'm okay?"

"I don't think that's a good idea, Gerome might hear. We can't have anybody finding out who we are and what your dad's up to before it happens."

"But they'll be worried, they'll be looking for me," I implore.

"You should try to forget about them."

"How?" Who is this heartless woman?

"Well don't ask me! I'm still here, aren't I? I've lost count of the number of times I've told your dad I won't marry him, but he's wormed his way into my heart, and I can't quite let him go. Especially when he can connect me to you. You wouldn't know it, but we used to watch you dreaming sometimes when you were little. He was able to dream-walk into your dreams, but hide so he didn't change

249

anything, and then I could sleep on his chest and see too. You were so adorable. You used to dream about jumping in puddles of magic water which could change your outfit into a princess dress, and of a big hairy guineapig whom you could talk to in squeak-squeak language."

"Cute," I say. And completely unbelievable. She told me they weren't together, that she tried to lose me in a scalding hot bath, and yet now she's saying she slept across his chest to watch me dream as a kid. It doesn't add up. This imposter is letting her teammate David down. I cannot trust her.

"You were adorable. I know we can never make it up to you, but I hope that by keeping you safe now, we can at least move in the right direction. Perhaps after all this, we can meet up from time to time and get to know each other?"

Before I can answer, the building shakes and I grab hold of the bedframe until it stops.

"Oh my God, what was that?" We don't have earthquakes in England. Was that what it was?

"Errr, I think that may have been your father…" She stands and excuses herself from the room. My father can cause earthquakes?

I head to the ensuite to try out the shower. I find a folded pile of clothes beside the basin which aren't what I would ordinarily choose, but at least they're fresh. I want to burn these cheap pyjamas I've been living in.

Adam

It's like a scene from the film '2012.' Car alarms blare from all angles as cars are abandoned, some are smashed up, some perfectly fine. Car doors are left open, their owners unconcerned about theft. People are scared, running for their lives.

"What the hell?" I turn to face Kyle as we stop in the never-ending line of traffic.

"Turn on the radio, isn't that what people do in the movies?" he suggests. I press the button then press down through each saved station. There's nothing, just static. That can't be a good sign.

"Well, what are they running from? Why is everyone panicking?" I ask him.

"As if I know any more than you do! Ask someone!"

I open my door and try to get someone's attention but nobody's interested. They're hurrying, screaming, dragging children by their clothes. It's a real panic zone out here.

"Hey!" I say, making my way towards an overweight man, moving slower than the rest. He looks up but doesn't stop moving. I jog to catch up and walk alongside him.

"What's going on? Why's everyone running?"

251

"Didn't you see?" He looks at me like I'm the crazy one. "They're coming! The aliens are coming! We have to make our way to the coast. We need to get off this godforsaken island as quickly as we can! The government have sacrificed our country for the aliens. For the future. We need to go before we become their number one food source!"

Trust him to be concerned about food sources, I think to myself.

"Where are you going? There aren't enough boats for the entire population."

"I don't need there to be enough boats for everyone, I just need there to be enough for me. Which is why I'm in a hurry. Get out of my way!" He shoves me and increases his pace.

Clearly, he's the type of kind gentleman who was busy getting into a lifeboat when they were calling for woman and children on the Titanic. Selfish prick. Deranged, clearly, but selfish. I make my way back to Kyle.

"He seems to think the aliens are coming," I tell him.

"Yeah, so did another woman with kids."

"You think it was Dad?"

"Who else would it be?"

"So what, he's trying to clear the country now? Cause mass panic and evacuation so he can have the entire country to himself?"

"Maybe for all of us, Dream-Walkers?"

"Hmm, nice idea. But I don't see anyone staying calm, do you? It seems to be everyone, humans and Dream-Walkers. The question is, how did he do it? Where is he? How did he project his dreams to so many people? This is like the beginning of the end out here."

"Shit, do you think Ella's behaving like this too?" Kyle asks.

I hadn't even thought about that. What if she's also rushing around? Someone might kill her in a desperate act to get on a boat. Or she could be abandoned locked up somewhere, the person who took her now distracted.

"We need to find Dad and put a stop to this madness. Wherever Ella is, that will make her safer. Where do you think we should look first?"

"So we're agreed the aliens are bullshit then?" He smiles at me.

"The aliens are us, you prat. Now where would Dad be, that he'd have a good view of all this chaos he's created?"

"Somewhere high up, perhaps?"

We make our way against the crowds towards the nearest tall tourist attraction. The Sumpton 360. One of those places with a zillion stairs, or a lift you pay extra for, viewing platforms and a small clear section of flooring you can walk over and look down. Luckily, we're only a couple of miles away from it. Of course, there's no saying that Dad's even in this part of the country anymore, so we could be completely out of luck with no way of driving anywhere and a very good chance the trains are also out of service. But I'm keeping my fingers crossed that luck is on our side. It has to be. Good always triumphs over evil.

We are 'good', aren't we?

Two miles feels like 10 when you can't walk in a straight line and keep getting shoved. One woman elbowed me so hard in my chest, it brought tears to my eyes.

"I fucking hate walking," says Kyle.

"Chin up, it's not far now," I tell him, feeling determined. I can see what we're aiming for every time I look up at the sky, and I try not to notice the dark clouds.

"It's going to rain," he states the obvious.

"No shit."

"It's going to make them panic even more if it storms. They'll think the aliens are coming."

253

"Thank you," I try to ignore his completely rational fears.

Of course it will get harder to move if it rains, which is why we need to keep moving. I don't know what makes me think he'll be there, but I do. I feel it in my heart. He wants us to find him, even if he's annoyed about what we did and what I nearly did. That won't have been the end of his plans for us. There'll be more. He'll be waiting for us. And if he knows anything about where Ella might be, he'll be expecting us to turn to him for help and information.

"How are we going to get in?" asks Kyle as we get closer.

It looks funny without the usual line of tourists queuing around barriers to enter. The barriers have all been knocked over, and the building stands alone, silently looming over the city. The doors are locked, sensibly. For some reason I'm suddenly overcome with the image of King Kong climbing the Empire State Building.

I look at Kyle. I think he shared my thought.

"No, Adam. No."

There are some ropes hanging from the top, probably from the last group of abseilers before the madness broke out. They must be fixed securely. We could climb...

"No," he repeats, shaking his head. "What if it's a trap? You get halfway up, or higher, and then someone releases the rope, and you plunge to your death?"

It's a fair point.

"Okay, well, what's your idea then?"

"We find a way to smash that ultra-strong entrance door. After, of course, looking at the camera on the off-chance Dad is sat up there waiting for us and feeling kind."

"Ugh, fine." We approach the door. I give the door a shove and Kyle stands in front of the camera, waiting for anybody inside to check. Nothing happens.

254

We give it another few minutes, and I keep shoving at the door, just in case.

"Alright, brute force it is." I say, hoping Kyle will help me to charge at the door with something heavy. I've eyed up a metal bin and a picnic bench nearby.

"Unless he's not in there and this is a total waste of energy," Kyle suggests.

I want to scream at him. This is our only chance right now. He has to be up there, holding all the cards, grinning because we're right where he wants us. I know it. It's just the way the world works when Gerome Clarke is free. He's up there, he's just biding his time.

And if he's not, well, at least a tall building should keep us away from the madness down here. It's not like we can just jump in the car and drive around looking for him anymore. We're in a bloody apocalypse now.

We ram the door, oh, ten times or something, before we stop and sit down, panting and sweating. I haven't worked out in forever. That was hard work!

As we sit there, mopping our brows and trying to catch our breath, we hear a short sharp beep come from the door. Then again, and again.

I leap up and push the door. It opens.

"Oh for fuck's sake!" shouts Kyle, "he was watching us, wasn't he? Watching us tire ourselves out. What a bloody dickhead!"

"Come on," I say, walking into reception. Of course the lift is marked 'out of order.' Fuck. I'm not sure either of us have the energy to make it up that many stairs. Our legs are going to be pure jelly by the time we reach the top. We won't be able to fight anyone, we won't even be able to stand up.

"Shall we wait a bit?" I ask, looking at Kyle.

"Hell no, I'm not giving him that satisfaction. Come on," he marches ahead.

We're about halfway up, out of breath and a little dizzy, quads burning, when I grab the handrail and close my eyes. The ground tremors beneath us and I imagine we're in a tall tree, swaying in a storm. Shit. This is the worst place to be right now.

"Was that an earthquake?" asks Kyle.

"I don't know, it felt like something like that. Right?"

"But he can't control the weather, and we don't have earthquakes here. What the hell is going on?"

"Bad luck?" I say, "do you think it's safe to keep moving?"

"I don't think any of this is safe, but we might as well now."

We take the rest of the stairs two at a time, jelly-legs be damned.

Adam

"Well, well, well, look who finally came back to Daddy," he greets us at the top of the staircase. Dad seems to have converted the main viewing floor into a centre of operations. His minions are watching screens and writing reports. He moves to stand proudly in the middle of the area with transparent glass floor, at the centre of the action.

"What are you up to now, and where is Ella?" I demand.

"I'm well thanks, how are you?" he responds sarcastically. "Since you rather fucked up my plan of getting elected, I had to take things in a different direction. But I've hit a snag."

"A snag?"

"Yes, a snag."

"What do you mean? It's chaos out there, people are running for their lives, it's like a scene from a disaster movie." I tell him, it's the sort of scene he would normally revel in.

"Exactly, but it wasn't me! I'm trying to work out who did it. Somebody has got in the way of my plan. I was going to have them all killing themselves, not running to save their lives! I'm sure some will still die, but this wasn't my plan by a long shot."

I try not to smile as I look at Kyle.

"It wasn't you, was it? You haven't teamed up with someone have you?" he asks, eyeing us suspiciously.

"No, it wasn't us. We were too busy trying to find Ella. Was that an earthquake just now?"

"A large section of the M25 was ripped open, much like an earthquake might cause, but as you I'm sure you're aware, there are no tectonic plate boundaries in the UK, so it wasn't natural. Some bastard was showing off."

"And that bastard wasn't you?" asks Kyle.

"No! I need people to get to London! Destroying the M25 is not going to help me accomplish that, is it? Especially when the trains are already fucked after the drivers kept killing themselves." He pulls a face. "That I *did* have something to do with."

"Alright then, so your plans have gone to shit due to some unknown opponent. Where's Ella? Did you steal her back from Damian?"

"I have no fucking idea what happened to that bitch you're both obsessed with. Damian was supposed to move her to my next location and instead he took off with her. Before I could figure out where exactly, things started going wrong."

"What did you do with the others? Jeremy and whatsherface?"

"Ah crap, what is her name? I can't remember either!" He laughs. "What a disappointment! And I thought you two were bad enough!"

"So…?" I wait for him to get to the point.

"They're locked up safe, I believe. Probably safer than they would be if I let them out, now that all this is going on." He waves his arms around.

"And you have no idea who took Ella?"

"Oh, so she's not with Damian anymore then?" he asks, surprised.

"No, someone else took her from where he had her. Frankie said he was a well-dressed older gentleman."

"Frankie Parker? Oh boys you are in a pickle if you're trusting her! Bad blood, that one."

"We don't trust her, she was the last one to see Ella alive," snaps Kyle.

"Do you think this suited and booted gentleman might be the man who's messing up your plans?" I ask Dad.

"Well I have no idea who I'm up against, so it's possible, though why he would have any interest in that bitch is beyond me, unless he thinks I still need her for something. But if this person knows me at all, they know my plans would never hinge on something so weak. They'd be wasting their time taking Ella, and judging by the scenes outside, they've not wasted much."

"Stop calling her that." I try to contain my anger.

"What?" He raises his eyebrows, mocking me and enjoying my reaction.

"Stop calling her that." I repeat.

"But she is. You know what she was up to when I took her from the hotel, don't you? You can't trust her. She's a whore. How about that? Do you prefer that word? Whore."

"Dad, stop it," says Kyle calmly. My fists are clenched, I'm ready to deck him.

"Sir!" A short mousey woman interrupts, standing up from her desk. "I've been digging around to find out who might be strong enough to pull this off, who is a serious contender for you, and I think I've found something."

Dad storms towards her and we follow quickly behind. Kyle gives me a nudge and mouths at me to calm down. As if it's that simple.

"Did you know there are some Dream-Walkers who are not kept on the record? Even when their skills are confirmed, they remain unlisted on the database. For centuries, a small number of families have been paying for privacy. They have zero intrusion from the Human Justice Department. They are allowed to practise and multiply in secret." I gasp. Dad is shaking his head.

"That can't be true! After all I went through, you're telling me that some of us never even have a blood test? How could the HJD agree to that? They have no idea what other advancements these people may have figured out in private. They could be stronger than me! They could be dangerous!"

"It says that these people were outstanding members of aristocracy in the beginning, and they have always had a reputation to uphold. The Department believed that was enough to trust they wouldn't behave irresponsibly."

"Well clearly somebody has decided the time has come to showcase their skills, haven't they? They've seen what I'm up to and they've decided to hunt me down." If I didn't know better, I'd say Dad is scared. "So what else do you know? Did you find any names? Anything else to go on?"

The woman's face creases.

"No, not really. But I do have another idea." We all look at her. She stands up straighter, her confidence growing.

"Well, as the man who took Ella was wearing a suit, I believe it's not too big of a jump to assume that he is likely to be one of these 'private' Dream-Walkers. So, if you can give me the address that you know he took Ella from, perhaps we have caught some footage of him on one of our drones? If we can find a good image of him, we might be able to find him elsewhere. Not on the HJD database, but perhaps in a human newspaper or something."

"Drones? You have drones now?" I stare at Dad incredulously. "You were locked up for what, ten years? Fifteen? And yet you know about and own drones now?"

"Damian filled me in on the technological advancements before my escape," he says quickly. "Do you have the address?"

I look at Kyle. We silently agree we have nothing to lose. He leans forward and tells the woman what to type in.

A bird's eye view of the mansion appears on her monitor.

"How many of these things have you got?" asks Kyle.

"Never you mind."

"I'm just saying, it's pretty coincidental you had one flying over there, out of everywhere…" he replies sceptically.

"If you must know, I had it down as an area of interest because of that family's connection to my daughter. I thought she might end up there if she escaped."

The woman presses rewind on the footage. There's not a lot to see, and the drone keeps getting too close to trees which obscure the view. Finally, we see ourselves.

"Okay, she was gone by then, it can't have been too long before this though."

She rewinds and what happens next, none of us were expecting. Whoever took her didn't travel in a car; didn't travel in a helicopter, or even a motorbike. Whoever took her arrived and departed in a horse drawn carriage. What the hell?

The woman rewinds to just before his arrival and then lets the footage play out.

He appears to be alone, with silvery hair and a smart grey suit as described by Frankie. He walks inside calmly, as if he has all the time in the world and knows exactly where he is going. He is inside for a short while before he is seen carrying Ella over his shoulder as if she is weightless and placing her inside the carriage. Then they depart.

But, instead of making their way down the forest road back out onto the main road, just before they go out of view, the carriage disappears. They only trot ten or twenty metres before disappearing.

"Erm..."

261

"Well that was weird." Kyle says what we're all thinking.

"Where was the next drone? Could another one have caught their next moves? Perhaps it's a glitch," asks Dad.

"There wasn't another drone for another hundred miles, and we don't know which way they were headed," the woman answers quietly.

Dad is fuming, he knocks some paperwork off the desk next to the woman and then shouts as a stapler lands on his foot.

"So whoever I'm dealing with here, is magic?"

"Or there's a glitch." I remind him of his own suggestion.

"No, you saw it as well as I did. Whoever took her vanished, perhaps even teleported. I can't do that, can you? We are dealing with someone or something we know nothing about. Who knows what else he can do!"

Once again, he appears afraid. It's funny what potentially not being the most dangerous Dream-Walker alive can do to a man. In this case, it's made him jumpy.

"It still doesn't explain why he wanted Ella. If he's out to destroy you, why bother taking her?" I ask, not really expecting a response.

"Perhaps she's more important than you think," the woman pipes up.

"Excuse me? I know how important she is. She's my girlfriend. There is no one who is more important to me."

"Cheers bro," jokes Kyle.

"I meant in terms of our society. I heard that she's a P.I.N.S.? Perhaps that's significant," the woman continues, blushing scarlet.

Dad scratches his beard. It's grown considerably since we last saw him and is now in the transition period between rugged and homeless where it will soon need a trim.

"Of course your bitch is important! It would explain why you're both besotted with her. She's probably been playing you both from the start. Trying to get close to me, to destroy me with whoever she's working with."

"She was carried out of there; she was hardly working with them," Kyle retorts.

"Okay, so she didn't know then, but she does now. I bet she's playing happy families right now, plotting against us and laughing. I bet she has one of those sickening girly giggles. What did you tell her about me? How much does she know?"

"She knows less about you than the rest of the community does, I'd bet. Now quit jumping to conclusions and help us come up with a plan!" I raise my voice.

Are we on the same team now? We want Ella back, and this potentially magical man who might be a secret elite Dream-Walker who is out to destroy Dad has her so, temporarily at least, our motives are aligned. But, this bastard is strong. There's no reason to believe he's any more trustworthy than Dad. He does appear to have caused the disaster movie situation outside after all.

"What else can you find out about these secret Dream-Walkers?" I ask the woman. "And what's your name, by the way? We weren't properly introduced," she blushes again.

"I'm Amelia. And um, I don't know. I can try, but the whole point was not to document them. Perhaps I can find when the first generation made the pact with the Minister of the time, but it'll take a while. I'm not sure we have time."

Dad has moved away from us and is now sat in a director's chair on wheels.

"Boys, boys, boys. You are missing the obvious here. Do I have to do everything for you?"

We turn to face him.

"Ella. She's a P.I.N.S., she was adopted, ergo, her birth parents might be Dream-Walkers, one, or both of them. Wouldn't they seem to be the top suspects in the role of stealing her to protect her from me, whilst simultaneously destroying me?" He seems proud of himself for this idea.

"Except her birth parents are dead." I inform him.

"Since when?" asks Dad, frowning.

"Jeremy, the Minister's son told us."

"But I spoke with them, I offered Ella a deal to meet them!" he exclaims. "What do you mean they're dead?"

"They died not long ago, since you've been out. It wasn't you, then?"

"Of course it wasn't me! I couldn't care less about that bitch's parents, I don't just go around murdering random people! I reached out to them as a way of getting Ella on side if needed, so that I'd have something to offer her. Not that I needed them in the end, Damian did a great job of impersonating you, Adam. It's just a shame he fucked off with her instead of sticking to the plan." He picks up a bottle of beer and holds it up to the light to check if it's empty. "Anyway, who the fuck would want to impersonate that bitch's birth parents?"

"What were they like, the couple you spoke to?" I ask.

"Hmm. David and Shelly, I think. The man was well spoken. I never saw them in person, just spoke over the phone."

"Well her mum's name was Elaine, not 'Shelly.'" I say, trying to remain calm.

"Oh, perhaps I misremembered. Tell me what you know."

"David Watt, Dream-Walker and greengrocer, Elaine Robertson, P.I.N.S. and prostitute." Kyle fills in for me. Dad smirks.

"Her birth mum was a prostitute?"

"Yes," I answer, grinding my teeth.

264

"Wow, you sure can pick 'em." He continues to grin, deliberately aggravating me. I clench my hands into fists and glare at him.

"Okay, okay, we're getting off topic now," says Kyle, trying to diffuse the situation.

"Yes, we're supposed to be figuring out who took Ella. Can you do facial recognition on that drone footage?" I ask Amelia.

"No luck I'm afraid, we didn't get a good enough angle." She shows the zoomed in blurry image.

"But this could be the 'David' guy Dad spoke to, couldn't it? Do you have a phone number at least? Something we can trace?" Kyle asks. Now that's a good idea. Finally!

"Wait! If Ella's parents are regular Dream-Walkers or P.I.N.S., why didn't Ella have any matches on the system when she went to court then, hey?" Dad asks smugly. It's a good point.

"Well, her mum might not be on there, P.I.N.S. aren't exactly well known of, or she might have an incomplete record... But fine, that's a good point. Her dad should've been on there. Why wouldn't he come up on a search?" I look at Kyle.

"Maybe someone didn't want us to find out who he is. Someone on the inside could have hidden his file. It doesn't have to mean he's some super elite Dream-Walker. Maybe it's adoption protocol or something." He shrugs.

"Well either way, the real guy is dead. Jeremy saw the paperwork." I add for Dad's benefit.

"And you trust this Jeremy character?"

"I trust that he wouldn't lie about that," I answer. I do not however trust that he wouldn't try to steal Ella from me if given the opportunity. But I'm sure as hell not going to share that insecurity with my dad.

"Maybe we need to think about who would want to pretend to be Ella's parents? Who might have killed them, to take their place?" Amelia suggests.

"Like one of those secret elite Dream-Walkers," says Kyle. "Someone out to destroy Dad using their secret abilities. Maybe he doesn't realise that Ella isn't important to you," he tells Dad. "You did have her held hostage, it's an easy mistake to make."

"Does anyone else feel like we're just going around in circles, or is it just me?" I ask, finding myself a spare office chair and taking a seat.

Jenny

By the time they've tracked down Gerome and I am finally helicoptered into the vicinity of his current hideout, my nerves have been replaced by stress. Why couldn't it have been as simple as picking up the phone? We had to call everyone, including Tasha, who still hates me, in order to narrow down their location.

But this is it, I'm here. I'm ready to make my grand entrance. I stand at the bottom of the building and look up into the security camera and wait to be let in. Francis reckons they may be able to hack into the system to let me in if it comes to it, but he's hoping Gerome will be pleased to see me. He needs him to believe what I have to tell him.

The door beeps and I head inside.

They could have warned me about the stairs, I'm an out of shape housewife. By the time I make it to the top my face is beetroot, and I can't catch my breath.

"Well get the woman a chair!" Gerome's voice booms, making me jump. A petite mousey woman rolls a desk chair over to me and I sit down gratefully, rolling myself away from the top of the staircase. Adam and Kyle Clarke are also here, and there are other people working on computers behind a partition.

"Jenny, darling, it's great to see you." Gerome continues, as Kyle glares at me. I wonder if anyone filled him in about Jeremy and the rest of my lies. I smile, feeling awkward. This wasn't how I imagined our reunion. I feel like I'm about to be interrogated. I don't know what to say.

"Jenny, the clock is ticking. I believe you have some information for us, from our mutual friend, the Minister?" Gerome prompts me and Adam and Kyle's eyes open wider. Do they not even know why I'm here? Does Gerome really keep his cards that close? Still?

I try to compose myself. So this isn't going to be a pleasant reunion, so I'm not going to get the answers I wanted, so Gerome really doesn't love me, I still need to deliver the message. If I owe anyone, it's Francis Krunk. And Jeremy. My beautiful boy. I clear my throat.

"I know where Ella-Rose Thompson is, and I know who took her. Their names are David Goldsmith and Michelle Symonds. Here," I pull out a crumpled piece of paper with the address on. Gerome snatches it from my hand and passes it to the woman who brought me the chair.

She types it into a computer and announces,

"It's not far, it's walkable."

"Brilliant! Come on boys, you have a girl to rescue, and I have a man to put in his place!" Gerome claps his hands, excited.

"Wait! Don't you want to know more about these people? They're dangerous! The man, he might try to capture you, and the woman, she's like a modern witch, she makes potions…" My voice trails as they leave the room. The other son, Adam, looks back at me with earnest eyes,

"Thank you."

I relax back into the chair feeling resigned. Gerome really doesn't care. He used me before, has used me again, and now Francis has used me too.

"Do you want a drink?" The mousey woman asks in the silence of their absence. "I can make you a hot chocolate, you look like you could do with some sugar," she smiles.

"I would love a drink," I agree. "Do you have anything stronger?"

She grins at me with a mischievous glint in her eye before unlocking a box at the side of one of the desks.

"How about one of these?" She pulls out a beer. "It's Gerome's secret stash, but something tells me he won't be coming back here anytime soon."

I nod eagerly,

"Yes please."

She takes the cap off and hands it to me, it's chilled and goes down a treat. I haven't drunk beer since, well, since 1992, probably. Since I lived with Gerome. I didn't like it then, but now it's nostalgic.

"I'm sure he is grateful," she tells me, sipping from a water bottle.

"I'm not so sure."

"But you are Jenny, right? The Jenny from before? He told me about you." She smiles again. Who is this woman?

"Really?"

"Of course, he looks back over those years like his highlights reel. He loved those days. I think maybe he loved you?" she asks uncertainly.

"Ah, I used to think that too. But no, Gerome doesn't love anyone. He used me, repeatedly. I was a fool. I did love him though, that much is true." I tell her, honestly.

"Well don't be too hard on yourself, he's a complicated man. But seriously, if he has ever loved anyone, and maybe it's not even possible for him, but if he has, I think he loved you."

Why is she being so kind? How does she know what I long to hear?

"Thank you for saying that." I gulp down more beer. It's like it tastes better, knowing it's his.

"I'm sorry I have to do this," she says suddenly, reaching for my beer.

"What?" I haven't finished it yet.

"I really am, it's just... Oh never mind, you'll figure it out soon enough. All of this is so much bigger than Gerome and your history together. Just know that I am sorry for what is about to happen. Truly. But you understand, right?"

And with that, everything goes black. No, I do not understand.

Ella

"Kristina, is that you?" I gawp into the intercom beside my door. I didn't even know I had an intercom in here until my fake mum told me to look behind the photo frame. This place is so strange.

But there she is! My tall, insanely chatty and outgoing friend from my old job, whom I haven't physically seen since we went out to celebrate me quitting my job. How did she get here? Did they call her? I suppose this is the surprise my so-called mum was hinting about - friendly company to make me stay longer.

I have so much I want to tell her, but I can't, can I? I can't tell her about the dreams that weren't random at all. I can't tell her about the HJD and my time in a Medical Investigation Unit and the Minister who offered to harvest my eggs in exchange for my silence. That he's also Jeremy's father.

There's so much she doesn't know, but I can't tell her because I swore to keep the Dream-Walker secret.

Before she reaches my bedroom (or effective cell) I quickly ring my bedside bell to get someone's attention. 'Mum' appears smiling with glee.

"Your friend's here!"

"Yes, that's why I called you."

"Are you pleased? Do you want me to make you both some drinks?"

"No!" I say a little too quickly. "I just wanted to check, I'm not allowed to tell her about any of this stuff, am I? Nothing about people who can get into your dreams, or anything that's going on in the world outside right now? The reasons behind it? The truth?"

"Well, I suppose that depends on how much you trust your father." She scrunches her nose. "He can protect you both, should you choose to divulge."

I nod slowly. A man I don't know is willing to protect me and my friend from the HJD as well as Gerome Clarke, and all because he says he's my father. But I know he's not. Probably.

I can't tell her. What if I piss him off and he decides to throw me to the sharks? I'd rather not give them any more reason to come after me. If I behave, I stand a small chance of reasoning with the Minister. I know he has a heart. We could come to an agreement. Let's face it, he was prepared to take my eggs last time. Perhaps he would offer that again. It's not the worst idea in the world.

Kristina knocks on my bedroom door with big bold taps, and I spring to open it quickly, hearing it magically unlock.

"Well hello stranger! Fancy seeing you here!"

"Ella!" She responds, enveloping me in a big hug. She always was a hugger. "Wait. What are you wearing?" She pulls a face at my frilly white blouse and below-knee floral skirt. "Never mind!" She pulls me towards the bed and sits down, tapping the space in front of her.

"Tell me everything!" She beams at me. She's so happy and upbeat. I've missed her energy. I feel like I've been dragging myself from one drama to another ever since I found out the truth about Adam, and I've slowly been running out of oomph. It's to be expected, I suppose, when

I'm surrounded by powerful people, and my newly discovered skill is useless for anything other than getting rid of unwanted company in bed.

"Go on, how is everything? Are you still with Adam? What's new? Do you live here now?" She asks, looking around at my luxurious living quarters. Where do I start without saying what I'm not allowed to say?

"I'm still with Adam, but we've definitely had our ups and downs and it's been kind of a crazy journey." She nods, looking at me from an angle with her ear facing the door like a dog, listening for her owner. I frown at her. "Are you okay?"

She holds up her hand counting down three, two, one with her fingers. Jazz hands on zero.

"Okay, now I am."

I frown at her even more.

"You won't believe the morning I've had! I wasn't sent here to keep you company like you think. Well, I was. But I was approached by some other people first."

"Who?"

"Jeremy and his father, the Minister of something or other. They needed me to get inside this place and check you're okay and tell you what's going on. I don't know how they knew I'd be contacted, but their plan came together brilliantly."

"Wait, you know what's going on? You know about them?"

"Who exactly? Adam? Kyle? Jeremy?" She grins. "Yeah, that Minister guy has given me an official pass. They needed me to be prepared so that if I was brought here, I could fill you in on what's really going on. They formally introduced me to the Dream-Walker society. It was a very enlightening morning. Did I mention they woke me at 5am and I've had seven coffees so far?" She pulls a funny face and I laugh.

"And to think we used to believe my dreams about my dream man were just normal dreams, that meeting Adam and Kyle was some absurd coincidence. It's a crazy world, right? Now go on, what did they ask you to tell me? Is it about these people I'm stuck here with? I'm pretty sure they're not my real parents, but I haven't dared confront them about it."

"You're right, they're imposters. But like, not just any old imposters. They only know a little bit about the woman, but the man is a special kind of Dream-Walker from a line of Dream-Walkers who have been allowed to flourish away from the Human Justice Department. They don't appear on databases, and they don't go in for check-ups like the rest of them do, apparently. Who knew?" She expresses with her hands. "Anyway, this man, his real name is David Goldsmith and they believe that he is some kind of super Dream-Walker. He can do what the rest of them can, but other stuff too. Like teleportation and whatever that earthquake was. I guess you felt that here too?"

She babbles on and I let her voice wash over me. It's so nice to see a friendly face, hear a friendly voice. I miss normalcy.

"But why has he brought me here? Why the charade about being my dad?" I ask.

"Well, apparently, he's also a 'Collector.' Capital C. They think perhaps bringing you here was a ploy to get Gerome Clarke – I think that's his name? – to come here to get you. But he might also be trying to collect you too, given your situation. They hope his motives will become clearer once they figure out who the woman is and what she's capable of."

"Oh God," I cover my mouth, "they told you about my 'situation'?"

"Yup." Well, at least I don't have to explain it.

"So, um, how was Jeremy, when you met him?" I ask, thinking of how close to death he seemed when I last saw him.

"Very concerned for your wellbeing, desperate to save you. If I didn't know any better…" She raises her eyebrows suggestively.

"No! Don't go there!"

"Alright, but you did ask. And he has gone out of his way to get me here, so clearly he cares," she teases. "Maybe you care too?"

I can't stop myself from blushing.

"I love Adam, okay. Jeremy is just… Jeremy." I roll my eyes. "Did he tell you he's like me? Did he share his theory with you, too?"

"No? What's the theory?" I can tell she's trying not to smile.

"He did, didn't he?" I narrow my eyes at her.

"I don't know what you're talking about, you'll have to tell me." Her grin escapes.

"He wants to have sex with me, to find out if we counteract each other, or whatever." I try to keep my voice steady.

"Makes sense to me! A logical scientific experiment," says Kristina.

"But I can't do it, obviously! I love Adam. I could never!"

"Even if doing it could stop the P.I.N.S. effect for good? Meaning you could then go back to Adam and have a normal – or, as normal as possible with a Dream-Walker – relationship?"

"Yes! I can't do it, because no matter what the outcome, Adam would never have me back. He still hasn't entirely got over what happened between Kyle and I in our dreams!"

"Okay, but are you sure you want Adam?"

275

"Did Jeremy put you up to this? You know I love Adam! And besides, Jeremy's old!"

"I mean, he's not that old," she widens her eyes, "and he's like you…" She shrugs.

"Oh my God, stop! I can't talk about this right now!"

"Alright, I'm just saying…" She laughs and pulls me in for another hug. "Just because you loved Adam first, doesn't mean you're meant to be with him forever. Just bear that in mind. Don't instantly dismiss Jeremy because he's a posh twat. I know he's annoying, but he really does seem to care for you. There might be something there that's worth exploring."

"And you swear he didn't ask you to say any of that?"

"I promise. I was only sent to talk about these imposters who may or may not have killed your birth parents. I just couldn't ignore his obvious concern for you." She smiles. "Honestly, girl. He likes you."

"How did you get here anyway? I don't even know where I am!" I ask, changing the topic.

"I'm not entirely sure. Helicopter? Horse drawn carriage?"

"Horse drawn carriage?" I raise my eyebrows at her.

"Yeah, I don't know. All I remember is agreeing to come and keep you company. A strange man, possibly your fake dad, told me you weren't feeling well and needed to see a friendly face – and then I think we got into a carriage. I went along with it because Jeremy had already told me some guy was likely to turn up and ask me to visit you, so I didn't ask any questions. But the roads are blocked everywhere, so that doesn't make any sense." She frowns.

"Oh, yeah, I saw it looked a bit gridlocked out there, but I haven't left this room since I got here. I don't know what's going on." I glance over at the window.

"It's madness. People are saying that aliens are coming! Most people are rushing to the coast to get into boats. The

Minister reckons we have your fake father to thank for that."

"Really? Not Gerome?"

"Nope. Gerome is apparently furious. He seems to have a real competitor in your fake father. He's really screwing with his plans."

"So what happened after you got in the carriage?" I ask.

"I don't know. The next thing I remember, I was pressing the door buzzer and you were speaking through the intercom." Kristina stands, peering out the window. "Um, Ella?"

I stand up to look out too.

"Is that Adam?"

Standing on top of an abandoned car, holding a spray-painted street sign over his head, his biceps trembling, is Adam. I think. Or it could be Kyle. Or Damian. I always forget about Damian.

"Yes, I think so."

The spray paint has run a bit, but the message is clear.

HE IS NOT YOUR FATHER

I look at Kristina.

"I guess Jeremy and the Minister aren't the only ones who have figured that out then. But if I'm not his daughter, then why is he protecting me?" I think aloud.

"Who says he is?" Kristina eyes the door. "Can you leave if you want to?"

I shake my head,

"No, they keep locking it."

"Sounds like we need to escape then."

"Probably, but it's nice here, it's comfortable. Seriously, that bed is amazing. Can't I just stay in blissful ignorance? They haven't hurt me yet and, if he's so powerful, any escape plan will fail. Can't we just have that girly gossip

277

session I thought you came for? I need to know: did you get with Daniel?"

"Ella, wake up. We need to get you somewhere safe, somewhere none of these freaks can get to you."

"Nowhere is safe Kris', Dream-Walkers will always find you eventually. You can't hide, unless you can keep your eyes open forever. I'm up to five minutes."

"Seriously?"

"Yes. And somebody's avoiding my question," I tease.

"Fine, I'll tell you, but then we leave." She holds her hand out for me to shake it.

"Deal," I say, shaking her hand and sitting back on the bed. It really is so comfortable. My bum just sinks in.

"Yes, I slept with him, it was possibly the lowest point of my romantic escapades. But you know what? It really wasn't that bad. Nowhere near as bad as you'd think. I just kept his mouth busy away from my face, if you know what I mean." She giggles. Daniel was a colleague of ours back when we worked together, with a terrible smelly breath issue.

"Oh my God! So that must have made things in the office..."

"Mega awkward, yes. And he was insufferably confident after that. But, 'unfortunately' we all got fired or redistributed when they decided to close our site at the end of last month, so I was finally able to 'lose' his number and change my own, and I haven't heard from him since."

"Oh no! Where are you working now then?"

"Only the next nearest office. It's near a train station so it's not too bad, I was one of the lucky ones. Daniel was made redundant with next to no pay out since he was still relatively new, and Hannah was offered a job 90 miles away."

I wonder if Jeremy had anything to do with my friend getting such a convenient job offer when the others didn't. Would he do that for me?

There's a knock at the door.

"Ladies, I've brought you some refreshments. Are you enjoying your chat? I miss girly chats. Do you mind if I join you?" My fake mother asks, carrying a tray of what looks like cocktails and biscuits. An odd combination for 11am.

I look at Kristina and then agree. Perhaps she can help me figure out what motivates this woman and why she is helping David; what's she got to gain?

She joins us on the bed, carefully positioning the tray of drinks between us. They look delicious. I reach for a glass and take a sip. Mmm, it's a Tequila Sunrise, I think. I imagine I'm sat on a beach somewhere exotic. I nod at Kristina, and she takes a glass too although she seems more hesitant to drink it. I smile at her reassuringly. This imposter woman provided me with a delicious breakfast, why would she poison me now? She seems intent on making me feel comfortable here.

"This is delicious, Mum. Thank you."

"Aw, I love hearing you say that. I never thought I would, you know. I never thought I wanted to, either. But all of this, it really brings you together, doesn't it? The madness outside. You have to hold on to what you have, like family." I keep drinking and I see Kristina seems to be enjoying hers too.

"Mum, what is going on out there? What's Dad up to? How long do I need to stay here? I'd really like to get a message to my boyfriend."

"But you have company now, you don't need a man!" she says, smiling.

"No, I don't need him, but I want him. I like having him around." I explain.

279

"He's not good for you, Ella. His family," she looks down at her hands, "you shouldn't mix with people like them."

I finish my drink and place it back on the tray.

"People like them? Are they not the same as Dad? Dream-Walkers?"

"Your father is not a Dream-Walker, he is much more. He is everything. He is… No, I can't say, I mustn't, he'd never forgive me." I make eye contact with Kristina. Did this woman basically just confirm what she told me? That my fake father is a super Dream-Walker who can do so much more than dream-walking? "Are you okay? You're looking a little sleepy," the woman sounds concerned. "Here, lie down, let me move this tray out of the way."

I watch Kristina's eyes struggle to stay open as my eyelids get heavy before we both fall back onto the soft pillows. My so-called Mum picks up the tray and hurries out of the room. I faintly hear her whisper the words 'it's done' before the door locks behind her.

Ella

Where are we? What is this place? The walls are multicoloured like someone has put a funky filter on my eyes. We're in a tunnel, Kristina and me. Though she's yet to open her eyes and move. The edges of my vision flicker like a bad recording. What is going on?

"What the fuck?" *says Kristina from her position on the ground.*

"Oh thank goodness you're okay," *I say, bending down to see her. I offer her a hand to help her up.* "Ordinarily, I'd say we're dreaming, but I don't know. I've never seen a place like this before."

"Wow," *she says, looking around at the multicoloured tunnel.* "It's like we've been drugged."

"Maybe we have," *I agree.*

"The cocktails!" *we both say together.*

My 'mum' drugged us, but why?

"What are we supposed to do?" *asks Kristina as she tries to touch the wall, which proves impossible despite looking within grabbing distance.*

"Wait, I guess."

"You're very calm," *she says with a nervous laugh.*

281

"It's not the first time I've been in a strange realm that's beyond my control." I shrug. "You know, with the dreams, they actually fooled me into believing I could control them for a while. Well, Kyle did. Or Damian. I forget, it all got so confusing in the end. But they made it seem like I could fight back, undo what they were doing. I felt so strong. Then it turned out, it was never me at all."

"So we're stuck here?"

"Yep. Until we wake up or whatever."

"Well that's crap." She sits back down.

Yes, it is crap. Especially since I don't think we're dreaming. I think this is something else. And if we're not dreaming, how can we wake up?

Adam

I can't believe I'm saying this, but it's all thanks to Jeremy that we know where Ella is and who the man pretending to be her biological father is. And based on what Jenny started to say about the woman, I also have a vague idea what type of woman she is, too. A witch. A potion master. I suspect she might have something to do with why I can't find Ella and Kristina anywhere.

Dad and Kyle have taken the lead on trying to get close to David Goldsmith. Dad has not been put off by the news that this man is forming a collection of supernatural beings and that he's apparently stronger than us, something 'more' than a Dream-Walker. Instead, he wants to meet him and prove him wrong. He wants to fight. I wished them luck and left them to it.

I've found my way up to the room Ella and Kristina were in before, when they saw me from outside, but it's empty. I know this is the right room though, I can feel it. Damn, my arms are achy. Why Kyle couldn't just find some cardboard, I'll never understand. A road sign, honestly!

I look at the bed. It's still a little creased from where they had presumably been sat chatting. In fact, the more I look at it, the more I feel like I can see the dips in the covers, as if they are lying there, invisible. As if the duvet is being squashed by their weight. I narrow my eyes and step closer, my fingertips reaching out towards the pink covers.

An almighty scream stops me in my tracks. I spring around as a woman charges at me with a lamp and I duck out of the way. What the fuck? Is this her? The woman who has been helping David Goldsmith? The witch?

She doesn't look like anything special, but she's not giving up. She comes at me again. I push her away and she falls back into a chest of drawers.

"Ella! Kristina! Can you hear me?" I shout. If they are here but not visibly here, perhaps they will still be able to hear me. I stare at the duvet covers for any signs of movement. Nothing. The woman is getting back up again. I need to get rid of her so I can work out what's going on.

Before I can approach her with a scarf I've picked up from the side, something hits me on the back of my head and I fall to the cushioned carpet below. It doesn't feel so plush now. And the pressure in my head... Soon all I see is darkness.

Kyle

"It's not working, Dad. Whatever this guy is, he's too strong for us. We should go and get reinforcements!"

"And admit that someone out there is stronger than me? I don't think so boy; we're going to do this now. One way or another." He grits his teeth.

"But if he's got a fucking magic chariot, isn't he just going to disappear the moment we get close to him?"

"Not if he wants to prove himself, he won't." He tightens his grip on the post.

We're trying to get into what we believe is some kind of lab. It's a part of the building which is heavily reinforced, and, with zero guards around to manipulate, we're having to use brute force to gain access. I hope Adam had better luck getting to Ella.

We push harder.

"It's starting to give!" I grunt then hold my breath again as we push. Finally, a click. The door releases. We drop the post, and it narrowly misses my foot. "Jeez, Dad, careful! I'd like to keep all my toes."

"Shut up and follow me," he orders, storming into the room like he means business.

285

In the centre of the 'lab' is a hologram of the man we are looking for.

"Hello gentlemen," he says to us, before straightening his tie. "Welcome to my home. I'm sorry I couldn't be there to give you the full tour, but I'm sure you understand why I have decided to distance myself from you at present."

"Because you're a wimp," snarls Dad.

"Quite the opposite. I'm far stronger than you could ever dream to be. Haha, get it? Dream… You have no idea who you're dealing with."

"No, *you* have no idea who *you* are dealing with!" asserts Dad, puffing his chest out.

"Oh really?" The man mocks him. Then his hologram is replaced with images from Dad's life and headlines about things he's done; clips and words that sum up the beast he is. He's done his research, that much is evident.

"Close your eyes and say that again!" Dad threatens.

"See that's what I mean, you think you're so powerful, you think you can get your way through invading people's dreams, manipulating their rare moments of escape from this horrible world we live in. It's so weak, it's pathetic."

"Nobody calls me pathetic!"

The hologram laughs. "Oh but you are. You're the ape and I'm the human. Evolution. You don't stand a chance against me."

"Well come down here and fight me like a man then! Put your money where your mouth is!"

"I don't need to. Gerome Clarke, do you see that small cubicle to your left? Stand in there please."

I watch astounded as Dad makes his way to the cubicle. He steps inside and closes the door. The lights around it change from green to red. I suspect that means he's now trapped inside.

"Now then, what are we going to do with you?" The hologram turns to me. I put my hands up.

286

"Hey, I'm not part of this, I'll walk away and leave you to it, okay? I only came here because he made me. You don't want me, I'm nothing special."

"So self-depreciating! Adam was the same. 'Save Ella, please, save Ella', he mock-whimpers. What is it with you two and that girl, eh? I know why I want her, but why do you? Why do you want your brother's girlfriend?"

"I don't answer to you," I reply stubbornly.

"Okay, you don't want to talk about Ella. How about Izzy then, isn't she the reason you released your dad from that MIU? Because you wanted revenge on her killer? How's that working out for you? It doesn't look like it's going to plan…"

"Shut up and show yourself or let me go. I've had enough of this shit for one day. I need a drink." I turn to look at the way we came in but, of course, a brand-new door is now firmly in its place.

"Alright, I'll show myself to you. But only if you make me a promise." The hologram appears to look me straight in the eye.

"What do you want?"

"You let me keep Ella and your dad, and I will let the tall lady go, and you won't speak of this to anyone. Nobody is to know what happened to Gerome Clarke. He vanished. And, to sweeten the deal, I'll also help you get your revenge."

"Why would you want to help me?"

"That man is scum. I saw what he did to you, and I thought it was most unfair. I watched it like a soap opera, with a cup of tea and a pile of biscuits. It was most absorbing. And terrible. Of course."

"Why were you watching my life?"

"I was keeping an eye on you. I was alert for whenever Gerome might walk the streets again. I needed to be ready."

"But why do you want to keep Ella?"

"For my collection, of course. I didn't have a P.I.N.S. yet."

"And what about Adam, where is he?"

"Ach, never you mind about him, he was only getting in your way. If it weren't for him, you could have had Ella all to yourself."

"If it weren't for him, I would never have even heard of Ella."

"Well, if you're not interested, I can ask you to stay in one of my pods too…" He raises his eyebrows and I notice the other cubicles around the room, with green lights and doors open.

"No, thank you. I'm just trying to negotiate."

Dad appears to be asleep in his 'pod', completely oblivious to the world around him. Isn't this what we wanted? This isn't an MIU, but it's good enough. He's not able to cause any further harm.

"There will be no negotiation, you're not in a position to negotiate with me. I could destroy you, but I don't want to. I like you, Kyle. I like your style. My offer is simple: you agree not to tell anyone about me or this place, which will vanish as soon as you leave anyway; you deny any knowledge of what happened to your dad, or Ella, or Adam for that matter – you say you lost them and you don't know where they are; and you leave this place, with the innocent human. I'm not a bad man, like your father, see, I have no reason to detain innocent people."

"But Ella and Adam are innocent!"

"Are they?"

The hologram zaps off, and the room immediately feels darker. They are innocent. What has Ella ever done to deserve any of this? Sure, it turned out she has that unfortunate issue, but besides that, she's only ever been a victim. She's never hurt anyone. Right? Not on purpose.

288

And Adam, he's definitely a victim of circumstance. He wishes he was human, he always has.

But this man has been watching us, he knows things he shouldn't. If there is anything they've been keeping from me, he would know. He's like God or something.

Maybe Ella did cheat on Adam with Jeremy.

Or maybe she did try to kill her sister in that accident.

Maybe Adam knows more about what happened with Izzy than he lets on. He never was happy to see me happy.

But if I leave them here, what does that make me?

I was always the bad brother; I'll be living up to expectations. They'll hate me.

But if they deserve it, if they're not the innocent ones after all…

Okay.

OK.

Fuck it.

Fuck them.

They're in here together. Perhaps they'll be happy here.

I look up to where the hologram was moments earlier,

"Deal! Let me out!" My voice echoes.

The door opens and I step out into the afternoon sun, my eyes watering from the intense bright light. Beside me appears Kristina, Ella's ex-colleague. Together, we walk into the bustling road, back into the madness.

People are still running for their lives and cars are still parked everywhere, abandoned. It seems that even though he's caught Dad, he is still leaving the world in chaos. I suppose Dad will take the fall for that. I pull Kristina forwards as she hesitates.

"Wait, shouldn't we…?" She turns around to look back where we came from.

The building has gone. In its place, what looks like an abandoned church. She stares at it in confusion.

"But I don't understand! Where's Ella? I was with her in this tunnel…"

I pull her again, to get her to keep moving.

"She's with Adam. She'll be fine. We have to go."

"But she's in danger!" She wriggles free from me.

"We can't save them. You're welcome to try, but you'll fail. You'll die," I tell her, ignoring my conscience.

"But…"

"We can't."

We walk a bit further.

"I thought anything was possible in dreams," she mumbles.

"But we're not dreaming! Look around, woman! The world has gone to shit!"

"Has it though?" she asks me, looking around carefully. "Doesn't this all seem a bit *too* '2012' to you?"

I can't deny I do keep expecting to see John Cusack speeding around in a limo, but we don't have time for an existential debate right now. We can't be dreaming. We can't all be dreaming. That'd be insane, that'd be ridiculous. Impossible. Nobody could create such a scene. It's too detailed. Nobody is that powerful. Unless…

She looks at me, waiting for me to answer her.

"Okay genius, how do you propose we attempt to wake up?"

Before I can stop her, she runs fast into the crowds. I chase after her. She keeps running and running until she reaches the end of the abandoned cars. The road is clear from here on. I'm out of breath and wondering where the hell she got that stamina. Is she a marathon runner?

She starts running again until she finds a bend in the road, and then she positions herself right in the middle.

No!

"Kristina, stop! Get over here! What if you're wrong?" I yell at her, from my safe position on the pavement.

"What if I'm right?"

I hear the squeal of breaks and the thud of impact, and I squeeze my eyes closed, unwilling to open them and see the scene before me. I can't believe it. I couldn't save Ella, and now I've just let her only friend kill herself. I am a terrible person. I should be the one locked up.

I listen out for the sound of sirens, but of course they don't come. They can't get here, there are too many roadblocks. I still refuse to open my eyes. I don't want to see it, her body all misshapen. But, what if she's not dead, what if she's lying there in pain? What if she needs me? What if I'm the only one who can save her?

I open my eyes and the light blinds me for a second time. I can hear a beeping sound, not a car horn, a hospital machine. A steady heartbeat type sound. I blink my eyes to clear my vision. A face is leaning over me. Ella?

"He's awake!" the voice says. It belongs to a tall woman with long hair and a smattering of freckles. Do I know her? "I told you it was a dream, Kyle," she says, grinning.

"Where am I?"

"I have no idea!" She laughs. "But at least we're together."

"But Adam, and Ella? And my dad?" I rub my eyes and run my hands over my stubble.

"No idea. But I was right, we were dreaming, so…"

"So maybe we never left?" I finish for her. She tilts her head and frowns.

"Maybe, but it looks kind of normal outside, and not like the chaos where we were before."

I push myself slowly off the bed, detach myself from the machine, and go to look out the window with her. She's right, it looks normal out there. Except, no, that's not right, that's a foreign police car! We're not in England anymore.

"Kristina?" I say, hoping that's her name. "I think we're in Italy."

291

Her eyes widen and she looks outside again, paying more attention.

"Well, would you look at that! They're driving on the wrong side of the road!" I nod. "But how did we get to Italy? I thought we were dreaming?"

"Maybe we were, or maybe that was all real and we just got teleported once you were hit by the car. Maybe that triggered something."

"Who are you people?" she says, incredulous.

"Hey, don't look at me, I can't teleport!"

"Oh yeah, that's right, you just make sexy dreams in women's heads!" She laughs and I give her a playful shove. My reputation precedes me.

THE END

(UNTIL BOOK 3…)

Acknowledgements

Once again, I have to start by thanking Mum and Daisy. You are the only two people I trust to read my early-stage manuscripts, you tell me what I need to hear (even if I don't want to) and for that I am eternally grateful.

Dean, thank you for putting up with my writing obsession (again). It's not going anywhere so I'm grateful for your understanding when I spend 12 hours staring at my laptop and ignoring you. It's not personal, I love you. Oh, and thank you for reminding me of the word 'snatch.' I'm sure it made all the difference.

Marti, your enthusiasm about Duplicity and your help to spread the word was incredible, you really helped this introverted author step into the spotlight and say, "Yes, I wrote a book." Thank you. I hope you have enjoyed Complicity equally as much, if not more!

Dad and Andrew, thanks again for all your support and social media likes. I know these books aren't really your kind of thing, so thank you for ensuring that no post goes unliked, and for sharing them with other potential readers.

Jennifer Cyphers, wow. You are like my Instagram Mum! I love how we have connected over our books and our passion for helping our fellow indie authors. If any of my readers are into Sci-Fi, they should check out your novel 'The Cosmos in Her Hand' right now.

To anyone I haven't already mentioned who read and reviewed Duplicity, THANK YOU! It's probably because of you that people are reading this right now. (Seriously, reviews really do make that much of a difference).

And finally, I thank you, the person reading this today. Perhaps you fit into the category above, or perhaps you threw caution to the wind and dived straight in with 'book 2.' Either way, I thank you for taking a chance on this novel by a somewhat unknown author. If you enjoyed it, please leave a review to help others discover it too.

I'll see you in Book 3!

Chloë x

About the Author

Chloë is one of us.

She's that girl who reads on her lunchbreak, on the train, at the hairdressers; that girl who has bags under her eyes because 'one more chapter' rolled on and on until the book was finished at 3am, on a work night.

Chloë is also a writer and, until February 2022, she kept that pretty quiet. She hid her 'true' passion beneath her love of other people's books, by studying English and American Literature at University, and only ever talking about what she was reading, not what she was writing.

Many of her acquaintances were surprised to hear that she had written her first novel, Duplicity, and I daresay they will be even more surprised to hear she has released a sequel, Complicity, only six months later. But not those who truly know her. From a very young age Chloë filled notebooks with stories and now she's grabbing that childhood dream of becoming an author with both hands.

'Complicity (The Dangers of Dreaming: Book 2)' is her second novel, with a great many planned for the future.

FOLLOW ON

Instagram and Facebook
@chloeblythauthor

WEBSITE

https://chloeblythauthor.com

If you enjoyed this book, please post a review online to help other readers discover this new series. Even a few kind words will make a difference.

Thank you!

Printed in Great Britain
by Amazon